PAPER CLIPS
MERSEYSIDE

Short stories by writers from Merseyside

Edited by

SUZI BLAIR

NEW FICTION

First published in 1993 by
NEW FICTION
4 Hythegate, Werrington
Peterborough,
PE4 7ZP

Printed in Great Britain by Forward Press.

Foreword

New Fiction is an imprint born through demand.

Such is the popularity of writing as a pastime of today, the opportunity to get 'into print' is increasingly difficult. Competition is tough and plentiful - rising at about the same level as opportunity shrinks. In the midst of a market that proves financially rewarding and worthwhile to only the blockbusters and best-sellers, new and less well known or unestablished writers bear most of the burden of lack of platform.

New Fiction is achieving its twin aims of building such a platform for fresh talent and publishing stories accessible to a broad range of readership.

The Paper Clips collections gather together a diversity of stories by contemporary writers who succeed with the essential magic, that has made storytelling a part of life through the ages. It is intended that individually the stories allow a quick and easy injection of entertainment. Collectively, they should present a buffet of subject and style with much 'dipping into' potential. Ultimately, Paper Clips represents a 'thumping good read' from writers living in Merseyside.

Suzi Blair
Editor

To Joanne,
Hope you enjoy it,
Ron

Contents

The Final Count

by

Jean E Barnes

It was one of those tedious tasks that cropped up at the end of each school year, destined to leave a taste of futility that lingered into the summer holidays, but was, thankfully, forgotten by September. Bureaucracy dictated that Bill Appleton (and every other class teacher on the payroll of state schools) spent some time on the final afternoon of the Summer Term totalling the number of attendances for each pupil on his class-register. With a sense of relief, Bill reached the final name on the list, Webster. It didn't take long to work out that Webster (pupil number thirty) had attended school on a mere eight occasions that school year; five mornings and three afternoons. For the remaining 352 sessions, a series of noughts against his name spread across the narrowly lined pages. The roundness defaced the otherwise uniform strokes of herringbone above. Bill wondered how many pen-strokes he'd made in different registers over the past fourteen years. It must run into millions!

Bureaucracy reached its triumphant peak inside the register's dull front-cover, demanding that each entry be made in either blue or black ink, thus aborting forbidden flights of fancy which might evidence the proverbial two-fingered gesture at authority. Bill recalled one particular headmaster early in his career who had insisted on the same coloured ink being solely used throughout the entire year. Colour-prejudiced, you necessarily made your choice on the first day and were stuck with it! This dictum had many a time caused him to stifle muttered obscenities on those frequent occasions he had the wrong pen and a roomful of restless youths impatient to 'get their mark' and go - some to join the noisy throng in the overcrowded corridors, some to enjoy a last minute, illicit cigarette in the 'bogs' and others to slip undetected through the outside doors to the waiting freedom beyond.

So often Bill had reached pupil twenty nine in the column of names, sure in the knowledge that number thirty would be absent again. (It had become an unconscious reflex to alter his pen stroke to form the usual nought). The class had made a joke about it, whooping with derision and shouting unflattering remarks on those few occasions when Webster had put in an appearance. It was a one-sided onslaught that petered out, unfuelled by any rejoinders.

For some irrational reason, Bill had felt a continuous sense of guilt about the boy, as if he were personally in some way partly to blame for such non-attendance. It was irrational; after all, he scarcely knew the lad. Eight quick sightings had scarcely put them on speaking terms, let alone a long-term acquaintance!

Outside the room, the lesson - bell erupted, echoing along the corridors and prompting doors to burst open. Overstrained hinges and handles came under threat as the klaxon spawned a thousand and more youngsters, who surged in opposite directions. Regardless of their ultimate destination, the wise and the weedy moved with the human tide; the unwise and the unruly against it! In the centre of the maelstrom, the usual scuffles broke out as tempers flared over briefly - held territorial rights. Bill had long since realised that it was expedient to ignore the whole proceedings. It made sense to reserve his energy for the challenges he would have to face within his own classroom. That way you stood a fair chance of some success!

The noise muted with the slam of doors and Bill's own empty domain regained its temporary calm. He picked up his pen and wrote the final figures in the column against the name of Webster; sessions attended: 8; absent: 352. Bill tried, rather half-heartedly, to picture Webster, to put a face to the name. The image proved unexpectedly elusive and this annoyed him. He'd always prided himself on his memory for faces, on being able to identify every pupil he'd taught, past and present. Number thirty: Webster, Alan David. Bill's eyes ran down the last few names on the list - Stott, Turner, Varney, Webster. He visualised each boy's face in turn, until he reached Webster. Why couldn't he place Webster? Even on those eight occasions when the boy had attended over that year, he hadn't been faceless, for heaven's sake! Bill knew he could check it out easily enough. A brief glance through the school records would solve the enigma, for each of the dog-eared, faded, blue files carried the relevant inch-square photograph. But that was to admit defeat, admit that his memory was at fault. It was simply a matter of greater concentration.

Instinctively, Bill's eyes wandered to where Webster had sat on those few, isolated occasions. Desks were allocated in alphabetical order. Third from the back, fourth row, by the window. From where he sat, Bill could see the shabby, wooden surface, pockmarked with innumerable initials. Even the desk had an air of vacant neglect about it, while the ugly, grey, plastic chair (with its spindly, spider legs) was straight and tidy, in marked contrast to its angular counterparts sprawled around the room.

In spite of this increased effort of will, Webster's face refused to materialise. Bill closed the biscuit - coloured folder, pushed back his chair and made his way to the staff room. Unexpectedly, it was empty. Ignoring the newly-placed anti-smoking signs, Bill lit a cigarette and picked up a discarded newspaper from one of the tables. A brief glance showed that it was one of the local papers financed by advertising and circulated free of charge. He looked with disinterest over the front page - straight into Webster's face! With a sense of shock, Bill recognised the pinched look and the jagged strands of dark hair framing the forehead. The boy had good, straight teeth and the hint of a dimple in his chin. Funny, Bill mused, he'd never particularly noticed either feature.

Whilst acknowledging the likeness, Bill's subconscious refused to register the headline beneath the photograph:

'Alan Webster - found dead' and in larger, heavier print 'Mother finds truant son dead at home'. Bill felt he should be shocked - and was mildly surprised to realise that he wasn't. He read the short account. The quiet tragedy unfolded in the few paragraphs. Half-huddled in a sleeping-bag, the boy had been discovered lying on the carpet in his own vomit. The pity of the mother's words rose from the page: 'I came home from work and just saw him lying there. I knew he was gone.'

A fitting obituary, Bill thought. 'I knew he was gone.' Just as I had known that he was hardly ever there. Elusive to the last. The mother's words lingered, voiceless in the stale air, until they evaporated in Bill's cigarette smoke. The rest of the details were sparse. Alan had been playing truant a lot, his mother had said, but that was his only problem. He'd never seemed depressed, the report continued, and was due to leave school anyway the following March.

In his mind's eye, Bill saw again the row of noughts in the register. Where had Alan Webster been on all those absent half-days? The hopelessness of it all washed over him in the realisation that the forgotten face was now more familiar to him than it had ever been. At the very moment that he had penned one of those negative entries in the register, Alan Webster had already departed this earthly life. The shape of that final nought against the name of pupil number thirty seemed to elongate in Bill's imagination, coalescing into the image of a slight figure, half-huddled in a sleeping-bag. At the final count, Bill realised, Alan David Webster had eluded them all.

Private Detective

by

Tim Clarke

'What do you mean, a private can't be a detective?'

'I was a private at the time and I can tell you I solved a crime that had been baffling the best detectives in France. - Don't believe me? well, see that emerald that my wife is wearing, couldn't afford a duck-egg like that on a squaddies pay I can tell you. Well that's how I got it.'

I waited while another round was set up.

'It was the time of that revolution in Monte Carlo, remember, about five years ago? Well, as soon as it started our platoon was flown out there and told to commandeer a vehicle and rescue any Britisher we could find.

'Not many trucks on the road, but we found one old boy who was loading a dormobile with furniture, looting I guess, so we grabbed that van and drove down to the seafront and collected half a dozen bathing beauties in bikinis and such. Before topless beaches were invented, I'm afraid or we would have done better still. The girls had fled off the shore and only had what they stood up in, and that wasn't much I can tell you. Anyway we managed to squeeze them all in the van together with the old boy's loot.

'The Sarge said it would be cold when we got up into the hills away from the firing area, and suggested that each girl chummed up with one of us and shared our greatcoats. Some didn't need no invitation, in fact, Gable, had already rounded up a couple for himself. There's two Clark's in our platoon see, me, I'm Nobby, and Gable. He thinks it's because he looks like a film star, but he's got a face like the end of a house really. Still the dames seem to like his brickwork! Well I got fixed up with this little blonde in a green polka dot bikini.

'Bodger didn't bother, he said he rather fancied the desk he had found in the van and propped his book up on it to do some serious reading. That's why we call him Roger the Bookdodger, even topless dames wouldn't have disturbed his reading.

'So there I was, sitting on a hard kitchen chair with this little blonde, Vicky, on my knee, and my greatcoat round the pair of us, as the driver bumped his way up into the hills. Don't know how she stuck my bony knees and rough serge uniform rubbing against her bare skin all those miles but at least she was warm.

'Eventually we pulled into a railyard and Sarge says, 'Grab any furniture you want and get the girls into that rail truck'. Well I had only my kitchen chair and a five foot blonde so I was first out and into the truck. By moonlight I could see it was nearly empty, except for an old treadle sewing machine in the corner and another old codger sitting on a pile of sacks. 'That yours?' I signalled to him, pointing to the sewing machine. A shake of the head, so I deposited Vicky on it and started to grab some sacks to make a softer seat. The rest of the lads were still struggling to get their stuff out of the dormobile; I remember Bodger didn't even have a girl to help him with his desk. Then into the doorway stepped a

4

strange woman, long black hair, black beret, black coat. She was staring at Vicky and me, 'This yours?' I asked her in my best schoolboy French, indicating the sewing machine. But with a shake of her head she disappeared through the door.

'As I reached for more sacks I noticed a light flash outside the truck window, and could just make out a gendarme, and of all things, a British Female Military Police dame.

'They had a little walkie-talkie and I could just make out her saying, 'We've recovered a bit of silver but not found any of the jewellery, nor the thieves yet.' I sensed someone watching and there was the lady in black again. 'Sure it ain't yours?' Again a shake of the head and she was gone. As I turned to pick up another sack my number tens kicked the treadle, and off fell a bit of the works, or so I thought until I picked it up. It was a black tube about a foot long, but taped at each end, as I lifted it there was a rattle.

'Now my detective instincts were aroused, so I slipped it through the window, where it fell right at the feet of missus M P.

'As they undid the tape and shook out the contents, I could see a handful of rocks, reds, greens, blues, good as the crown jewels.

'I signalled them to silence, jumped up beside Vicky and pretended to be asleep. Everyone settled down, and soon, through my half closed eyes I saw the lady in black sidling towards my corner.

'She came right up to the sewing machine and started fiddling about under the 'works'. Then I grabbed her round the waist, lifting her so that her black shoes were thrashing about in free air, and I shouted through the window to the French arms of the law, who doubled smartly round and snapped on the 'cuffs'.

'Several days later I was told to report to the local cop shop, where a well-dressed franko and his missus thanked me in their strange foreign way. On the desk were all the jewels they'd found stuck under my sewing machine, and they told me to chose one for my reward.

'Well, as I'd already discovered, Vicky's eyes were green, it had to be that emerald. Don't you think it suits her?'

Whatever Happened To Archie?

by

Valerie Clegg

How happy they were at Hawthorn Cottage when they awoke to see a shaft of light beaming through the window. Mrs Walkendin was going off to stay with her sister in the Hebrides, and the weather there could be somewhat unpredictable. It had been three years since the two sisters had been together and the very thought of this reunion was the cause of great excitement and joy. Today looked as though it was going to be gloriously sunny which would, of course, herald the start of a carefree holiday.

The car was duly packed with all kinds of paraphernalia including, of course, Mrs Walkendin's home-made cakes and jams (for which she was renowned). Her husband was only driving her to the station; she was to continue the rest of the journey by train and boat, alone. What a wonderful feeling it was to be leaving, at last. The elderly couple settled themselves firmly in their seats, checked that everything was present and correct and moved away from the house.

'The sunshine must have brought out the best in everyone,' said George as they drove along through the village, 'it certainly puts a better light on things.'

They passed the milkman who waved, in what they thought was a friendly gesture. *This* was *most* unusual as he was usually quite glum at this time of the morning. A sullen chap!

'Old Smeddles', a jolly old soul who lived at the corner house, and who was crippled with arthritis, waved his stick madly, which looked really comical, and certainly drew attention to himself. He was well known for his strange ways and eccentricity, so the Walkendins did not take too much notice of his antics, but drove on. A little further along the road they caught sight of Joe Potter, the local Policeman; he had a quizzical look on his face as they passed him, and when George looked into his rear mirror he could see the 'Bobby' almost toppling off his bicycle as he turned round to watch them go by. He waved. George waved back. 'Such a friendly lot,' he said, 'good lad, Joe.'

The station came into view, the car was unloaded and George, with much difficulty, humped the cases and packages up the walkway to the platform. Bill Jones, the Station Master, exchanged greetings with the pair, and remarked on the truly lovely weather they were having lately.

Eventually the train arrived, 'bag and baggage', were deposited in the compartment and after the usual farewells, the carriages and engine disappeared along the track in a cloud of smoke.

Now George could settle down to a bit of peace and quiet. No little woman pestering him to mow the lawn or mend the cupboard door. He could settle down to listening to a good day's cricket, knowing that there would not be a background of endless chatter. What bliss!

Madge rang that evening to say that she had arrived safely. George hesitated before he spoke and thought that perhaps he ought not to tell his wife that

Archie, their cat, had not appeared at the normal time for his dinner. No . . . he wouldn't alarm her, as after all, the monster hated his mistress leaving him and he was probably, at this very moment, sulking under the blackcurrant bushes.

Two days later, George was panic stricken - no Archie. 'Where on earth is that damned cat?' said George. 'I'll break his scraggy neck when I get hold of him.' He didn't like the cat anyway and he liked him *even less* now that he was causing all this disturbance, when, had things gone well, he would have been having a well deserved rest. The search was on, the bicycle was dragged out of the shed and a rather disgruntled fellow started his check of the hedgerows and surrounding fields. Neighbours were alerted and the task of making enquiries about a missing cat was treated with great disdain and put a permanent frown on George's face.

After three whole hours of fruitless searching, it all got too much for 'Old Walkendin' and he decided to seek respite in the 'Horse and Groom'. A pint would make him feel much better, he thought. 'Hello there George,' said Bill Swithens who was leaning against the bar, merrily puffing away at his pipe. 'I thought you had gone away for a few days, but I didn't expect you to take the cat with you?' he said, laughingly.

'What the hell are you talking about?' said George, 'what cat?'

'Well . . . you passed me on the lane last Friday morning and I looked up, and on the top of the luggage rack, sat this furry traveller; the whole thing looked so amusing.' Now . . . the 'cat was *really* out of the bag' (so to speak).

Despair set in; sleepless nights. There would be 'murder' when his wife got home. What had been Archie's fate? Was he wandering around like a nomad in a starved and dishevelled state? Madge was due to return home tomorrow; what would she say? Had he to go out and get a replacement he thought. He decided against it and resigned himself to whatever ill may befall him.

On reflection, it had been a pretty miserable week. Small chance he had had of spending leisurely hours in the deckchair and I suppose Madge would have been having a *wonderful* time.

Ah well. The twist of the story is that . . . on the eleventh hour, when all thoughts of solving the problem of the missing cat had long since gone, Archie reappeared. *Not* the emanciated little wreck that one would imagine, after seven days absence, but a *very fat* 'aristocratic cat' who swaggered down the road looking altogether as though he was wearing a full evening dress attire with his black coat and white front, and there . . . tripping along beside him was the prettiest little feline figure you ever did see, her white, long haired coat, giving the appearance of the rather lavish furs of the film stars, and her whiskers almost sweeping the ground as she glided along. Archie had obviously been 'putting on the Ritz' possibly with a trip on the Orient Express thrown in, mused George.

'All's well that ends well' and Archie has settled back in the old potting shed at the bottom of the garden. 'Honey' his little mate has nested in beside him and is now obviously pregnant with her first litter and we are no longer wondering 'whatever happened to Archie?'

The Homecoming

by

D Eckersley

Rebecca slowed as she approached Leyton Avenue. Her parents' house was only a hundred yards away, and she was still very unsure of her reception. She had not contacted her parents since she had run away. She had left no note, no explanation. They knew nothing of her reasons for fleeing. How could she explain to her kind, trusting, moralistic parents that she was going to be a parent herself?

Panting slightly, Rebecca paused at the corner. Despite her obvious advanced pregnancy, any casual observer could see she retained her poise and style. Her hair, always her best feature, was long, black and glossy, and her sinuous legs turned heads, even now. She knew her looks belied her position - homeless, penniless and, - worst of all - lonely. A momentary weakness pervaded her, causing her to gasp and lean against the nearest garden wall. How long was it since she had eaten? She had missed breakfast, wanting to get an early start on the long journey home, and it was now well past midday. Not good for her or the infant.

She hadn't dared to return home before now, and it was only the severity of her situation that forced her to continue along Leyton Avenue at this moment. What if they made her give the child up? Even now, she was frightened of the pressure they might bring to bear on her to abandon the baby after the birth. This, she told herself, she would never - could never - do. She prayed for the strength to fight them, whilst hoping for some forgiveness and compassion. She knew they would be - what? Shocked, disappointed, worried about finances, even. 'Please let them understand, so I can keep my baby,' she thought.

She would bring the offspring up alone; that much she had faced up to. Tom may have been many things - handsome, charming, plausible - but he was certainly not cut out to play the role of doting father. This fact he had pointed out to Rebecca in no uncertain terms that terrible evening when she had fled her parents' home and gone to him.

Now she had reached her own home. Nothing had changed. The front garden was spick and span, the square lawn neatly bordered by pansies and gypsophila, evenly spaced, no weeds daring to show their face. Could a baby possibly fit in here? She would soon find out.

Suddenly, before she had reached the front door, it swung open and a middle-aged couple emerged from within. It was the woman leading the way, who saw Rebecca first, standing on the path, frightened and apprehensive, her pregnancy obvious.

'Eric, Eric, it's Rebecca,' she exclaimed. 'Oh my goodness, you're . . .' There was silence for perhaps half a minute, then Rebecca decided on the best course of action known to her. She walked towards her mother with her head held high and gently rubbed the side of her sleek, black body against her mother's legs, whilst looking up at her, beseechingly.

'Oh, Eric, Rebecca's going to have kittens. I know we said we didn't want any more cats, but we can't turn her away now. We must look after her. Please, Eric!'

And from the softening of her father's features, and the slow spread of his smile, Rebecca knew everything was going to be all right.

The Talking Spiders

by

L Hardy

The six spiders continued spinning their webs outside, their work could be seen through the half opened window.

Mrs Williams was standing by the washing machine with her friend Mrs Dobson discussing the white lace dress she was planning to make for her eight year old daughter, Suzy.

In the interval Mrs Williams went to London to buy some material to make the dress, but when she arrived home she realised she had left it behind.

She tried phoning and writing to the shop and leaving her address, but she didn't get anywhere, there were no arrivals in the post.

Every day the spiders watched outside the window fascinated at Mrs Williams, but to their disappointment she hadn't started yet.

'I wonder what's holding her up? Perhaps she can't think of a good design. I think we should get to work, and make an outline of a dress,' they thought. So, they set to work very busily.

In no time at all they had formed a beautifully detailed web.

Exactly six weeks after losing the material, it was returned to her through the post. She immediately took it into the sewing room and was very surprised when she saw the largest, and most beautiful spider web she had ever seen outside the window. Was she imagining it, or did it form the faintest outline of a dress? The rain drops which clung to it added to the design's undeniable charm.

'I think I shall try to copy it,' she thought. In about two days time she had completed her task - which was the fastest time ever. It was the loveliest dress she had ever seen.

She wrapped it up in the prettiest wrapping paper she could buy from the stationers, and gave it to her daughter the next day.

'Mommy, this is the nicest present I have ever received, it reminds me of the beautiful spider webs outside your sewing room window.'

'Funny you should say that, my dear. I was very much inspired by them when I worked out the pattern for the dress.'

'I think I'll go and look through the window and see if the webs are still there.' her daughter said. She followed her mother into the sewing room, and sure enough, the webs were still there.

Later on her daughter went outside to closely inspect the spiders.

'I hope you like your birthday present. It was from an idea of ours,' said the six tiny, squeaky voices together. Her daughter gazed in unbelievable astonishment around her. In about ten minutes she realised that the spiders had been talking to her, since there were no other creatures around.

'Yes, very much so, I shall always be grateful to you spiders.'

'You are a very nice little girl,' said the voices again.

'The spiders actually spoke to me, Mommy,' she said when she arrived back in the house.

'How marvellous my dear. I have seen other animals talk in some of the Walt Disney stories, but not spiders, but I imagine they could do so, if they put their minds to it.'

'I would like to take you outside and let you see for yourself.' her daughter said. Sure enough, they went outside and the spiders did talk to her Mother.

'I know it is not my imagination now, those spiders really did talk to me.' she said.

Needless to say, all the little girls around the neighbourhood were ecstatic when they saw her dress.

Then, the spiders and their webs suddenly disappeared from outside their window. For weeks Suzy cried her eyes out, she missed them so much.

One afternoon, a month later, the little girl from around the corner came to see her. 'You'll be glad to know that we have spotted the spiders and their webs outside the room where my mother does her sewing. When the vivid golden light shone on the webs yesterday evening, a faint pattern of a dress was formed, it glistened with all the colours of the rainbow. In all the places the colours shaped into the form of flowers, and my Mother is going to make a dress according to the pattern. I am going to wear it to my birthday party, which is in two weeks time and you are invited.'

One by one, the spiders visited all the little girls houses on the street, and disappeared from each house as before, but each little girl knew that they were at another house doing their work.

One dress looked like it had been dotted with silver, because the rain drops had dropped onto webs at a particular house, and others had rainbow coloured patterns in different shapes and sizes all over them. All the girls wore them to Sandra's birthday party, and a very happy time was had by them all.

The Old Maids

by

Rachel B Manning

My story is about three sisters. Next door neighbours. They became part of my life for almost one and a half decades. I was born in 1930. Life was so much slower paced than now. Summer seemed to consist of long hot days, cricket and my longing (never materialised), to own a white tennis dress, trimmed with red. The endless quest, when summer trod on the heels of autumn, searching for and picking blackberries. Eating half, setting off for home, fingers and mouth stained purple from the juice. Happier children couldn't have been found anywhere.

I lived in a row of cottages, eight cottages in all. Side on to the road. To get to them entailed going into the field, along a dirt track. We had a large front garden, no rear garden at all. Indeed, no back door, just a front door. The kitchen window overlooked a farmers field. Chickens strutted there. Working class people were very poor then. A chicken would be hauled through the window. Never to be seen again. This was usually around Christmas time.

The three old maids lived in this row. Not next door at this time. The eldest, Ellen, Big Ellen, Big Push, she was known by all three names. As the name suggests, she was tall and angular. Small wire spectacles, perched on a long thin nose, small thin mouth, forever twitching, as if she was having a conversation with herself.

Maggie, the middle sister, was very small, similar features to Ellen, but behind the wire spectacles, one eye looked in a different direction to the other. She was cross-eyed. Again, she always appeared to be muttering to herself.

Mary Jane, the youngest, was similar to the other two, but her whole expression was gentle and kind. She didn't wear spectacles, but had a large sticking plaster across her nose, so large as to hide it.

All three dressed in long black cotton skirts or dresses, down to the ankles. On their feet, 'Granny' shoes, black bootees, laced over the insteps, through little studs.

Over iron grey hair, was worn white cotton bonnets, such as toddlers wear out in the sun, with a piece of material covering the nape of the neck.

Sometime in 1936, these cottages were condemned, and we moved 'en masse' to newly built council houses half a mile away. Here we became next door neighbours of the 'Old Maids'.

My first memory was of Mary Jane.

As I played in the long back garden, she would sometimes be pacing up and down their garden. She did try to be friendly and speak to me, but, as I was always intimidated by the sisters, and was a shy, timid child, I didn't know how to handle the few kindly words, (unfortunately she died shortly after we moved into our new homes, the large plaster covered a nose, rumour had it, that was being

12

eaten away with cancer.) The eccentricity of the remaining sisters increased with the years.

We now had electricity in our homes. Not so the 'Old Maids' only the flicker of candles and oil lamps could be seen on dark winter evenings. Maggie had the disconcerting habit of lurking, with a black shawl over her head, down the side of the house. The paths to our side door were adjacent. In the blackout, (due to the war), she would be invisible. When I heard rustling, I knew she was there. I would run into my house, as if the devil himself was after me. My lively imagination had me grabbed and dragged into their eerie and mysterious home, neighbours never entered their abode.

A Catholic priest called occasionally, a tradesman came once each week, knocked and left a carton of groceries at the front door. These cartons, empty? could be seen, stacked in the middle of the front room, (they lived in the back room), through a gap in the lace curtains shrouding the window.

Once each week, Ellen would don a black straw hat, an ankle length black coat, and with a straw basket over her arm, strode purposefully, looking neither to right or left, to the nearest bus stop, to journey to the nearest small town. Maggie would hover at the front door, until she was out of sight.

They instantly became angry anytime children were playing. Whatever game was played, it was wrong.

The net curtains twitched, as if bewitched, as we played. Piggybacks! If our partner tumbled off our back, and we used their garden fence to hold as we crouched, out of the front door would emerge this 'bat out of hell?' Black clothes flapping, a stick raised to hit our fingers. We ran away like a shot out of a gun.

When we had a ball game, we played to the chorus of two voices as one, as to what would happen if the ball broke their window, or went near their home. As the law of averages are, once in a while it would go into their garden. Instantly our ball game was finished. The offending ball was gleefully grabbed and taken inside, quick as a flash.

Long summer evenings, Ellen set off on another journey. The village police station, complaining about us, she wasted her time, the village 'Bobby' knew them too well.

Eventually they stopped troubling the law, after smugly putting a 'Wilful Damage' notice in the front window. This never made a scrap of difference, no-one wanted to go near their house anyway, certainly not to do any damage.

That notice stayed in the window until it yellowed and faded with the sun. Part of the 'Old Maids' as was the stack of cartons, flickering lamp light and half open doors. Exit or entering, their doors were ever only partially open.

Our back gardens overlooked an open landscape. On summer afternoons, from my bedroom window, I have watched Ellen stride to the bottom of the garden, lift her voluptuous skirt, climb, and cock her legs over the five foot high fence. Down the field she would stride, until just a small speck in the distance. Sometimes stooping as she loped along. An hour or so later, I would hear her querulous voice, (It used to strike terror in my heart.)

'Maggie! Maggie!'

Maggie would scurry down the garden. Ellen wore a large apron made from sacking material, known as a brat. This was full of pieces of wood. This fire wood was the reason for her trek over the fields. Now this was passed over the fence to Maggie. Transported in relays into the house. Ellen would then clamber back over the fence. Maggie and she would walk up the garden path, muttering in undertones. Nodding to each other. Well pleased with the afternoons work, like two conspirators.

One particular day, I was very brave. I had reached fourteen years by this time. A boy whom I was 'sweet' on, was visiting neighbours. He came from Wales. We were kicking a ball, one to the other. Horror! Over the gate it went, into the 'Old Maids' garden. The first time ever, I beat Maggie to the ball. (I must have been very keen on this boy to do this, and get his ball back.) In my fourteen years, I had never been thru' that gate. What a wasps nest I disturbed. Noone had ever beaten them to the ball before. There was much shaking of fists, and I am afraid I was called a b - - - - - - . It took all of thirty minutes for them to quieten down. They were so angry and frustrated. When peace came at last, Maggie was posted 'On Guard', pacing up and down the path. A soldier on guard duty. One never knew when she actually looked at one, as of course, one eye looked one way, and the other eye, the opposite way. As a child, I found this very disconcerting.

The end of life next door to the 'Old Maids', was in such a way, I wouldn't have imagined in my wildest dreams or nightmare. By this time, I was sixteen years. My best friend's father was cousin to them. Maggie died, they were both in their seventies now. One dark winter's evening, I was at my friends home. Her mother decided she would go and pay her respects to Maggie, and visit their home. I was invited to go with them. I must admit I was curious to enter a house, which as a child, had petrified me. Their home was spotlessly clean, although sparsely furnished. A bright fire burned in the grate, an oil lamp stood on the table. Its flickering light gave almost a cosy glow to the room. So different to my childhood glimpses, through windows and half open doors. The same room had looked sinister and eerie.

When greetings were over, (I got a curt nod), we all trooped upstairs. In the front bedroom, Maggie was lying in state in her coffin. The four of us looked down at this small old woman. The room in darkness, lit only by the flicker of an oil lamp, which Ellen carried.

These two old women, of whom I had spent one and a half decades terrified, (in my child's mind they were two witches, ever ready to lean over that dividing fence, on dark winters evenings, to drag me into this very house where I now stood). One dead, the other a frail bony old woman. Suddenly I felt the fear leave me. I saw them for what they were. Indeed two Old Maids. never to have known a man's love, or a child's tiny arms around them. Their whole world had been this cheerless, bare, house and each other. They had protected their home and boundaries so fiercely, that had put the fear of the devil into this quiet, timid child, who just happened to live next door.

Maggie hadn't finished with me yet.

Ellen stood at the door with the lamp. My friend's mother walked with the aid of a walking stick. So slow was she, through to the bedroom door, I stood alone beside Maggie's coffin, in the dark, for what seemed to be an eternity.

The message was, 'Don't get too cocky, I can still send a chill down your spine.'

Shortly after, Ellen moved into a Catholic home, quite a distance away. She died peacefully a couple of years later.

In time, another 'ordinary' family moved into 'their' house. However, it had lost its character.

Fifty years later I still sometimes pass. Smart and trim as it is, I conjure in my mind's eye two lonely old maids, peeping through yellowed net curtains. A pathetic 'Wilful Damage' notice hanging in the window.

An age dead and gone. Dead as the three Old Maids.

It's An Ill Wind

by

Stella Worden

Madge lay sleepless in the tousled bed, her gaze caught by the movement of the faded curtains as they swayed gently in the breeze from the open window. She was conscious of the huge bulk of her husband, Brynn, pressing into her side, feeling the heat from his body, but gaining no comfort from it. Turning over and taking the duvet with him, he emitted a raucous snore, which made her whole body stiffen with irritation. Resentfully, she glared at his back, and yanked the quilt back over herself. Grey hair stuck up in greasy tufts on his head and the grubby, off-white vest that he always wore in bed, gleamed darkly through the shadows. Why couldn't he wear pyjamas in bed like everybody else, instead of pressing his naked, hairy backside up next to her?, she wondered. Twenty years of this she'd put up with, and how may more would she have to endure. She was only forty four years old now. The prospect of her dreary life with Brynn loomed endlessly before her. Her nostrils twitched, something was rising above the usual smell of stale sweat, Oh no, the dirty pig had done it again! The rotten egg odour threatened to suffocate her, and she leapt out of bed and put her face near the open window. Where are the cigarettes? Ah. here they are.

After lighting one up, she sat at the dressing table, inhaled deeply and looked critically at her face in the mirror. In the dim light, she saw the glossy, black hair, with no sign of grey, thanks to 'Midnight Glow' as applied by her hairdresser, but quite a lot of lines, lines of discontent dragging her mouth downwards, crow's feet and frown lines on the forehead, and big, brown eyes, once her best feature, now just looking sad, dull and listless. Pushing the stool backwards, she posed before the looking glass, and saw her trim little body, no fat there. Only five foot two inches tall, she'd always been determined to ward off the flab and she'd been successful. On the rare occasions when she'd been able to tidy Brynn up, and they'd gone out to a club for the night, people had stared at the odd couple, she so petite, slim and dainty, he so tall, gross and rhinoceros like, swilling the ale back as if there was no tomorrow. They didn't go on nights out nowadays, as it was no fun trying to drag a giant, drunken lump of a man back home in a taxi. All he seemed to be interested in was drinking and eating to excess and it nauseated her. Take yesterday dinnertime, he'd eaten three quarters of a large loaf with his beef stew, then polished off a full Swiss Roll and a whole pint of custard!

Madge went into the bathroom, threw the stump into the toilet pan with a plop, where it fizzled out quietly, then flashed around the bedroom with the 'Fresh Air' spray, 'Not that it would do much good,' she reflected and got back into bed. Just then, a double trumpet resounded in the dark, followed by a belch. Madge reached for the cigarettes again. She'd rather have the smell of burning tobacco in her nostrils, that Brynn's own 'perfume'. They should never have moved into this bungalow she thought, at least in the other house there'd been two

16

bedrooms and she could have retreated to the other room there, but here she was trapped. Resentment of her sleeping husband rose up in her breast.

Switching on the low overhead light, she began to flick through a magazine which had been lying next to the bed. Taking a deep drag on her cigarette, she glanced at Brynn's fat back rising and falling with his now gentle snoring. She could see where his vest ended and the fleshy, goosepimply buttocks thrust upwards indecently. Remembering the novel she'd finished reading the day before, a wicked little thought took shape in her mind, as she contemplated the glowing end of her ciggy. 'Why not', she mused. He was well insured, think of a life without Brynn, and with money. What a laughable idea, but it would never work, would it? When she'd read what happened in the book, it had seemed hilarious, but of course it wasn't quite so amusing for the cow. Well, she could just try, couldn't she? It would give her something to do all night, because she knew she'd never get to sleep now. So she waited, just smoking her cigarette and holding her lighter in her right hand. At last, it came, the 'ill wind' that blew nobody any good, least of all Brynn, and she acted swiftly. With her feet she thrust the quilt down the bed, flicked the lighter and the flame ignited the gas, 'Just like lighting the oven,' she thought. What happened next was mercifully a frenzied blur of action and reaction. Whenever Madge tried to think about it later, there was always a blankness of mind warding off reality.

Suffice it to say, the widow Madge, (after she'd told her story to the police of her husband's digestive problem and her smoking in bed prior to it setting alight), was met with great sympathy all round. She gave a terrific performance because she was, after all, in a great state of shock, as she had never really imagined that her strategy would ever work.

All went smoothly at the inquest; The Coroner gave a verdict of Accidental Death and implored the hapless widow not to blame herself for the tragedy, and just to be thankful that she'd escaped only slightly singed after heroically trying to extinguish the blaze.

There was just one, small, niggling anxiety for her. She couldn't find the book. Silly to worry really, but she would have liked to have disposed of it. Anyway, after all the Insurance policies were sorted out, leaving her forty thousand pounds better off, she sold up, moved to a new district and started to live life to the full.

However, things changed one day about six months later, when she answered a knock at the front door to a very presentable young man. This same young man incidentally, had a wife, two toddlers and a large overdraft (though he felt that he might have access to the means of reducing the latter in the very near future). His face seemed vaguely familiar, but she couldn't place him until he introduced himself to her.

'Don't you remember, I came with the Forensic boys the night of your late husband's unfortunate accident. I've been meaning to get in touch with you because I borrowed a book from your shelf that night, 'The Trials and Tribulations of a Vet'. Madge looked up at him in sick horror.

'You know,' he continued, 'the one with the story in it of the vet called out in the middle of the night to see to a cow with stomach problems. The said vet then passes a flatus tube to release the gas from the bulging bowel.

17

Unfortunately it was dark in the barn, so he decided to light a candle, the worst thing he could have done. The naked flame went too near the gas and set both cow and barn on fire. And we both know what happened then don't we Madge? Fatal for the poor old cow. Remember?'

She remembered all right. He shouldered his way past her into the hallway of her pleasant bungalow.

'I think you and I will be seeing a fair bit of each other in future, don't you Madge?'

Chill Factor

by

William Spencer

As fridges go, it was too big for one person, but I liked the way the small top freezer shared a circular recessed handle with the large bottom half, very neat, very eye catching. Pity there were no release catches fitted to the inside.

It didn't cost me anything though, because my plastic bounced and the repo. man never called to collect it. Probably because some of their cheques bounced too, after they did a flyer, leaving behind much bigger debts than mine. So maybe that's why somebody decided to supernaturalise my fridge, as a morality lesson. Now I wish they had repossessed it, and I'll tell you why.

I'd lain awake for a couple of hours this particular night, too hot and tired to sleep after watching the TV late film, it was an old style horror film, but don't jump to any conclusions about an over-active imagination. What happened, happened.

As I said, I lay there, thinking mostly of my last can of lager in the fridge, all tangled up with the empty holes in the plastic holder where the other five cans had been until, inevitably, I stood up with my hand on the kitchen door. I'm still not absolutely sure how I got there, I've no memory of getting out of bed. Dream walk? Could be. But what was to follow makes it pretty unlikely.

I opened the door, reached for the light switch, but didn't press it. There was no need to. The bottom door of the fridge was wide open, spilling out a misty bluish glow that shimmered across the floor in front of the fridge until it reached my bare feet, which felt as if they had been hammered down with icicle nails. I couldn't move an inch, although I really wanted to. Believe it. I felt both stupid and very frightened. It's true what they say, your hair does rise, but only on the back of your neck, maybe my hackles rose, as the storytellers put it. Neither was I in a dreamlike state or trance. Every detail was perfectly clear. Completely aware of where I was, that I still had a strong thirst, and was feeling much colder than I should have felt.

The kitchen was absolutely silent, no noise from the fridge's compressor, nothing from the outside, just an unnatural stillness, the illuminated floor space and a peculiar shape almost filling the lower fridge cabinet, a shape with a very pale blue face above a child's curled up body, knees drawn up to its chest and looking very babyish with a thumb in its mouth. No way could I turn my eyes away from the almost transparent closed eyelids which slowly began to open until they reached their widest, allowing two of the most reproachful looking eyes I have ever seen, hold my own in a frightening stare that seemed endless, increasing my sense of fear until something in my mind told me I had taken enough, and I lost all sense of awareness. maybe I fainted.

Somehow later, I got back to my bed, a shaking heap under the blankets. I can't remember getting out of there, just a frantic dash up the stairs with a mind in turmoil as I tried to make some sense out of it, what did it mean if it was meant to mean anything, and why me, I mean I'm totally disinterested in kids, marriage too come to that, so what was I trying to read into it?

Friday morning came without sleep. I managed to get back to the kitchen door. It was shut, so I must have had enough presence of mind to shut it. Reluctantly, very reluctantly, I opened it. The kitchen was filled with light. A really bright sunlight bouncing off the shiny unit tops and doors. Especially the fridge door, now tightly shut. Who shut it though? Not me, I can promise you that, but now I opened it very slowly. Nothing. Except the usual under-defrosting round the two star freezer door, items with sell-by dates so old that carbon dating would be the only way to read them, and my solitary lager. And a toddlers dummy. That did it. That's all I needed. Because I had just begun to disbelieve that anything had happened at all, but that impossible appearance of a semi frozen dummy gave me such a shock, I made an immediate decision to get rid of the damn fridge. Prize possession or not, albeit dishonesty, it had to go. I was also left in no doubt whatsoever that some kid had died in it.

I wondered if the discount store knew anything about it. Had it been sold before? Maybe the tragedy occurred soon after the installation and that's why it looked new. I wouldn't have put it past that store manager to take it back into stock for re-sale, keeping stum about its history.

I made a hot, strong, black coffee, drained it in one long draught and felt ready to do what I'd made up my mind to do. The main door was to come off before it went anywhere, to ensure that the same kind of tragedy couldn't happen, because by now I had reached the conclusion that I'd been sent a message from the beyond. A message that read : This refrigerator became a coffin and it would be sacrilegious to re-use it as a fridge. Maybe you wouldn't agree with my logic, but that's the way I saw it and still do. In fact the idea of removing the door was partly due to my own built-in brand of the same logic, ie. one corpse, one coffin. So perhaps I'm not all bad after all. And who knows? maybe I'll chalk up some merit marks for my after-life.

Just one problem. I couldn't find the bloody hinges. They were cleverly concealed somewhere at the top and bottom of the smoothly swinging solid door. So what did I need to do next? My natural innate cunning gave me the obvious answer : get someone else to do it for me. The disposal experts of course. I phoned the local free-of-charge-disposal council office, who assured me they would collect it that afternoon, so I 'phoned my office, pleaded temporary incapacity, had a pub lunch, returned feeling a sense of wellbeing that hadn't all come from a couple of pints of best bitter, and waited.

They came. Two hefty lads with a pickup truck and built-on small crane. No trouble at all for them to tilt it back on to a hand trolley and wheel it out, minus the contents of course. I couldn't have touched anything out of it after what had happened, so I binned the lot. Couldn't find the dummy though. Completely disappeared. Somehow, that didn't surprise me. After all, the point had been made.

Before they drove off, I noticed the red haired one looking down the side passage of my house. An opportunist I thought; so I deliberately/accidentally stepped out of the kitchen door into his path.

'Owt else you want to go?' he ad libbed. I told him no, sizing him up as a very devious opportunist and wondering if he had any ideas about where the immaculate fridge would finally end up, so I spun him a tale about it having a failed compressor unit that just wouldn't be worth any repair cost. But whether or not he was taken in, I couldn't be sure, because he seemed to be sizing me up until his mate shouted, 'Come on Robbo, two more pick-ups yet.'

Sunday lunch found me again at the pub bar. Across at the bar opposite stood Robbo. We stared, his eyes had a haunted look. Now I was sure where the fridge had gone. Especially after he left without finishing his pint. So did I soon after. I soon realised I had taken a wrong turn and the lane became a narrow path that led to an unofficial tip. We were green when seen. But why had I turned off the main lane? I looked ahead and saw it gleaming in the shaded clearing. How? The answer came immediately . . . Robbo. He also must have had a vision, only he couldn't take it to the official tip because it wouldn't be on his worksheet Saturday morning or maybe the tip was shut that day. Serve him right for nicking it.

I experienced a feeling of deja vu when a cold familiar feeling travelled from my feet to my hackles. My hand of its own accord lifted to the circular handle and pulled open the door. There he was, the same little boy. The same colour but without the shimmering light and very much in the dead flesh. This time I felt only pity. He looked to be asleep with his thumb in his mouth.

Now what I want to know is who was to blame? Was it a divine intervention that misfired? Or was it a time slip? Did I bring that kid's death forward by getting rid of the fridge too soon? I mean what really came first, the vision or the tragedy?

Egg or chicken? Chicken or egg?

The Blackbird

by

Ivor Cowdy

When at five that afternoon Stewart glanced from his son's wide open bedroom window, Mather was still sitting upright next door on his folding canvas chair. The old man sat unmoving in the middle of his dry lawn, his head fallen a little to the right, a book he had been reading slipped to the withered grass at his feet. By his side an empty glass sparkled in the hot sun.

'I don't like it,' Stewart murmured to his wife, his brow furrowed. 'He's so still, hasn't moved for hours.'

'Aren't you imagining? Let me see.' Margaret also spoke in a low voice, afraid their talk would carry - and leaned cautiously past her husband on the sill of their young son's brightly painted den. She sighed. 'Probably asleep. He is old and it's very warm. The heat's enough to make anyone nod. Why's he wearing ear phones though?'

Stewart glanced again. The bedroom they were in despite the heat was relatively shaded at this time of day. Outside, making the room darker, the sun glared off a spread of neat drought-hit suburban gardens. The old man was indeed wearing a pair of bright yellow ear-protectors.

'I suppose they're to cut out the radios. Everyone's outside.'

'That's going a bit far . . .'

'Why? He lives alone, he has fences. No one sees.'

'Still seems weird,' Margaret insisted.

'Only got himself to please. Who wants a noisy garden?'

'Even so, d'you think he's alright?' Margaret now was a shade more worried, fretting slightly. She added, 'I don't like to interfere - but why not call out - to make sure?'

'Leave it a while,' Stewart said. He was a little embarrased, having started the matter. 'He wouldn't hear anyway.'

Margaret sighed again and turned from the window and Stewart, perhaps to justify himself further, said, 'I'll see later if he's still there. After all we hardly know him. What's for tea?'

Mather had padded out to his garden after a frugal lunch. He carried folding chair, book, glasses, ear-protectors and a soft drink and slowly and solemnly set up camp with his back to the house. He muttered a little about bad taste in neighbourhood music but was not unduly bothered, knowing his ear-protectors shut out what he termed 'jungle drums' and the assorted sounds of do-it-yourself tools and grass-mowers.

For a while he blissfully read a book on classical music, complacent that the noise all around was at bay but then, heavyheaded with the heat, laid his book face down on his lap and decided to rest. It would be for just a few minutes.

22

Removing his glasses, Mather reached down to place them neatly by his seat. That was several hours ago. Now the old man had had a stroke and was dying.

So it finishes like this, came the mild thought. I'm amazed I'm not shocked. In fact I'm quite unastonished, unable to move yet it all feels so peaceful, right. There's no pain. No nervousness. It just seems absolutely certain, sure, that I musn't worry, perhaps couldn't even if I tried. (Mather, in his head, smiled to himself.) I wonder even if I would worry if I could. It certainly seems unlikely, also pointless. What an end though - so quietly, after all the fear, after the speculation. What an end. It's not hurting either. It's just drifting, without harm, letting go, like a sort of swimming into warm seas, on a day like this too. What a day. Even the heat doesn't bother me any more. And of course I can't hear a thing. And I've no regrets. Plenty of unfinished business - or have I? - but nothing I feel a need to try to fight back to life for. I hope no one tries a rescue. (Is that now possible? Am I too far gone?) I just want to go. I'm not even tired, just beautifully at peace with things. Not a care. How tranquil, how lucky. It comes to this then. 'Death where is thy sting . . .?' 'Death be not proud' et cetera, et cetera, et cetera. How blissful. How warm. This seems to be it. I'm going.

'That man next door's very still,' chimed young Robin, jumping down two steps of the stairs at a time.

'Mister Mather to you. Don't spy on people,' Stewart said shortly.

'But he's very still,' the boy insisted. 'He was there when I washed for tea and he's not moved since.'

Stewart and his wife glanced straight-faced at each other across the lounge.

'I bet he's forgotten it's tea time,' the boy continued. 'I bet he's hungry though.'

'Go and play,' Stewart ordered. 'At the front. I don't want you disturbing people. Why don't you go down the avenue, play with your new friend at number eleven?'

The boy, as though fired from an invisible bow, shot towards the front door.

'Don't be late!' Margaret desperately shouted - but the boy was gone. The front door of the house slammed and crockery on the dresser vibrated instantly.

Husband and wife looked again at each other.

'Think I'll take another look,' said Stewart. 'Can't do any harm. I don't like being nosey but . . .' Dropping the evening paper he started to rise from his armchair, pretending casualness. The chair creaked once in protest.

'Might as well look,' said Margaret. Her face was slightly pinched with worry. She gulped. 'What shall we do if anything's wrong?'

'Don't start presuming,' said Stewart, trying on a smile, keeping his voice steady. 'As I say, I'll just take a look.'

He started to run up the stairs as lightly as he could.

Slowly, pensively Margaret went on clearing tea things, listening hard for any sound above. In the heat none of the family had eaten much of the salad she had made. Now she scraped messes from plates.

In a few moments Stewart was back, his face showing a smile of relief he tried to hide without success.

'It's all right,' he announced. 'Just as I got to the window I'm sure I saw him move. He's alive all right.'

'It's still a long time,' said Margaret, unconvinced. 'He's been an awful long time out there.'

'Nonsense. Lovely day like this. Who wouldn't want to make the most of a nice spell of weather?'

Evening shadows were reaching out. Despite protests young Robin had just been put down and his parents were resting briefly in their adjacent bedroom, a little ruffled from the nightly struggle, all the upstairs windows still wide open in the heat. A last radio poured popular music out nearby. A not-too-distant mower hummed and whined and fretted.

'I can't see well from here,' said Margaret, her nose amid abundant white lace curtains which stirred faintly in the hint of an evening breeze. 'He's still there though.'

'Could have been in and out of his house a dozen times,' Stewart said manfully. 'We haven't been watching all the time. Must have taken at least twenty minutes for tea ourselves. Perhaps he ate then.'

'Perhaps,' said Margaret. She remained unconvinced and sensed her husband was just as worried but trying to be brave and masculine and keep up a good front.

Outside, the breeze was growing. It was Midsummer's Eve. Next door Mather's thin white hair stirred in the draught.

Suddenly a late blackbird was on the grass: dark, intense, yellow-beaked, its eyes watchful, alert. The couple next door gazed down. The bird pecked and darted, seemed to listen, stared, pecked and darted, cocked its head, ever ready for cats, predators, its head jerking, looking enquiringly round every few instants. On the lawn it was vulnerable and knew it. Ignoring the old man it circled near his feet but then came close to him. Just then the last radio stopped. The silence was complete, as though the whole world had been told to hush.

'I'm going down,' Stewart said abruptly. In a rush he was tumbling downstairs. A faint dismal cry came from Robin's darkened room.

In a moment, calling out once ahead, Stewart was clambering clumsily up the high wooden fence between his own garden and next door. His shoes banged and slipped on the wooden panels and he barked one shin. Muttering nervously he gained the top and leapt awkwardly to a flower bed. Stems cracked. Margaret's head was thrust from the window above, white lace framing her face, making her nun-like.

With a staccato 'dik-dik-dik' the blackbird took off along the garden on a long low swooping flight before rising and beating swiftly away.

'Is he alright?' Margaret's low voice came.

Stewart had reached Mather and was bending, looking intently. He did not touch the old man. Then he straightened and glanced towards his wife, remembering to shade his eyes from the low late-evening sun. His smile was a little wan.

All he said was: 'Who do you phone when someone's dead?'

Madam Rosie

by

Naffousa Turner

Rosie had poured herself a cup of strong black coffee and was sat back in her chair, just staring at the breakfast she had prepared only minutes earlier. Now however, her appetite had disappeared along with her sense of well being.

That July morning had started well, in Blackpool, where she lived and worked as Madam Rosie. The sun was shining as she climbed out of bed, and slipped her feet into her slippers then pulled on her dressing gown. She opened the bedroom curtains of the spacious flat she shared with her daughter Nadine. She opened her bedroom door and padded her way down the hall to Nadine's bedroom, to wake her up for work. Nadine got up straight away, but took her time in the bathroom as usual and was now on the last minute. She came into the kitchen and helped herself to a piece of toast.

'Mum, you've not forgotten I'll not be home tonight, I'm staying at Julia's for the weekend.'

'No, love I haven't forgotten,' she drawled out in her Spanish accent. But you take care now,' she said as she followed her daughter down the stairs and through the shop, to see her off to work.

Rosie closed the door after her daughter had left, and proceeded to straighten the chairs and the magazines that were on the table in the middle of the room, as the people came in for a consultation this is where they sat and waited. The walls in this room were full of photographs of Rosie and her husband Ramon when he was alive, with many many famous people who had come for consultations from Rosie. She was a very famous psychic, and fortune teller.

The sign outside Rosie's shop read: The Past and The Future as told by Rosie. She was from a long line of fortune tellers. She had made her way back upstairs, when suddenly she shuddered, the air was thick suddenly, and she had a strong sense of foreboding. Once she was back in the kitchen, she had made herself the breakfast she was now staring at. She had finished her coffee now and decided she would go and do some shopping to try and shake this feeling she had, she took her slippers off and put her shoes on, followed by her jacket. She picked up her handbag and shopping bag and made her way downstairs and out the door.

The sun felt warm on her face, giving it that glowing feeling, as she reached the shops, soon her time was taken up with shopping, and so she forgot for a moment the feeling she had sensed earlier.

After shopping she made her way to the hotel where her best friend Polly worked. She made her way into the coffee house area. As she entered, Polly spotted her and made her way over. Wearing a grin from ear to ear, and carrying a coffee. Rosie flopped down into the first welcoming chair she came to.

'Hi, Polly, oh, my feet are killing me,' she said, slipping her shoes off under the table.

'How are you? Did you go dancing last night as you said you were?' Polly was just saying she did go and had a good time, when a crowd of men piled into the coffee shop.

'Oh drat, it's those seminar people,' Polly murmured, 'they're here for the week. I'd better go and see to them, see you later.'

Rosie sat up stiff, and *shuddered*, she felt it *again*, the *foreboding*. It was *here* and *now again*, but this time stronger. She looked at the crowd, it was something to do with them.

Three of them were talking, two were trying to calm the other one down.

'It's only a game . . . management games . . . you shouldn't have lost your cool like that, you lost to Carl, the moment you blew up, and started shouting,' Dave said calmly.

'Game or no bloody game, he's not going to make a fool of me like that,' Tony said with ferocity.

'Anyway,' Mike said, 'forget it now, schools out. I'm going to get some lunch. Then tonight . . . it's Friday night . . . my time for hitting this town in a big way! Who's for it?' he shouted out to the room full of men. They all cheered and agreed with him.

Rosie finished her coffee, and went over to say goodbye to Polly explaining, that she had to get back and open up.

Rosie worked right through until six o'clock that Friday afternoon. She closed her shop door, and made her way up to the flat. She was feeling ravenous now after missing her breakfast and only having a sandwich for lunch. She made herself a big dinner, using the fresh Haddock she'd bought that morning.

She sat watching the television all evening, until twelve o'clock, then made her way to bed. She'd not been asleep long or so it seemed to her, when she suddenly awoke. She put on the bedside light so she could see the time. Three thirty the clock registered.

Rosie tossed and turned after that, she couldn't understand her own restlessness. It wasn't like her, usually she slept like a top. But now she couldn't find sleep, it totally escaped her.

In place of sleep, were those flashes. A red scarf. A hand with a strawberry birthmark on the back of it. She got up and made herself a drink of coffee. She knew there would be no more sleep for her tonight. The following day she was lazing about the flat, catching up on the sleep she'd missed out on.

That Saturday afternoon, Polly came hammering on the front door full of excitement. Rosie let her in and they made their way back up the stairs with Polly jabbering on so fast Rosie couldn't make head nor tale of what she was saying. She sat her down.

'Now,' Rosie said. 'Slowly, tell me what's happened.'

'Well, the police came to the hotel about two o'clock, this afternoon and they've arrested a man called Carl. As word has it, in connection with a woman's death in the town. Apparently they've found a letter from this Carl to this woman called Sandra after she'd broken off an affair with him, saying he couldn't live without her and if he couldn't have her nobody else would either.' Rosie and Polly talked for about ten minutes further, then Polly left saying she had to get back to work before anybody missed her.

Later that day, when Rosie had closed the shop, she was watching the news when it came on about the local murder. The Chief Inspector in charge was a friend of hers. He'd asked for her help on more than one occasion. She'd give him a ring later. In fact she wouldn't ring him, she would go to the station first thing in the morning.

She changed her mind after sitting there thinking about it, and gave Chief Inspector Marsdone a call.

'Hello Rosie. What an unexpected pleasure. What can I do for you.'

'Well . . . er . . . I don't exactly know how to start now,' she said.

'Come on Rosie, it's not like you to be lost for words. Out with it.'

'Okay. It's about the case you're working on at the moment. Has the man you've arrested got any visible marks on his body, only last night. . .' Rosie went on to tell him about the red scarf, and the strawberry birthmark, 'And there was one more thing,' she explained to him.

'Oh . . . I see, Rosie I know in the past you've been spot on, but are you as sure about this one.'

'Positive, absolutely positive,' she said adamantly.

Dave and Mike had left the hotel and called at Tony's house, concerned about how he was taking the news of his wife's death.

All three were sat in the lounge, with Tony wearing the suit he had worn Friday night out on the town. It was the first thing he had put his hands on when they got him out of bed to tell him about his wife's murder.

The Chief Inspector knocked and was admitted into the house, along with his number one, Jenkins, and began to question Tony in front of the other two men who looked on in disbelief. About his movements on the Friday night.

Tony laughed and said: 'We all went out together; except for Carl who said he was going to the pictures.'

'Is that the suit you wore on Friday night?' the Inspector asked. 'Only if it is we'll want to have it checked out with forensics, against the red scarf, found at the scene of the crime. I really am sorry to put you through this.' He carried on. 'But it is our duty you know.'

Tony laughed. 'You can't be serious Inspector, of course there's bound to be some of that fibre from the scarf on some of my clothes. My wife wore it lots of times.'

'Well, that'll be all for now, if we need you we'll be in touch.' He turned as if to go, then turned back. 'Oh, there was one more thing. Did your wife wear false finger nails?'

Tony's face turned white. 'Yes she did, why do you ask.'

'Well, apparently when we found her she had one missing. Jenkins, look in his turn-ups.'

Jenkins pulled down Tony's turn-ups and out fell one ladies *false finger nail*.

Inspector Marsdone, muttered under his breath: 'Nice one Rosie,'

Tony was arrested.

Somewhere Different

by

E Spenwood

My husband and I dined out last night. As the mist was still hanging over the 'ills, we had a change from our usual haunt. I use the word haunt intentionally in this instance. We went to a place t'other side of Todmorden. Now, Tod has a reputation for being a 'back wood', and this was definitely back of Tod.

Friends had been there and told us the bar snacks were of the hearty, filling quantities and they had Taylors on tap. Fine. Interesting. Worth trying we thought. We tried.

We were warned that the car park was before the pub. It was. One hundred yards before. Up an 'ill, park the motor, down some steps and along and along and along a path to a stone building set into the 'illside. we entered. Inside it was dark and rustic but it had a bar which Ian made for. Nice lady served him and we also ordered a steak sandwich, salad and chips. Not too pricey.

It wasn't even busy so we had a fair choice of seats. The rooms seemed to go back forever, it had obviously been a row of cottages at one time which had been knocked through. I wanted to go to the far end to see how far back it went but Ian saw a fireplace and we sat by the window in that room. No fire though.

Decor included framed spiders - Blue Blackbird Eater, Tarantula - and a Blue Nymph. Now I was always under the impression that a nymph was a fairy-like creature, on the lines of fair maids and perhaps fair men. Tree nymphs flitter from tree to tree through woodlands and glades don't they? This nymph had a definite appearance of a beetle - a big beetle. Gone off nymphs.

Other wall adornments were heads of deer, buffalo, stags, badger, 'quaint' Gothic written rhymes about the pub and lots and lots of bedpans. Someone must have had a fetish about bed pans - they were in all shapes and sizes and conditions. One was even in its original packing - nailed in and stuck on the wall next to the tarantula! Fancy sitting on that.

The rafters were decorated with ancient saws and hammers and taps and other such manual work-type reminders so we didn't look too much towards the ceiling.

It was around this time the cold began to seep through to us. There were radiators which were fed by pipes that felt warm - I felt one that ran along the wall beside me. However, they were not having much effect on the temperature in the room. The food arrived as we were beginning to look around for a warmer corner.

Big bread rolls filled with hot beef slices, salad, and lots of crispy chips. Hearty indeed. Accompanied by a good pint - and a half - of Taylors. Happiness! If the temperature surrounding the food had been higher maybe the food would have stayed warmer longer. As this was not the case, the food quickly cooled. We ate as long as it was warm - fortunately we had our fill.

Having had our fill of food, we began to look around for seating away from the window. We went to a bench at the other side of the room where we felt warmer - slightly. Unusual table in front of this bench - the top was cut from a tree trunk and it was obviously the first slice off as the surface had a more than slight curve. Care was needed when placing glasses on this table top.

As Ian went to the toilet, I settled back to listen in on surrounding conversations - as is my habit. One can assess the clientele in this way. I had already noticed that I was overdressed - in skirt and jumper. Not dressy but not tatty was my mistake. This was definitely a place to dress down for.

The accents were not local either - slightly plum in mouth and most surely educated - I could tell by the references to colleges and schools and education in general. Definitely a trendy pub for the intellectual. I now began to feel overdressed and under intelligent.

Ian returned and began to tell of his adventures. The light was not excessive in the main area but it got darker on his way to the Gents. His first problem was deciding which was the Gents and which was the Ladies. The doors were marked but it was so dismal he had difficulty seeing which was which. He had to get close to the doors to peer at the signs - hoping that the door he was peering at wouldn't be opened by a lady coming out of the Ladies - this would have indicated which door was the wrong one but his position could have been misconstrued. Luckily it didn't and wasn't. He went into the Gents and did what he had to do against what he hoped was the correct wall - it still being not overly light.

Ian liked the beer. It was flowing down well. We chatted - quietly to hide our local accents in this local pub. Not that we would have been ridiculed - the type of people that go into this type of public house respect the locals and like to listen to their views and accents. All part of the 'getting to know life as it really is and not as they live it'. Served me right for looking down on Tod!

The end of the evening came and, as Ian went to shed surplus fluid before we went, I had a final look - upwards was the area I had so far neglected. The lights were interesting. Wooden structure hanging from the ceiling, three lights hanging from the wooden structure covered - almost - by lampshades. On studying them I came to the conclusion that the tatters of these lampshades were held together by the webs of the framed spiders - or similar creatures.

Ian returned. I commented on the lampshades and the place in general. One felt one was in another era - if not another century. Not quaint - while the bare stone walls were not filthy they had a definite murky appearance. The tables were obviously of the put together variety and the faded curtains and flagged floors looked original, not just for effect.

Carefully placing his empty glass on the convex surface of the table, and with a grin on his face, I said that not everything was olde worlde - he had looked around more this time in the Gents and seen a condom dispenser on the far wall - containing 'fruit flavours'.

Splitting Image

by

Doris Kirby

Of humble parentage, in fact, of the Venetian Plain Glass Company, and sold from a tray marked 'imperfect', I was taken, as I thought by chance, in the shabby handbag of a singularly unattractive woman to the Island of Murano. We were watching a demonstration by craftsmen glass blowers.

'Please ladies,' their spokesman called, 'hand in your unadorned hand mirrors. Ten thousand lira are at stake for the one of us who can transform the plain in to the most exquisite of glasses. No charge at all to you, only the price of a velvet-lined case to protect your embellished mirror from breakage. Our work is a gift from us to our visitors.'

Ugly and undistinguished, I was in keen demand for I offered the biggest challenge. As we stood absorbed by the men's skill, the greasy odour of the melting glass mingled with the noise and heat of the furnace's fury. The spectators strained forward marvelling.

The temperature was Hades-hot, and I feared for my survival, but my ordeal was rewarded. Valentino won the money from his work on me. Ruby and gold flowers garlanded my edges. Then onlookers gasped at my transformation. 'It is beautiful, exquisite,' they cried. 'Changed into a treasure.'

But when I was being handed back to Maria, my rightful owner, with a request for several thousand lira for a case befitting such a valuable object, she had to refuse it. 'I haven't got that sort of money,' she protested. 'I am just a poor wait-ress on my day off. You will have to take it back.'

Tears were in her voice.

A stetson-hatted tourist nudged forward.

'Will you take eighty dollars for it, Madam? My daughter back home would be real glad to have it as a little souvenir.'

She shook her head. 'I am hoping that it will be worth more than that to me, even without its case.'

'For its beauty?' the man queried. 'It's certainly real pretty.'

'No,' she murmured sadly, 'for a private reason.'

'A hundred dollars, then?'

But Maria edged away. 'There will be others. Just wait for the next demonstration.'

In full view of the audience she moved towards the cash desk and offered back the case. 'I'll just take my mirror. You heard my position.'

I heard too, with great surprise, what the cashier whispered to her. 'You did well today, Maria. There are many mirrors and many potential buyers present. I will send your commission on to you.' Then, in a voice intended to be heard by all he persuaded her to take me and my fancy box free of charge. 'We can't leave this little signora both glassless and moneyless can we?'

The audience murmured their appreciation of his generosity, and implored their Tour Guides to allow them stay for another demonstration, with a chance to buy examples of this delicate craft.

The American followed Maria and me from the glassworks into the burning sunshine.

'A hundred and thirty dollars then.'

She hesitated and then agreed. 'Oh, all right then. The money will be useful to me.'

Now cushioned in my velvet-lined receptacle, I almost cracked with pride. I was no longer 'imperfect' a 'reject'. For the first time in my life I was coveted.

I was sad in a way that my ownership had changed. I had been sorry for Maria. She, too, was plain and unattractive. I had felt empathy with her when she had discovered me in a shabby, discarded handbag. Then we were both unfavoured by the Gods. She, gaunt and graceless, I, just a piece of common glass. But now, I had been embellished and felt romantic. If only by an act of magic my new beauty could have been reflected onto her plain features as she looked at me. But it was not to be. For while my purchaser was still poised on the Bridge of Sighs, she passed into the shadows of a crumbling palace.

I never saw her again.

The man now unlatched the container to take another admiring look at me. 'Some trinket this,' he said appraising me. 'A real humdinger. Pearl will think this mighty cute.'

But at that moment, a sightseer jogged his elbow and I was catapulted through the dazzling Italian sunshine landing safely onto the black robes of a Nun sitting in a water-bus as it emerged from beneath the bridge.

'Sister Philomena look, oh look, our prayers are answered again. It is a present from Heaven. It is saleable and will provide another meal for our orphans. God works in a mysterious way indeed.' Two pairs of white hands were raised in a prayer of gratitude.

I was a little dazed by my all but unbroken and delighted that I was to stave off the children's hunger. To achieve this, I was sold to an English surgeon who was spending a few days in a retreat in Assisi.

'A perfect gift for staff nurse Cameron. She is a worthy member of the Burns Unit in our Centre of Excellence. She will truly appreciate it,' he ruminated.

'I will never part with it,' she promised when it was given to her a fortnight later. 'It is exquisite, unique.' And looking up into the doctor's face she searched for a more personal reason for the present than merely of her skilled nursing.

He was uneasy now wondering whether he should have bought it for her. He was singularly devoted and loyal to his wife, Anita. Staff nurse Cameron propped me up against a white vase of pink carnations on her desk, looking frequently into my face searching for an alchemy which would stir the doctor to see her for the first time.

I would not be a part of her plan and clouded myself in condensation.

No mirrors were allowed in the Acute Burns Unit. Charred faces, frightening disfigurement, mutilated features must not be seen by the patients until they had their skin grafts and pedicle replacement treatments. The ordeal of staring at their terrifying reflections would be too traumatic, too daunting even to the most courageous of victims.

I had heard this and tried to keep a very low profile, but one day Flt/Lt Mason knocked on the staff room door, and before I could be whisked out of sight, he had entered the office.

'I heard you had one,' he choked through his missing mouth. 'Let me see.'

Snatching me away from the white vase, he looked deeply into my pretty countenance and screamed.

'Hideous, unbearable, grotesque!' he cried. 'I can't live with it.' And he fled into the night. But not before he had flung me against the wall.

I lay splintered into a cruel carpet of jagged pieces.

I would have done less harm if I had stayed in the 'imperfect' tray.

Micky

by

Bernard Byrne

Little Billy loved his dog Micky; they went everywhere together. When Billy came home from school, off they would go into the fields for a run. They spent many happy hours this way. Always, they would come home both tired and hungry, and many times dirty, but always happy.

One day, however, Billy came home alone; he was very upset, sobbing fit to burst, and trailing the dog's lead behind him. His mother took one look at him and said, 'Billy, what on earth's the matter? Where is Micky? What has happened?'

Billy shook once more in a fit of sobbing. He couldn't speak for some time. 'He, he's d-dead, mum,' he managed to blurt out, 'two greyhounds savaged him, I, I couldn't do anything to stop them. Oh mum, it was terrible.'

'All right, Billy love, just try and tell me what happened.' And so he did.

They had gone off for their usual walk, he told her, and everything was fine. Micky was having lots of fun running this way and that across the fields. Suddenly, two men appeared, each with a greyhound on a leash; they had come to exercise their dogs. They slipped them off their leads and let them have a run. Micky spotted them and ran over to join them. He wanted a bit of fun. They seemed quite happy, all three of them chasing each other and barking with obvious delight.

Then without warning, one of the greyhounds turned on Micky, grabbed him by the throat, and shook him like a rag doll. The other one, scenting blood, rushed in and sank its teeth into Micky's hind leg, and off they ran, dragging the howling, helpless dog between them tossing it in the air and pouncing on it as soon as it made a move to run away. The two men were powerless to intervene and could only stand and watch, with horror, the savage spectacle.

Billy's heart sank. He turned away in despair and began to trudge wearily back home, convinced that he had lost his best friend.

His mother tried to comfort him, but he was too upset and lay on the couch, remembering all the good old days he had spent with his dog and now, he was alone.

There was a knock at the door and Billy's mother went to answer it. Billy was half listening to what was being said. Two boys from further up the street had seen the closing stages of the fight and later watched as Micky had half walked, half dragged himself into a nearby park and was lying under a tree nursing his wounds. Billy couldn't believe it at first but when the boys described the dog he knew it must be Micky. He shot up from the couch and went off to find his dog. Sure enough he was where the boys had said he was. Billy went up to him and looked at his pet. He was a sorry mess. His hair was matted with blood, his throat and back legs had several deep gashes on them. He coaxed him to his feet and led him home. He was so happy he cried all the way and he kept

33

turning around to make sure he wasn't imagining things, and that Micky really was still alive.

The vet took care of Micky and after a few weeks the scars began to heal and he was soon able to go out and about with Billy again. He was never quite the same dog after that, but Billy still found delight in his company. Micky did pass away a few years later from old age, and Billy was by this time old enough himself not to be upset by it. After all, he thought he'd lost him before and he did get a second chance to be with his dog.

Misheard

by

Mary Meadows

I was just putting on my lipstick, to complete the finishing touches of my beauty treatment, which I was hoping might attract the attention of some suitable male company at the pub that evening. A girl may have her dreams! The doorbell rang and I hurried downstairs to let my friend, Jenny, in. 'Are you ready then?' she said, 'let's get going before the Cock-up gets too crowded.'

The Cock-up was the name of our local pub, at least that's what we called it, its real name was 'The Broody Hen'.

As we walked into the pub, we realised it was overflowing, but we managed to find a seat in the corner that wasn't occupied. 'I'll get the drinks,' said Jenny, 'what are you having?' As she walked away to the bar, I saw, sitting at the next table, the most attractive man that I have seen for a long time. A Chippendale look-alike. Tall, dark, handsome. He looked at me and my knees went to jelly. I smiled at him. Then Jenny returned. 'Did you see him?' I whispered.

'Who?' she said in a loud voice.

'Don't turn round,' I said, 'but there's the most gorgeous man sitting at the next table and he smiled at me.' Of course Jenny had to turn round. How embarrassing your best friend can be!

'Would you like me to disappear?' she said.

Which was quite nice of her really. After she had gone to powder her nose, I glanced at the next table, and he was still there, and he smiled and said in a deep husky voice, 'Has your friend gone then?' I nodded, although it wasn't strictly true. 'Would you like a drink?' he said. From then on it was absolute bliss. He told me his name was Garth and that he had just finished with his girlfriend. We had a wonderful evening together, although the pub was crowded and noisy, I hardly noticed. Then just before the pub was about to close, he said something to me that sent my senses reeling. 'I'm thinking of having a sex change,' he said. I looked at him in disbelief. How could such a magnificent male contemplate such a thing? Well you can imagine, I made an excuse and got out of that pub in double quick time. I didn't dare go back for a couple of weeks and that was after Jenny made sure he wasn't around.

I was curious to know what had happened to him, though, so I asked the barmaid.

'Do you remember a bloke that was here a couple of weeks ago, called Garth? Do you know where he went?'

'Oh, do you mean the Chippendale look-alike? He was a great guy, pity he moved on. He said he was thinking of going to Essex for a change!'

An Unwelcome Guest

by

Tim Shearer

'She doesn't want to know you,' said the man. 'Not after what you did to her.'

She tried to remember what she'd done, but all she could remember were details: a man's voice shouting at her, accusing her of something; Peggy complaining that the windowsills were so dirty you could grow cress on them.

'I only want to talk to her, for God's sake.'

'Well she doesn't want to talk to you, so you'll - don't try and force your way in, now!'

'You'll not get your way with me.'

'I wouldn't want my way with you, not a cranky old woman like you.'

He pushed her roughly away and slammed the door. A shower of dust broke out along the hall; a woman shouted angrily down the stairs; in the upper part of the house a baby began to cry. The object of the man's rudeness, however, appeared quite unperturbed. It didn't surprise her in the least that a man she'd never met before should call her a cranky old woman and slam a door in her face.

She laid her ear against the keyhole and listened. She could hear the old lady moving about her kitchen, the rubber grips of her walking-frame scraping on the linoleum, a cupboard being opened, a table being laid. 'Peggy?' she said, knocking softly on the door. 'It's Norma . . .' But the door remained closed. 'This is crazy,' she murmured in exasperation. 'Crazy!'

She sat down on the floor and lit a cigarette.

She was a tall, thin, frail-looking woman, with long grey hair and a long grey face. Her clothes, too, were long and grey, a flimsy cotton dress that was too loose round the waist and a shabby cardigan whose frayed sleeves trembled on her wrists like tiny throbbing veins. She'd preserved her figure, but it was not, she considered, a figure that was worth preserving. It was lanky and angular, a figure of fun.

The door opened and the man with the pimply face reappeared.

'Are you still here?' he said angrily.

'Could you just tell Peggy that Norma's here?' she said in a placatory voice, thinking that perhaps there'd been some misunderstanding, that he'd confused her with someone else.

'I've told her. She doesn't want to know you.'

It suddenly occurred to her that she had in fact met him before. He'd been at Peggy's flat one day last week - it was his voice she remembered shouting at her. 'You bought - or she paid for?' she remembered him asking her. She seemed to remember, also, that he'd been rude to her on that occasion as well.

'This is private property,' he was saying now, 'and you're an unwelcome guest. If you've not gone in ten minutes, I'm calling the police.'

It was quite dark now outside; the light of a streetlamp washed in through the windows of the porch. In the house opposite, a family was sitting down to its evening meal; a smell of cooking drifted across the street, and a memory came to her of her own family. It was Christmas; she was in the kitchen preparing lunch, humming as she did so the tune of a song she'd heard that morning on the radio. In the sitting-room Joe and the children were watching television. She could hear Joe mimicking the slow solemn voice of one of the characters in the cartoon they were watching, and the children shrieking with delight. The memory faded, and she had an uneasy sense that the significance of what she remembered had eluded her. For two weeks later, quite unexpectedly, without indeed her even suspecting he was in any way unhappy, Joe had left her.

She opened her handbag and took out a bottle of whisky. She listened to the rain tapping against the windows. She fell asleep.

She was woken by a man's voice, 'What's your name, love? . . . It's all right, I'm not going to touch you . . . How did you get here? . . .'

She closed her eyes again.

'Well?' said the policeman.

'I want to go home,' she spoke quietly, almost inaudibly, but the words seemed to echo in her mind, mocking her like a taunt. Again she thought of Joe, and again she had an uneasy sense that the significance of what she remembered eluded her. In a letter she'd received from him a couple of weeks after he'd left, he'd tried to explain why he felt unable any more to live with her; but the letter hadn't made sense, referring as it did to a staleness in their life together which she had neither felt nor, looking back, could see any sign of.

'I want to go home,' she said again.

She felt suddenly lonely and scared, her heart began to pound as at some impending danger. She opened her eyes. The man with the pimply face was in the hall again. He was talking to the policeman, but she couldn't make out what they were saying. In the light of the streetlamp their faces gleamed garishly, like faces in a waxworks.

'Where's home, love?' said the policeman.

'I don't think she's got anywhere,' said the man with the pimply face. 'She used to clean for the lady in this flat.'

'Used to?'

'She did the dirty on her.'

The policeman nodded. 'Where's home, love?' he said again.

'I've got a lovely home, a lovely sem . . . '

'Well what are you doing here, then? You can't stay here all night. This is private property. Listen,' he said, bending towards her confidentially, 'there's a women's hostel down the road - I'll give them a ring and see if they'll take you, shall I? Just for tonight . . . then tomorrow you can give your friend a ring and sort everything out. All right?'

'I'm not going in a hostel.'

'Look,' said the policeman, beginning to lose patience, 'I don't care where you go, but you can't stay here. This is private prop . . . why are you taking your shoes off?'

'I'll stay here. I'll be all right, I'm tough.'

'You? Tough?' said the policeman. 'Don't make me laugh!' Then suddenly, 'Have you been drinking?' She shook her head. 'What's the smell, then? Somebody's been drinking . . .' She shrugged her shoulders, but he'd noticed the bottle of whisky. 'What's this, then?' he said, tapping the bottle with his boot. 'A coconut?' His voice, all of a sudden, was harsh and hostile; she said to herself, I must be dignified, but something about him daunted her, something implacable and relentless. Hardly aware of what she was doing, she picked up the bottle and, unscrewing the top, lifted it to her lips. But her mouth was numb with cold, and the liquor dribbled onto her dress. The policeman, grave now, and dispassionate, like a doctor conducting an examination, watched her silently. She lowered her head so that she couldn't see his face, but she felt his eyes moving over her, scrutinising her, appraising her . . .

'What are you staring at?' she snapped at him. 'Do I owe you something?' She glared at him, but beneath his hard relentless gaze she felt as bare and exposed as if he'd stripped and searched her.

She looked away and gazed out of the window. Rain was falling heavily now; the street was deserted. Her heart began to pound again; the hall seemed to sway. 'Words could hardly tell you,' Joe's voice said suddenly in her mind, 'no matter how I tried, of all the things you've meant to me, since you became my bride.' They were words that often sounded in her mind, though Joe had not in fact ever spoken them to her. They'd been printed inside a card he'd given her on their third wedding anniversary, a card with a picture of an orchid on the front. Recalling that day now as she looked out across the street, she felt as though she was recalling something she'd read in a novel, so remote did it seem, so strong was her sense of dislocation.

'Right,' said the policeman. 'You've had your last chance. Put your shoes on - you're under arrest. I'm arresting you for creating a disturbance. Do you understand? You're . . . under . . . arrest.'

She continued to gaze out of the window, watching the rain fall, surprised at her own tranquillity. She'd be taken to some grimy police station, and in a room that reeked of disinfectant and stale cigarette smoke she'd be advised of her rights. A policewoman would search her clothing, a record would be made of her arrest. Then she'd be taken to a cell and locked up for the night. In the morning she'd be charged. And yet she felt no sense of injustice, no indignation, no anxiety or fear. She felt, as she watched the rain falling relentlessly on the dark deserted street, nothing.

Second Line Of Strategy

by

W Price

It ain't my fault, but I suppose it's true I've got the biggest ears in Kate's Grill. Mebbe that's why the regulars pour their troubles into them. So I ain't surprised when Bumps Carter flops at my table, gnashing at a sardine sandwich in a sorta gloomy frenzy.

'Woman trouble?' I ask.

He looks at me, like I am talking about some rare specimen of plant life from Upper Orinoco.

'It's Winifred,' he groans.

After he has knocked my tea over, trampled my feet under the table and stuck his clumsy great elbow in my steak and kidney pudding, Bumps unburdens himself.

This Winifred, it seems, is an Amazon-type bird, full of jousts and javelins, and all that jazz. What is more to the point, she ain't impressed with Bumps, who is a local yokel from the nearby hamlet of Bugs Hump, and looks every inch of it. Bubonic sorta - or is it bucolic?

'Strategy, that's what you need,' I suggest. 'Suppose you were able to demonstrate your courage to this Winifred?'

'But how, Jigsy? There ain't no dragons about these days.'

Difficult ain't it? See what I mean about this bucolic business?

'You've got pals,' I explain patiently, 'so - two of three of them stage a phoney attack on you and the chick. You make a great show of beating them off - and bingo - the dame is all over you.'

Bumps shudders from the crown of his massive nut to the soles of his great feet. 'No perishin' fear,' he snaps, 'Winifred is five foot ten and a judo black belt.'

Jigsy my boy, I say to myself, you are nonplussed. But my grey matter is in good shape and I am soon plussed again.

'Right then,' I say, 'we must fall back on our second line of strategy - the fake rescue. Every good general has a second line of strategy.'

'There ain't nobody with your brains, Jigsy.'

Bumps is as subtle as a polar bear in a school of seals; but I gotta admit he is right. Not that it means much. A half-wit would qualify for the intelligentsia in Kate's Grill.

So I am involved and we get down to discussing ways and means.

The following day, about seven in the evening, I am running an unfriendly eye over the river which Bumps has selected for our stratagem. Water ain't my favourite element, even when under control of the municipal taps. Still, I see this ain't a big river, as rivers go. I reckon a good athlete could jump across without getting his feet wet and Bumps assures me it ain't nowhere deeper than four feet.

We scout round for a spot suited to our purpose and decide on a sharp bend with a thicket of hawthorn hiding the approach. Bumps departs for his bird and I take up my position in the hawthorn. A dead uncomfortable position it is too, on account of it being midsummer and the insect life is foraging at full strength.

An hour drags by on the fleeting feet of a sluggish dinosaur. At last I see two figures approaching in the distance. Soon they are near enough for me to recognise Bumps. The chick by his side is big and beautiful. Especially big. She looks as if she has stepped outa the pages of one of them physical culture magazines.

This is it. I flash a glance of distaste at the river. I ain't ever seen water looking so wet. But Jigsy ain't the man to let a friend down, and I take the plunge. Up to my ankles at first and I sure get cold feet. When the water comes up to my chest I rest on my laurels. Enough is enough.

I hear a murmur of voices and Bumps and his bird come into view round the bend of the river. So I go into my act, splashing and screaming like a nervous old lady who is being chased by Jack the Ripper into the arms of the Phantom of the Opera.

'Save! Save me!' I bellow. 'Help! Help!'

The water is bitterly cold and I am sure feeling distressed, so there is a strong note of realism in my histrionics.

The big doll is caught off balance, too surprised to act. Bumps of course, knowing what to expect, is right on the ball. He charges down the footpath like an enraged rhinoceros.

'Keep your head up,' he cries, 'I'll soon have you out!'

And then he crashes on top of me with a mighty splash and we are tangled together at the bottom of the river.

'You lumbering great nit,' I splutter, 'I can't swim.'

'Neither can I,' he bubbles.

Me and Bumps are clinging tightly together like we are each other's last straw. Which I guess we are. Everything is a sorta soupy green twilight. There is no pain and I am waiting for my past life to flash on the screen, like they say happens to a drowning man.

Suddenly, I feel a strong upward movement and my head breaks water. I guess I am heading in the right direction and I am gratified that my attempts at clean living ain't been overlooked.

The first thing I see is a pair of luscious golden legs topped by frilly white panties. Jigsy boy, I say to myself, you've made it. This is Heaven, sure enough.

Before I can sit up and take notice, violent hands are laid on my and I am pummelled and thumped something atrocious. From afar I hear a voice.

'He is coming to. I thought artificial respiration would do the trick.'

Then I am myself again. I see Bumps bending over me with a face full of dismay. The long golden legs come into view and I see they belong to Bumps' chick, who has tucked her frock into her flimsies, like little girls do when they go paddling.

A horrible suspicion is niggling at the back of my mind. The dame musta yanked me and Bumps outa the water. I feel myself go hot and cold at the thought. Rescued by a bird. It's mortifying.

40

Winifred takes charge, like she is Bodicea and me and Bumbs are a couple of serfs beneath her chariot wheels.

'Briskly now!' she cries. 'Back to the village and get out of those wet clothes!'

It ain't easy to be damp and dignified; but I ain't taking orders from no dame. I draw myself up to my full height and stare her straight in the bosom. I open my cakehole; then I close it again. My peepers are wide with a swelling rhythm of roses on the patterned frock and I see why Bumps is anxious to win this Winifred chick.

The moment passes and me and Bumps are being hustled along the path, lashed by the bird's tongue.

'Turn off here,' she calls imperiously, 'there is a short cut to the village.'

I see a five-barred gate and a narrow track beyond leading into the fields. Winifred takes the gate in her stride, with the ease of an Olympic vaulting champion. Me and Bumps tumble after her like a coupla wet codfish. There are two stiles where we repeat our individual performances and then we come to another gate. The bird sails over in good style. Then almost in the same movement she sails back again, trembling in terror.

Brushing my dripping hair from my eyes I peer over the gate. There is a massive black beast blocking the path.

'A - b-bull!' gasps Winifred. 'We've got to turn back.'

The bull fixes me with a red malevolent eye, and I am with the dame. At the same time, I am glad to see she is behaving like a normal female-type. Bulls, I guess, are her Achilles Heel.

Bumps ain't wearing none of this. 'I ain't turning back for no bull!' he roars, male aggression oozing from every pore. He clambers on the gate and I think mebbe his mental faculties are waterlogged. The bull lets out a blood chilling bellow, the bird begins to whimper, and I picture myself giving evidence at the coroner's inquest.

Then like in a dream, I see the bull is moving away and Bumps is holding the gate open, dead nonchalant like. Winifred clings to him like a little girl lost, pouring her adoring peepers all over him, like he is Tarzan and El Cordobez all rolled into one.

They walk along all lovey-dovey and I squelch along behind them, pondering on the mystery of life. All my brainwork gone down the drain and the mission accomplished by a mere quirk of fate. Sorta inscrutable, ain't it? Mebbe Omar Khayyam coulda sorted it out over a coupla figs and a noggin or two, but it is beyond me.

Later on, after we have dried out in the village, I am getting ready to start my jigger, when Bumps dashes up.

'Thanks a lot, Jigsy,' he cries, 'everything is fine.'

He crushes my fingers in his massive fish and treads on my toes by way of bonus. He has just seen Winifred to her bus. His eyes are shining and I guess there are wedding bells, as well as bats, in his belfry.

'I must dash off now,' he says, 'I gotta take the bull back to the shippun.'

'Sh-sh-shippun?' I stammer.

'On my father's farm. That bull is as tame as a tabby cat. He wouldn't hurt a fly.'

He closes one eye in a slow, sly wink.
'Like you said, Jigsy: Every good general has a second line of strategy.'

A Traveller's Tale

by

Ronald Makin

Going on holiday can be such a strain, like last year's jaunt, when I set off for sunny Spain. It started to go wrong, even before I left home. When I washed my hair, by accident, with a bottle of bath foam. I must have looked quite a remarkable sight. Certainly I gave the neighbours a fright!

Then halfway to the airport, I realised I'd forgotten my case. You can well imagine the look on my face. Too late to turn back, at least I had my passport. I suppose I can pick up some clothes when I reach my resort. The good news was I'd be travelling light. Just my holdall to worry about on the flight.

I got to the airport with no time to spare. Pulled on my hat to cover my hair. At the check-in desk, I joined a long queue. That sort of resembled a human zoo. The usual thing, no great surprise, people tripping over luggage, dropping like flies.

Before long, I realised something was drastically wrong. Everyone else's baggage was labelled 'Hong Kong'. I shuffled over a bit, trying to look discreet. Politely smiling as I stepped on people's feet. Desperately hoping I hadn't missed my plane. With my luck, the Costa's have probably had six inches of rain.

As luck would have it, we were delayed for three days. That I managed to sleep at all, never ceases to amaze. The first night I was woken harshly, by a slap across the chops, while I was sleepwalking with my basket, through the duty-free shops. Next night I was strip searched, as I strolled through the 'Red Channel', waking up to find my embarrassment covered with a flannel!

Finally the time came, we were ready to board the plane. I struggled up the staircase, my body racked with pain. As I dropped into my seat, I was in no mood for fun. Why was it so uncomfortable? I was sitting on a gun!

To grab the steward's attention, I waved it in the air. Someone screamed 'Hijacker!' My God this isn't fair. Next thing I knew, I was under attack. Thrust to the floor, someone's knee in my back.

I tried to explain, 'It's all a mistake, some kid's lost his gun, it's only a fake!'

Looks like my holiday's suddenly come to an end. But the good news is I'll have no postcards to send.

Vowing never to go away again, it was at least a year later, when I once more felt the yen. This next excursion was to be a corker, sun, sea and sickness in Majorca. The topless dancing, that was quite a thrill. But too much squid made me quite ill. Mind you, my stomach was already used to the pain, from what was loosely described, as food, on the plane. I really wished I'd stayed at home with mummy, was this the start of my Spanish tummy?

We went along to the Flamenco night, all the hectic dancing was quite a sight. I thought I'd be safe with a bit of paella. But I think that's what brought on my salmonella. A few nights later, stuck for something to do, we took a carriage ride to a barbeque. It was only after several courses, I noticed our driver was missing one of his horses.

In the hotel, there food was no better. I complained to the 'rep', in the form of a letter. This was shortly before her strange suicide. Face down in her soup - funny way to have died!

A couple of days later, feeling much worse, at the medical centre, I consulted a nurse. She didn't really seem to understand. But I came away prescription in hand.

I soon found the chemist, just round the corner. But now I was sweating like I'd just left the sauna. The chemist looked at me as though I was mad. 'Zees tablet my seek dog 'as just 'ad!'

For a while it seemed these pills had done the trick. Until once more I started feeling sick. Getting very desperate now. Better find a cure. Don't suppose it helped too much, downing beers by the score.

Trying to take my mind off my plight. We went for a visit to the local bullfight. I missed most of the action with being so ill. But the final score was Matadors 3 Bulls 0.

I struggled back to my room, got as far as the door. Then collapsed in a heap in the corridor. Someone tried to revive me with a glass of water. Then shoved me on a trolley and left me for the porter. He wheeled me as far as the hotel lounge. Then waited to see what tip he could scrounge. He brought me round with the 'kiss of life'. A much better snogger than my wife!

In the last few years I've seen the world, and have many a tale to tell. But believe me when I tell you, nearly all have been trips to hell! On the nursery slopes in Switzerland, you can watch the novice skiers. Then see them later on, in plaster, now they too have become sightseers.

Italy's not bad I guess. If you're used to all that pasta. But if you're not an expert, spaghetti spells disaster. For all those poor Norwegians, it can't be that much fun. Waiting with their sunglasses on, to catch the midnight sun.

Germany's no fun at all, at any time of year. Full of chaps in lederhosen, swigging great mugs of beer. Have you seen those Greek young men, who dance while wearing skirts? Some people worry if they get too close, and kick them where it hurts!

Watching the Flamenco shows in Spain, can be a thrill. But don't go near the water, unless you fancy being ill.

Crossing the channel into France, wouldn't be quite such a wrench. If when you got into the country, all the people there weren't French! An eyeful of the Eiffel, in Paris, makes them drool. But I'd sooner have the bracing winds, and the tower at Blackpool.

Some people chuck coins in the fountain, after going all the way to Rome. But me - no more the rover. I'll save my pennies and spend my time at home!

A Fifth Kind Of Courage

by

Geoff Fenwick

Walkaway Jones they called him. He had earned that sobriquet because of his penchant for turning his back on an opponent and walking to a neutral corner immediately he had delivered a knockdown blow. There was no arrogance in the action, merely the certainty that the punch had been hard enough to ensure that his rival would not beat the count. The assumption was usually correct; a second knockdown was rarely required.

At nineteen John Henry Jones had become the youngest ever heavyweight boxing champion of the world. He had subsequently defended the title more frequently than the fabled Joe Louis and registered more consecutive knock outs than Black-Jack Billy Fox. He had become the longest reigning heavyweight champion and now, at thirty-five, was close to being the oldest.

A man does not become a professional boxer if he is unable to discomfort his opponents; but the most destructive hitters in the ring are those who develop the split second timing which catches an advancing fighter in the right place at exactly the right time. Walkaway Jones had acquired this skill very early in his career and it had not left him yet.

He had always been a popular champion, taking on the top three contenders each year and avoiding the mismatches and pushovers that had blemished the records of so many of his predecessors. A large proportion of the word's population watched by means of satellite television his progress around the great arenas of six continents, fascinated by his deft footwork, the swift left jab and most of all by the potency of the right cross which terminated so many of his contests in spectacular fashion. But as he approached his 36th year his audience had already begun to watch for something else, sensing the first hints of impending vulnerability. For an ageing boxer is like a trapeze artist or a rider on ;the Wall of Death; the excitement of his performance is heightened by the anticipation that sooner or later he will made a bad mistake.

The forty-ninth defence of his title, against Rocco Canzoneri, took place on a late September night at the start of the indoor season in Madison Square Garden, New York. Canzoneri was not destined to have a lengthy career. His style was too incautious for that. But his youth and strength had carried him through thirty-two contests without defeat and he as a worthwhile contender. Furthermore, there was the possibility that he might wear the old champion down. Such notions are the stuff of boxing promoters' dreams and, sometimes, their fortunes.

A blow by blow description of a prize-fight is the province of the commentator, not the writer. It is enough to record that for several rounds the champion's accurate left jab connected so often with his challenger's face that eventually Canzoneri was goaded into rushing forward without any semblance of defence in an attempt to pin Jones into a corner. At once he was caught with a right cross flush on the jaw. It stopped him in his tracks for just a moment. He shuddered and then, shaking he head like a young bull stunned with a club, he advanced once more.

The crowd was hushed. Perhaps it was not one of the champion's best punches? Three rounds and four hard right crosses later, there was no doubt. A great champion's artillery had finally started to rust.

Thereafter, Canzoneri was only momentarily halted when he was hit by the champion's best punches. Yet for all his relentless advance he was absorbing a systematic beating. Most of his own blows were smothered by Jones' gloves and arms. And all the time, the champion's accurate yet unspectacular left jab drilled into his face.

Canzoneri was caught again with a hard right in the eleventh round. It was no harder than any of Jones' previous attempts but this time he sunk to the canvas more from weariness than shock. He knelt there for several seconds before regaining an upright position. The referee looked at him closely. Canzoneri's face was cut and bruised but his eyes remained defiant and unglazed.

He was in trouble again at the start of the twelfth and last round. He went down once more, this time hauling himself up by the ropes like a fat man getting out of a bath. He leaned against them, steadying himself and waiting for the next attack.

Jones looked at the referee. 'No more,' he whispered.

The referee shook his head and waved him on.

Instinctively, Canzoneri moved towards Jones. The champion measured him with a sharp left and then brought over the last right cross. Halfway through its delivery he changed his mind and the blow slapped soggily and ineffectively into the challenger's face.

It has been said that to be a boxer, five kinds of courage are needed. The first is for simply getting into the ring; the second is for staying there; the third is for when the first bell rings and the fourth is for when constant punishment is being meted out. The fifth is for knowing when to stop.

Jones turned his back on Canzoneri, walked past the referee without a word, ducked through the ropes and was gone before the crowd could grasp what was happening. He was out of the hall and out of boxing within a matter of seconds.

There was no time for him to collect his clothes. Instead he walked out into the open air to where he knew his limousine would be parked.

His driver was listening to the radio, trying to make sense of what was going on inside the stadium. He switched off as Jones appeared.

'Put it back on,' said Jones, ' and get moving.'

The radio was vibrating noisily as the commentator tried to make himself heard over a pandemonium which was entirely of Jones' making. From time to time his voice was audible between upsurges of dull roaring.

'Walkaway really. . . this time. . . never in ring history. . . had the fight of his. . . will boxing ever be. . .'

They were well into the suburbs before the noise subsided and the singsong, show business voice of the M.C. could be heard intoning the result.

'On a retirement after one minute and five seconds of the twelfth round, the winner and new heavyweight champion of the world - *Rocc Oh Canz On Eri*

'That was the hardest fight, Charlie,' said Jones, 'there was never a harder one than that..'

Charlie pretended to concentrate on his driving. It was some time before he replied.

'Maybe, champ, we should wait to see what they say in the papers tomorrow.'

The sweat had dried now and the adrenalin had ceased to flow. Jones felt very tired yet surprisingly content.

'Once you're history, Charlie,' he said, 'tomorrow's papers are something you can do without.'

He wrapped the car rug around him and settled back into his seat.

Charlie said nothing.

A Letter From The Living

by

Jenny Roche

I died two years ago, when I was sixteen, but don't worry, it's really quite nice. In fact I could recommend it to anyone. The actual dying bit was messy, me being splattered all over the road and all, but once you get to heaven you'll see it's a wonderful place. Yes, heaven has an awful lot going for it. There's no pain or suffering, the weather's always fine and we don't have to bother about things like paying gas bills or whether we're going to be nuked by a nuclear accident. The thing I like most about the place is that I don't have to keep my room tidy, eat the proper foods or be home by eleven. It really is heaven.

My family weren't too pleased at my being taken so young. If they'd cried any more our street would have been looking more like Venice than anything else. Mum wailed, 'She had all her life in front of her, and it was the first day of the holidays and we couldn't get a refund.' That's my mother - always keeping her financial head no matter what the crisis. But none of them need have worried. Mum got a few quid when she sold my bedroom furniture and bike, and I'm really happy here.

When Mum and Dad were most upset I would have liked to let them know that even though I was dead I was being well looked after and didn't want for anything. I would have liked to boast about how well my wings were growing but we have to put our names on a waiting list if we want to get a message through a medium. You see, we have bureaucracy and red tape here too. It's a pity because I would have liked to let them know that my going off and dying wasn't just attention seeking, and I wasn't making a nuisance of myself. It was just that the Almighty was short of a few clouds stuffers and he thought I'd be quite good at the job. Nothing more spectacular than that.

I suppose I was quite lucky to get into heaven, because I hadn't led a blameless life. Perhaps not having lived long enough to get into being a rebellious teenager properly, saved me a bit, but when I was six I did pinch a Mars Bar from the sweet shop, and when I was three I put all the eggs from the nest in the hedge into my doll's house and the chicks never got the chance to be born. I hadn't remembered any of these things but St Peter, who keeps a kind of filofax on everybody ever born, showed me them all written down. He even knew about the crib sheet I had for my fourth year exam, and I'd kept that very well hidden. So you see, if the likes of me - a thief, murderer and cheat can get into heaven, you can too. God really is a forgiving sort of fella, but he did say children can't learn wrong from right if they don't know what wrong is and as I'd only ever done each kind of crime the once, and always been sorry afterwards. I'd been well on the road to being a good person.

Heaven took a lot of getting used to at first. Somehow I'd never imagined angels with beards, punk haircuts, hooped necks or wearing every manner of fashion from animal skins and crinolines to denims and saris.

I'd always assumed death to be the great leveller and in heaven everything would be equal, but it's more like Earth really. The Almighty is the big boss and then it goes down through archangels, saints, those who sit at God's right hand and right down to the lowly flawed things like me who have to be content with cloud stuffing whilst the more righteous have all the fun with the lightning and retributions.

You meet some very interesting people in heaven. Only last week I was asking Shakespeare why he couldn't have written in the kind of English that would have made it easier for children to pass their GCSE, but all he could go on about was what he could have done with the royalties from the texts.

As I was saying, heaven really is a wonderful place but I must say it's not as much fun as Butlins - in fact it's the most incredibly boring place ever invented.

You might think I'm being ungrateful but anyone who's being honest must admit there's not much to do here. OK, so I stuff clouds, a few angels twang harps, but apart from watching the world go by, which gets to be a bit like non-stop Coronation Street, there's nothing but mind-boggling boredom. After about six months of it I was in the right sort of mood for livening up heaven with some of the revelry that's normally found in hell.

I started a halo throwing contest with teams drawn from each century. If nothing else it proved that the modern world doesn't know everything because some of those cave women were an absolute whizz when it came to ringing the asteroids.

Then I found that if I overstuffed the clouds they made great trampolines. A few of us got quite good at it but we kept making holes in the ozone layer so perhaps it wasn't such a good idea.

As you can imagine it wasn't long before all this came to the attention of the Almighty. Not being a Deity given to having a bit of a giggle, he wasn't very pleased. It was hardly surprising. Until my appearance he'd had a pretty quiet and orderly house. Now he had angels gadding about like every night was party night. Myself, I think he was more annoyed at somebody having better ideas than him. So I think there could be some truth in God having made man in his own image - at least as far as egos go. He put a stop to the halo throwing and trampolining anyway.

It was too late. I'd already laid the seeds of discontent in heaven. St Cecilia asked for permission to turn the heavenly host into a pop group and somebody called Toscanini wanted instruments other than harps so he could have an orchestra and do the music making properly.

I could see there was going to be a lot of friction coming up and the finger of accusation could only be pointed at me. I applied to do a bit of haunting so I'd be out of the way. I might have known there'd be a waiting list for that too, Jesus, perhaps safeguarding his monopoly on resurrection, likes to keep a strict control on all the goings on from heaven. He says too many ghosts cluttering up Earth would only interfere with its workings.

I applied for reincarnation too, but there was only vampire bats and some sort of creature that lives on the bottom of the sea left, so I wasn't too keen. I had no choice but to face the music - or should I say the celestial chart toppers - and put my faith in absolution.

I was dutifully stuffing the clouds and trying not to notice a bunch of saints playing draughts with the black and white clouds when I got the summons to kneel. 'Damn!' I said, forgetting where I was.

I couldn't give one good reason for my behaviour. I admitted setting the ball rolling, but shamelessly pushed its continuation on the other angels. God said they'd had peace and harmony in heaven ever since creation. I said the place had been in the doldrums and needed a bit of life putting into it.

'So you think I don't know what's best?' he said. With all the effrontery that only a sixteen year old could have I called him an old misery guts. Ever so calmly he replied, 'Perhaps you're not suited to heaven?' I got a bit worried then. I thought I'd better do a lot of growing up very quickly.

I made all my apologies and promised that if I ever felt I had to have a fling again, I wouldn't do it with the halos. 'Yes,' said God, 'remember it takes a lifetime to earn one of those. And here's something to polish yours with, it's looking a bit tarnished.' And then he smiled. He's not such a bad fella really. Very understanding he is.

Anyway, I'm only telling you this so you'll know what to expect when you get here. Heaven's the best place to be dead in, but don't go expecting too much. It might be as well if you do all your growing up before you get here because there isn't much room for frivolity and childishness, and oh yes, don't forget how monotonous heaven can be so don't go stampeding to get in.

I've got to rush now as I've reached the top of the waiting list for a message through a medium and I want to make sure this letter gets through alright. I know Mum and Dad didn't fancy coming out tonight because the weather was bad, but if you happen to see them will you let them know I'm alright?

Allison's Dilemma

by

Rebecca Rae

It was a bright sunny morning as Allison drove the short distance to drop six year old Sean at school. He was his usual chatty self but Allison was quite disconcerted when he blurted out, 'You look nice this morning Mummy.'

'Well thank you sweetheart,' smiled a startled Allison, 'But I try to look smart every morning.' She *had* taken extra care of her appearance today thought Allison but it was a bit worrying to think her small son had noticed.

'Teacher says we should always look smart,' muttered Sean., losing interest and gazing out of the car window. They pulled up outside the school and Allison waved to her son as he entered the building.

Now off to work and the excitement of seeing David. Allison had been drawn to him from the first day he had come into the ward after emergency surgery following an horrific car accident. As he drove along the quiet road to the rear of the Hospital her thoughts turned to two years earlier when her husband John had died in a similar car accident, leaving her alone and Sean without the father he desperately needed. Was she being unfaithful to his memory? The thoughts plagued her as she stopped in the hospital car park.

Getting out of the car Allison put all these thoughts behind her as she smoothed down her smart nurses uniform over her trim hips and tucked a stray strand of blond hair under her cap. Taking a deep breath she headed for Ward 6A.

'Morning Sister, I'm glad to see you. It means I can go home to my lovely bed,' smiled Nurse Bellamy as they met in the Ward corridor.

'Morning Joanne, everybody had a good night, I hope?' queried Allison as she tried to see through the swing doors to catch sight of David..

'Yes everybody slept well, although David Conroy was a bit restless, he probably can't wait to leave us today.' With that she signed over her charges to Allison and left with a sleepy wave glad to be heading home.

Nurse Bellamy's good-bye's still ringing in her ears Allison strode through the swing doors into the Ward.

'Ah! here she is the beautiful Sister Nightingale,' beamed David smiling mischievously, one or two of the other patients nodded knowingly and Allison felt her cheeks burning as she tried to hide her confusion by being businesslike.

'You seem very lively this morning Mr Conroy. I shouldn't over do it or we might have to keep you in for your own good.'

David looked serious as she straightened his bed. 'If it meant seeing you every morning I don't think I'd mind too much.

He laid his strong hand on her small wrists as he spoke and Allison felt a quiver go through her body. She looked into his blue eyes wanting and yet not wanting to see what she knew would be there. 'Oh all the patients say that it must be the uniform,' she quipped trying to hide her confusion. She knew immediately she had hurt his feelings as his voice dropped and he quickly reverted to his light-hearted banter that had temporarily been abandoned.

'Of course that must be it, I say the same things to all the nurses.'

Silently she chastised herself as she went along the ward seeing to the needs of the other patients. He had said the things she had wanted to hear and she had foolishly made a joke of it, perhaps it would put him off altogether! The needs of the job overtook her thoughts until it was time for doctors rounds. When they got to David's bedside she held her breath. What if the doctor said he should spend a few more days in hospital, would she get another chance?

Her hopes were soon dashed as the doctor told him how pleased he was with his progress and that he could leave after lunch if he promised to take things easy.

The rest of the morning was a blur until finally the moment she had been dreading came, her heart missed a beat as she saw David pushing his way through the swing doors looking handsome in his 'civvies'. 'Well here I go, whatever will I do without my ministering angel,' his smiling eyes masking a hidden question.

'Oh you will soon find someone to look after you,' smiled Allison, the hesitation in her voice quickly transmitted itself to David as he plunged on.

'Seriously though without your sunny smile and reassurance it would have been a really bad time for me, let me take you to dinner as thanks,' David ended with an embarrassed stutter.

Allison had the grace to blush but she wasn't going to make the same mistake again. 'Well if you are sure, OK I'd love to,' she laughed and spread her arms in mock submission. They arranged to meet at a local restaurant the following evening.

The next day Allison went through the motions at the hospital but her 'date' was never far from her thoughts. She was also troubled at being unfaithful to John's memory and the evasive answer she had given to her mother-in-law when asking her to baby-sit went against her basic honesty. Even the thought of a 'date' with a man was daunting, she wondered if she would remember how to behave. The last man she had been alone with was her husband over two years ago. Then at last it was 5.30 pm and Allison flew home as if on wings. Sean had been collected from school by John's mum so all she had to do was get ready. Well should I try to look sexy or smart? This decision occupied her as she had a refreshing shower finally settling for smart.

Allison checked herself in the mirror and decided she looked pretty good for a thirty-four year old. She had a trim figure and her height of five foot eight meant she looked good in the long skirt with matching jacket and pink blouse. She was nervous on entering the restaurant but David was already there and soon put her at ease. The evening was everything Allison hoped it would be and was to be the first of many hours they spent together.

Several weeks later after a particularly pleasant evening they sat together on Allison's settee, David put his arm around Allison's shoulder and pulled her towards him, she felt warm and secure and when he put his hand under her chin and tilted her face they kissed without any reservations. When finally they breathlessly drew apart David looked serious. 'Listen darling we can't go on like this, you know I love you more than anything and I want to take care of you and Sean forever.' Allison's eyes misted over she knew he was right but how could she give herself fully to another man when she still loved John? 'Will you put me out of my misery and marry me please,' David's urgent voice broke into her thoughts.

'Oh David it's too soon I can't marry anyone.' She drew away from him frightened of her feelings and her thoughts in turmoil. David stiffened at the rebuff, it was as if she had erected a wall between them. The rest of the evening was spoilt and David left earlier than usual and Allison felt her world was crumbling around her. What should she do, who could she turn to? She decided the only person she could confide in was John's mum, yes she would understand and be able to advise her. She was excited at the thought of positive action and immediately rang and arranged to go for lunch the following Sunday.

The day soon arrived, lunch was quiet the conversation being stilted as Allison wondered what the reaction would be to her bombshell. She didn't have to wait long as Sean wanted to go and play in the shed which left them alone.

Allison took a deep breath and plunged straight in, her pent up emotions taking over. 'Mum you know I've been seeing a man for some time?'

'Yes dear I know,' replied her Mother-in-law rather stiffly, 'I hope you're not seeing too much of him and neglecting Sean.'

'No of course not, I wouldn't neglect Sean in any case,' bristled Allison.

Oh dear she thought this is not going to be easy. 'Well Mum he has asked me to marry him and I do so love him, but I also still love John and it is tearing me apart, what should I do?' There was a shocked silence until it was broken by Allison, 'Mum, please say something.'

'Yes I will say something,' was the terse reply, 'I am horrified that you should even consider such a thing, how can you be so unfaithful to John's memory?'

Allison was taken aback by the venom in her voice, 'But how can I be unfaithful to a memory?' she cried, but she knew in her heart even as she spoke that was exactly the trouble.

'Well you know how I feel, if you go ahead with this then you will no longer be welcome in this house,' screamed John's mother and strode from the room not waiting for a reply. Allison was left to rue the decision to have sought advice and left the house crying at the injustice of it all.

That night David came around to apologise for his petulant behaviour. As soon as Allison saw him much to his concern she held him and wept uncontrollably for what to David seemed an eternity. Finally she regained control of herself and blurted out the whole story.

David gently brushed the damp hair from her forehead with the back of his hand, 'Listen darling, if you marry me you won't have to worry about anyone. I know the three of us will be happy.'

Allison collapsed in his arms. 'Oh if it was only that easy,' she sobbed, but she knew in her heart she only really needed one person's approval.

The next day Allison took some flowers to John's grave and as she arranged them she felt a calmness coming over her, it was going to be alright. John always wanted her happiness and if it included getting a new father for Sean then it would have his blessing. There was a crunch of gravel behind her and turning quickly she saw David struggling to move his wheelchair along the path, an anxious frightened look on his face. She felt an overpowering love for him as he tried to reach her. Running to him she was laughing and crying at the same time, she fell to her knees and hugged him almost bowling him over in the process. 'Oh yes please I will marry you,' she sobbed, and as his arms embraced her she knew at that moment that John approved and happiness was hers.

Rocklight

by

J Sharman

Jane was just twelve years of age and very busy with music lessons, dance classes and helping her mother who was very house-proud. Jane helped by looking after her younger brothers and sisters.

Her father was a horse keeper at a very large stable where he tended about forty horses in the South end of Liverpool.

One day her father took her to see her grandfather who was working in a yard down at the Dingle about thirty minutes walk from where they lived.

Walking into the yard she spotted grandad beside a big wagon and surrounded by loads of wood and all kinds of tools. He had started to build a caravan on the wagon and Jane was amazed at her old grandad taking on this enormous task.

Jane went regularly to see how the work was progressing and each time she was more surprised. Then one day her father told her it was ready for the big journey, they were taking it across the river Mersey to Moreton about fourteen miles away.

The caravan consisted of a small hall, a bedroom and a living room all beautifully fitted out with furnishings and furniture and painted. Grandad had been a Navy man, and had decided to name the caravan after one of his ships, he had made an artistic nameplate bearing the name 'Rocklight' and there it was over the door, a permanent reminder of his seafaring days.

When it had been too wet to work on the caravan or any spare time at home, he was always pottering about making rope-soled shoes, handmade rugs and rope mats, and he worked in the name Rocklight on many of the items.

Now was the time for getting over to Moreton, so 'my father, is taking the outfit' Jane told her friends, and the word spread around the neighbourhood.

Jane's grandmother had never been a roamer, and had always preferred her own home. Never wanted any holidays or strange places to stay, so she made it clear that she would not be going to Moreton for any weekend breaks or Summer holidays.

The great day arrived, and Jane's father supplied four beautiful cart-horses to pull the caravan from the Dingle down to the Pier Head amidst cheers from people lining the roads.

It was a spectacular sight - four proud horses clop clopping down the gangway onto the Liverpool landing stage pulling a beautiful caravan, and then Jane's father guided them onto the ferryboat to sail across the river Mersey to Birkenhead.

When they disembarked, Jane's father led the horses up the steep gangway to start their long walk through Birkenhead, Bidston, Leasowe and finally down Pasture Road to a plot of land near Moreton Shore in the shadow of the famous lighthouse, built on Bales of Cotton;

Two horses were released and the remaining pair shunted the caravan into position. Then all four horses were fed and rested before their return journey the following day.

Jane's grandmother remained at home whilst grandad and his eldest son spent long weekends away. They built on an extra two rooms at the back of the caravan, a lovely veranda along the front and a set of steps with handrails. Then they built a fence all around the plot. It was beautiful, but still her gran did not stay in it.

Jane's mother often took them over for a few short breaks, and Jane loved it, timing the tides to go swimming - walks along the embankment, picnics on the Common, and shopping at Moreton Cross.

Then Jane met a young man and was very happy and became engaged on her 21st birthday and didn't visit the caravan because she was busy making wedding arrangements.

Two years later she married and the following year they had a beautiful baby girl, and three months later they all moved from Liverpool to a lovely bungalow in Leasowe, just a few minutes walk from the Lighthouse.

While walking to the village with baby in the pram one day, she met her grandmother.

What a surprise! Her gran in Moreton. It was really unexpected because grandad had passed away the previous year, and gran had now come over to stay at Moreton.

After that Jane visited gran regularly and learned that she loved being over here; although she was getting on in years, she was very active and Jane would take baby regularly for precious afternoon chats.

Gran loved 'Rocklight' and very much regretted not coming over in earlier years.

One afternoon she was on her way to a matinee at the local cinema, when she collapsed and died, at the age of eighty-nine years.

She had told Jane that she felt closer to her husband in Moreton, the place he had loved so much, and which she came to love.

They are both laid to rest at St James' Cemetery in the shadows of the Great Liverpool Cathedral.

Teething Pains Of A Parent

by

Sharon Woodburn

Parenthood is a catalogue of ups and downs, I've screamed, laughed and cried over my two boys, one aged eight (going on eighty) and one aged two.

I must admit I found the baby days very tiring. Motherhood was not quite how I imagined it to be.

There was the four hour feeding to adjust to, along with the colic and everything else that goes with it.

Then came the crawling stage, and my God, don't I know I've got a baby now. It's a case of, 'Quick grab the baby, he's heading straight for the dogs tail.' 'No baby, don't play with the ashtray.' 'Don't break mummy's favourite ornament.' If you thought the crawling stage was bad, *you ain't seen nothing yet!*

Next is the walking. My baby will only walk when he feels like, thus meaning when he no longer wishes to walk, he just literally falls in a heap wherever we happen to be at the time. 'Come on let's go and get some sweeties,' is my favourite bribe, but unfortunately bribery does not always work, leaving mummy carrying not only shopping but a 'look, I've got my own way' two year old.

Liam, this is my two year old's name, also has favourite hiding places. Where we almost always find the objects that have gone missing.

There's the tumble drier, or the waste paper bins or his favourite one of all is the mop bucket, usually when it's nice and full.

Daniel my eight year old has a mind of his own. He has an I'm nearly nine, I can do anything attitude.

But I must admit when I was very heavily pregnant with Liam, feeling sorry for myself for being fat, frumpy and ugly or so I thought at the time. Women that have had babies will know. The feel sorry for me phase, I'm talking about, anyway to get to the point, Daniel was very sweet and understanding in a funny sort of way. He would cuddle into me and say, 'Don't worry mam, you might be fat, but I still love you.' Well after such a lovely compliment what more can one say.

Another thing you find about children, is they speak their mind just when you wish they wouldn't. For example, while waiting in a bus stop children always notice faults with people, and aren't always quiet about telling you. So you stand in the bus stop praying to God the children don't notice the lady with a bit of a beard standing next to you. Then, oh no, Daniel spots her and begins to stare, you notice and try to get his attention.

'See if you can see your gran anywhere,' you say, but by this time he's shouting, 'Mam, mam.' You can just sense what's going to come out of his mouth next, so you tell him to be quiet.

Then he tries to be discreet, as he walks right over to you, staring at the lady all the while. Then quietly whispers, 'She's got a beard mam.' You grab him quickly and gently push his face into your shopping bag and tell him to look for his sweets.

Another thing you must never do in front of children, is talk about anyone, especially if you bump into them and the children happen to be with you. I have been in conversation with someone and suddenly Daniel has come out with , 'My mam was talking about you.' Try getting out of that one. It's quite an embarrassing situation.

Getting back to Liam. He has the face of an angel. But never judge a book by its cover. Because Liam is what could be described as a one man demolition team. His favourite trick is using the video recorder as a money box, meaning another trip to the repair shop. There's also the chocolate hand marks on the furniture after you've just cleaned up, and if you have any dishes of potpourri or ashtrays with anything in them, fear not, Liam does a good job of emptying them onto the carpet. These are just a few of the things a sweet innocent two year old can get up to in one day.

When children are old enough to play outside whether in the garden or at a friend's, beware of the 'my child does nothing wrong' parent, who will no doubt call on you to tell you your child has smacked hers, or your child has pinched little Johnny's car or worse still your child has sworn. So beware of strangers knocking at your door.

You also find with children, no matter how old you are, whether young or old, your children seem to think you are ancient. I am twenty-six years old and when Daniel is asking me questions for his homework or whatever, he always says, 'Did they have them in your days mam?'

No, I was too busy riding round on the dinosaurs Daniel!

It won't be long until you realise that being a mother is a very competitive job, especially when a child asks for something and you say no. Then you become a wicked witch, who is a bad mother and David or whoever's mum does everything for him, or Richard's mam bought him one. My goodness, my child is so badly done to. But don't try to compete by giving in and spoiling your children when you can't afford it, just to love your child is enough.

Never think for one minute you escape from children either day or night. You may well be one of the lucky ones who gets a few hours to yourself when the children are asleep. But when morning comes, more often than not, there's usually an extra body appeared in bed (yes, one of the children). I must tell you that this short story, of some of the fun you have with children, are just the teething problems.

The worst is yet to come!

A Cup Of Coffee

by

Beryl Makin

Emily sat down in the chair. She released a quiet sigh of relief. Her feet were aching after the endless promenade she had made through the countless shops. Not that she had actually bought anything, but it was fun to look.

She glanced around the bar, hoping to attract the attention of a passing waiter. Then out of the corner of her eye, she noticed 'him'. Not the waiter she was seeking, but a man sitting across the room, leaning casually on the counter. He looked to be in his late twenties. He had a beautiful golden tan and his hair was as black as coal. But what transfixed Emily's gaze were his eyes. So deep and dark. They seemed to be compelling her across the room towards them. Frightening but exhilarating, she confided to herself.

Emily felt her temperature rising and she blushed. Not too noticeably she hoped. She averted her gaze. She opened her handbag, and poked around inside. Looking for nothing in particular, but hoping that she could take control of her normally staid emotions, by this small diversion. She was sure that everyone was looking at her. In fact apart from 'him', only one young couple were in the bar, and they were too engrossed in each other to even acknowledge Emily's or anyone else's presence.

She closed her handbag, and turned towards the window. Even then her eyes focused not on the scene outside, but on the reflection of 'his' eyes. Still burrowing deep into her soul.

Her reverie was interrupted by the waiter.

'Madam,' he spoke, 'what can I get you?'

'Er. . . coffee with cream,' she replied, rather flustered at what she considered was being caught out in some sort of infidelity.

She turned once more towards the window. This time her eyes dwelling not on 'his', but on her own reflection. She didn't look bad for someone approaching forty, she mused. Her figure was good, if somewhat rounded. But 'breasts are back' she remembered reading in one or another woman's journal. That was something she could be thankful for!

The coffee arrived and she sipped it slowly. Yes, she reflected, she had tried to maintain her now fading youthful looks. She had her hair cut in a short style. Her sister had told her it made her look years' younger. She always wore her makeup, she felt naked and insecure without it. She was fortunate enough to be able to afford good quality, well cut clothes. Her husband, she had to concede, always made sure she had plenty of money to spend. However he never appeared to notice how she looked, or even cared how she felt. She knew that she was being a little unfair. He had a demanding job and worked extremely hard. Sometimes till late at night and at the weekend. Her life was full of material wealth. Yet what Emily really needed was love, romance and a little tenderness. Her husband certainly gave her very little of that. She did occasionally wonder exactly whom he gave his real affection to. But she dismissed such thoughts from her mind. Anyway, she wouldn't know what to do if she did unearth some secret affair.

She drained her cup and replacing it on the saucer, she looked over towards the bar. 'He' was looking at her, she was sure of it. Oh those eyes!

He smiled, and slowly rose from his place at the bar, moving leisurely towards Emily's table.

'May I join you?' His voice as deep and mysterious as his eyes.

Emily looked up and was once again hypnotised by his presence.

'Well, er. . . , I'm not sure,' Emily hesitated. 'I've just finished.'

'Let me get you another drink, something stronger perhaps?' he offered.

Before she could protest he had summoned the waiter and ordered two brandy's.

'I don't usually drink anything so strong,' she declared half-heartedly. Secretly enchanted that he had noticed her and was in fact, giving her so much attention. The attention she needed so desperately.

'On holiday?' he enquired.

'Yes, just for a few days, shopping and sightseeing, a present from my husband.' As soon as the last two words had departed her lips, Emily wished that she could snatch them back. Why, oh why, had she mentioned the existence of any husband. But even more importantly, why should she want to hide the fact of her marriage. Emily could feel the colour rising once more in her cheeks. She had on her wedding ring, it was no secret.

He seemed not to notice her dilemma.

'Paris is wonderful at any time,' he spoke with longing and love in his voice, 'but especially now.'

He smiled at her and she felt intoxicated by his close proximity. Or was it merely the brandy? No, it couldn't be merely the alcohol, she was sure of that.

They sat for an hour chatting like old friends. He made her feel so good, so important. Curiously, he didn't mention anything about his work, and very little about himself. He enchanted Emily however with his descriptions of the city. Telling her about the beauty of not only its more famous attractions, but describing the quieter, more secluded spots that even the most intrepid tourist failed to stumble across. Most importantly, for Emily, he appeared to take a genuine interest in her. The first person, even she had to admit, to do so in a long while.

To Emily it seemed all too soon, that he looked at his watch and announced that with deep regret he would have to leave for an appointment that he could not miss. He thanked her for her company and wished her safe journey home. She smiled, inwardly satisfied with herself. She watched him depart, following him with her gaze, until he disappeared into the crowded boulevard.

The waiter approached again.

'Anything else madam?'

'No, no thank you, just the bill.'

She opened her bag and reached for her purse. She fumbled around.

'One moment please,' she addressed the waiter, standing impatiently at her side.

She pulled a few odds and ends out onto the table. Perfume. . . lipstick. . . powder . . . tissues . . . pen . . . mirror . . . but no purse.

'Oh!' she exclaimed, 'my purse, it's gone . . .'

The police were very helpful, but didn't offer much hope of recovery. Fortunately she had enough money in the hotel safe to ensure that her holiday wasn't ruined. But how? when? who? She didn't know. What an awful end to such a lovely afternoon. Still the memory of that young Parisian would soften the blow and remain in her dreams for a long time. . .

In a bar across town, another woman sitting alone at a table, noticed a handsome young man, with piercing dark eyes. He, having counted the profit of his last encounter, had placed Emily's cash firmly inside his own wallet. He then tossed the purse into the gutter and without further thought continued with his work.

No Way Back

by

Margaret McHutchon

Sara Phillips was walking along Breckon Hill, with its large Victorian houses and long gardens, towards the entrance into Devon Close, the newer road where she had come to spend the New Year with her aunt. But, when she reached the place where she expected to find the junction, it was not there. Breckon Hill continued in a straight line, with no break anywhere to be seen. She looked round and realised that she must have taken the wrong turning when she left the library. Having spent most of her fourteen years in the country, she felt somewhat bewildered by the many rather similar streets in the suburbs of this northern industrial town.

The afternoon was becoming darker and colder. She saw a man and asked him the way, but he appeared to be deaf. She concentrated hard. Yes, that road to the left looked like Breckon Hill. There were old houses at first, as she expected, but again Devon Close had completely disappeared. Then she noticed a man in the drive of an old house where Devon Close - or so she thought - should have been. Maybe he could tell her the way home. She called to him but, like the other man, he did not answer. He was opening his front door and going inside the house. Quickly, she followed, calling to him again. He turned and hesitated in the doorway, but still he did not reply. Suddenly, she found herself in the hall. That was strange, because she had not meant to come quite so far. She heard voices coming from the back of the house. Almost as if someone were pushing her, Sara moved slowly towards a room where she found the man and a woman looking at a newspaper.

'I'm sorry to barge in like this, but could you - ' Sara began, and then stopped. They were ignoring her completely. She might have been invisible. And something else peculiar had happened. Outside it had been dark, but the light in the room was natural light, and a window looked onto a garden where the sun was shining and the trees were covered in blossom. How could there be daylight at 5 o'clock and blossom in December? Everything had an air of unreality, as though she were dreaming. Perhaps this was a dream - a dream which was not yet quite a nightmare. The couple were now sitting at a table, completely engrossed in an extremely frugal meal. Their voices were quiet, and Sara did not catch properly what they were saying, but she did gather that their names were Steven and Monica. The front doorbell rang, and Monica went to let in somebody, who could be heard running upstairs and then walking about in the room overhead.

Sara must have lost all sense of time, because she was aware of nothing more until she noticed that the room was becoming gloomy and cold. Steven drew the curtains, and soon he and Monica were sitting reading by a very dim light, one on each side of a newly lit coal fire. They had still not seen her and, oddly enough, she was not very frightened, but just puzzled and curious and conscious of the same unreal, dreamlike quality she had felt before. There was silence, except for the distant hum of traffic, occasional footsteps in the room above, a few unimportant remarks by Steven and Monica, the rustle of newspapers and the turning of pages. Then Steven looked up. 'Before I. . .' he began, when an unearthly wailing broke in, drowning all other sounds. When the wailing stopped, Sara tried once more to be seen and heard, but yet again she was ignored. There was a distant bang, followed by several others. The light went out, and the room, full of gigantic shadows, felt eerie in the firelight. Steven and Monica jumped, and Steven was saying, 'Since I'll be on duty tonight, you and Barbara must go to the shelter.'

Flying footsteps could be heard on the stairs, and a girl of about Sara's age burst into the room. The bangs were becoming noisier, and an aeroplane with a strange sounding engine was coming nearer. Steven, Monica and the girl were now in the hall, grabbing their coats. Steven pushed the other two out of the front door, which closed before Sara had time to follow. She could not stay in this ghostly house alone. Hastily, she grabbed the catch, desperate to open the door, but it was stiff in her shaking hands. She pulled harder, and at last it gave way. She almost fell into the drive, on which she thought a full moon was shining, until she realised that the light in the sky was manmade and came from searchlights and blazing buildings. Half the town appeared to be on fire. Steven and his family had vanished. She had no idea where to go, but she must escape from here.

Another of those terrible aeroplanes was approaching. She ran down the drive and had just reached the gate when there was a tremendous, terrifying crash. Turning towards the house, she was horrified to see that flames were leaping through the roof and the buildings on both sides were burning fiercely. A whistling sound was coming nearer and nearer, louder and louder. She waited, too frightened to move. The scene was becoming dimmer and dimmer. She felt herself falling slowly down - and knew no more.

Her eyes felt heavy, but eventually she managed to open them, and saw her aunt, anxiously looking at her where she lay on the sofa in the modern, attractive sitting room in Devon Close.

'Am I ill?' she asked.

'You'll be all right,' her aunt reassured her. 'You had a fall outside and hit your head on the gate. A neighbour helped me to bring you inside, and he's phoning the doctor now. I went to look for you when you didn't arrive back from the library.'

Sara could not remember arriving at the gate and falling, but, obviously, her very odd experience had merely been the result of her accident and she had not been lost at all.

The following week, Sara and her aunt went out for lunch. As they were sitting in a café, a tall, white-haired man appeared and walked towards them. Sara gasped. He was a much older version of Steven, the man she had seen a few days before. He said 'good morning' to Mrs Phillips, and he had Steven's voice. He looked rather searchingly at Sara, and then went to sit some distance away, out of earshot but near enough to be seen quite clearly. Sara shivered and wondered why he had looked at her like that. Her aunt glanced at her in surprise.

'What *is* the matter? You look as though you've seen a ghost.'

'I think that is probably what I have seen,' replied Sara.

'What do you mean?'

'Who is that man?'

'Oh, Mr Wilkins.'

'*Steven* Wilkins?'

Yes. How do you know?'

'I don't know really. But who is he? Where does he come from?'

'He lives quite near us. His wife and fourteen year old daughter were killed during the war, the same night that their house was bombed. He was fire-watching, and had persuaded them to go to a shelter, but the shelter and the house both got direct hits.'

'Where was the house?'

'Well, you must have noticed that Breckon Hill is an unusual road - old except for newer houses in the middle. The Devon Close houses are on the site of gardens belonging to houses that were destroyed one night in the war, during the worst air raid there ever was in this part of the country. I've been told that the Wilkins house was exactly at the spot where Breckon Hill and Devon Close now meet.'

Mrs Phillips looked across at Mr Wilkins. 'Mr Wilkins is staring at us, especially you. He almost looks as though he knows you.'

'He's never seen me before, but I. . .' She hesitated. She had nearly said that she had seen him before. But how could she have seen him and his house as they used to be more than half a century before? Had she perhaps in some way voyaged back in time, or else picked up the lightwaves of an evening long since passed? Was it possible that there was such a thing as re-incarnation, and she had, in fact, been here before and known him in those wartime days? Perhaps she reminded him of his daughter or even, maybe, was his daughter, who had died so many years ago when she was just her age.

Winning The War

by

John M Rimmer

It will hopefully be a small, contained fire. There will be no danger to me, or Sarah.

Our flat might get damaged - hell, the whole building may go up. But that's a risk I'm prepared to take.

Ideally, Forshaw's flat will be rendered uninhabitable and he'll have to find somewhere else to live. Possible, he will be overcome by smoke and die. I won't be heartbroken if that happens, I'm not intending to kill him, so it wouldn't be murder, would it?

On the kitchen table there is a milk bottle full of petrol, with a petrol soaked rag stuck in the top. I filled the bottle out of the spare can I keep in the car boot. All I have to do now is go downstairs and out of the front door, walk around the side of the building, put my lighter to the rag, and sling the bottle through his window.

Forshaw isn't popular and so there will be a lot of suspects; if I'm asked I shall simply say that I know nothing. I think the police would consider it unlikely that I'd firebomb the flat beneath my own.

I shall say nothing.

Sarah will be upset when she gets home from work to discover the danger I've been in. But I'll just tell her that I'm a little shaky with shock, relieved to have been out when the fire started. And as I say, hopefully the Fire Brigade will contain the damage and we'll be able to stay in our flat. It would be a shame if we had to move, because apart from Forshaw living below us, I like it here.

Forshaw. God, just saying his name makes me wince.

He was already living here when we moved in. I remember seeing him watching us through his net curtains as we carried our boxed possessions along the path. I nudged Sarah and we both smirked. We were moving in above a nosey-poke. Not a pensioner with nothing better to do, but someone our own age.

It seemed funny then, and I suppose if he had only been nosey it would have been all right. But he was more than that.

Right from the start he made living here a battle. Why he didn't annoy everyone else in the building as much as me, I don't know. He's too subtle, I suppose. And I'm usually sensitive.

'Don't let him get to you,' Sarah would say. 'He's harmless.'

She's more easy going than me. And also she was flattered that he fancied her. I'd seen the way he looked at her. So had she. A woman, no matter who she happens to be in love with, will always be flattered that someone else finds her attractive. So she would say, 'Don't let him get to you.' And toss her mass of blonde hair over her shoulder, unconsciously preening herself as he peeked at us through his nets, or through a crack in his door as we walked past.

How could he not get to me, though?

I parked the car about car-length along the kerb from the gate. So that any other resident who normally parked there wouldn't think I was stealing their space. I was being considerate.

And sure enough, that was Forshaw's old Escort. It was his space.

Then what happens? He parks his car in my space. So I have to wait around until he goes out, then move my car forward a length. And from then on, whenever he can, he parks in my space. He watches for when I go out and moves his car forward.

How childish can you get?

Then, we don't get any milk. It turns out that he's been putting a note saying No Milk Today in the milk bottles. So I have to put our empties out late at night, after he's put his out, and remove his note.

He doesn't say anything to me about it though, oh no. Sarah tells me that he'd complained to her that 'someone' was stealing his notes to the milkman, and he'd been getting milk when he didn't want any.

Accosting my wife and accusing me of theft, when it was him misleading the milkman in the first place!

She appeases him by saying that we'll put our empties on the left of the step and he can put his on the right, so that's what we've been doing. It's a solution, but it would be nice to be able to put things where you want. That's one battle he won.

And the music. He plays his record player at all hours. Loud. I bang on the floor and he turns it down. Sarah says that it doesn't bother her. Even that she likes most of the records he plays. She might like them, but not pounding up through the floorboards. She only says that to calm me down. So I have to put a record on to drown the thumping from below, even if I don't particularly want to listen to one.

On the few occasions that it is quiet downstairs I put a record on fullblast, just to let him know what it's like. And the cheek of him! He bangs on the ceiling.

Sarah says I'm being childish, but really I'm just trying to beat him at his own game.

And his nosiness isn't confined to watching me through the curtains either. Or peeping through the crack in his door. I've waited on the top of the stairs, sometimes for an hour or more, and caught him coming out of his flat simply to loiter around and spy on me. He spots me and quickly flees back inside. More than once that's happened, and he hadn't been leaving his flat for any reason, other than to lurk in the hall or creep up the stairs and listen at our door. I got the better of him there. Although I think i can sometimes hear the stairs creak at night.

Just last week I woke up in the middle of the night - something had disturbed me. Sarah wasn't in bed. She wasn't anywhere in the flat. I went to the door, opened it, and after a moment she came up the stairs. Seeing me she nearly jumped out of her skin. She had just her night-dress on and was clearly bothered. She told me she'd heard a noise on the stairs and had gone to investigate. Then I distinctly heard his door click shut. That had been a close one. Who knows what might have happened if I hadn't turned up?

66

So with that and the other things like him reading our mail, then resealing the envelopes and putting them back in the mesh basket behind the letter box. Telling friends who come to visit me that I'm not in. And above all, making Sarah nervy. I decided he had to go.

I make sure the rag is firmly in the milk bottle. Talk about tasting victory. I can already taste the smoke. Practically hear the crackling flames.

I look at the smoke for a while before I realise that it is actually there. There is smoke coming under the door!

I go to the door, pull it open and immediately stagger back. The outside of the door is ablaze. I drop the milk bottle and can only stare in shock as the flames waft in and drip onto the carpet. It's really hot. I daren't edge forward and retrieve the bottle.

Smoke billows all around. I can't tell if the hall outside is on fire - I can't see past the door.

I retreat to the window. Fire skitters across the ceiling, dances on the carpet. The sofa starts issuing black clouds.

Looking through the window I see people gathering on the lawn below.

There's Sarah! I bang on the glass and call her name. What's she doing there? She should be at work.

Forshaw appears at her side.

There's a pop! From behind me and flames spit all about. Drops of fire land on my arm.

Forshaw puts a hand on Sarah's shoulder, says something to her and she looks up at me. She nods her head.

I smash my hand through the window. Air blows into the flat.

'Sarah!' I scream.

She looks up without expression. Speaks to him as his arm slithers across her shoulder.

He laughs.

They're both laughing.

They're laughing at me. . .

A Pigs Tale

by

W D Cartwright

This is a tale all about a tail, a pigs tail in fact. Have you ever wondered how they got that quaint little corkscrew appendage, that is in all honesty a poor excuse for a tail, no? Well there is a very good reason of which I shall now tell you.

Long ago when pork sausages were a thing only dreamt about in the troubled sleep of Neanderthal man and read about in his sons' sci-fi books. Pigs as we know them today roamed the Earth free and unfettered, a noble beast. I say pigs for this is the name which we have given them of latter days a name much maligned and used to express derision. But the pig in days of yore was better known as Nocab . . . Strangely we find that this is an inverted anagram of bacon. It is an odd coincidence I know and probably speaks much of the wicked irony of life. Nevertheless in those ancient times when the last Tyrannosaurus Rex had finally submitted to the fact that sheer size and ferociousness alone did not dictate survival in the evolutionary pecking order and Homo Sapien as he was then still hung from a bough of a tree scratching what would one day be a forehead. Nocab was a fierce and proud hunter, brave and noble and was given a wide berth by the likes of tigers, lions and wolves and regarded with awe and suspicion by its possible prey.

Not for Nocab the inglorious free-for-all of the trough. No, Nocab enjoyed the thrill of the hunt and kill. Nocab of the noble brow and unwavering eyes, Nocab of the fierce threatening tusks and Nocab of the long, pointed, lethal tail. Yes, of all the weapons in Nocab's arsenal his most prized asset was his tail. (Oh that tail). Many a wolf or pack of wild dogs had been sent packing by an about face offensive from Nocab. That ominous grunt and snort from the midst of the long grass was enough to strike fear into all the beasts and fowl of field who vied for supremacy in the animal world.

With such awe was Nocabs' long, rapier-like tail held in by other feared predators in the animal kingdom that eventually Nocab had no known enemies or possible combat opponents. So Nocabs began to fight amongst themselves in an attempt to satiate his natural lust for action, for Nocab loved to fight. Duels were held much in the same fashion of our fencing today, Nocabs pointed and deadly tail used in a tense battle of parry-thrust, victory being decided by a lethal blow (for these duels were often fatal) or the warrior with the least blood lost.

The fighting went on and on for centuries and started to become more scientific and technical in its approach. A process known as hide thickening was introduced to avoid blood loss during contests. There were several ways of achieving hide thickening. One was for Nocab to run full throttle (or trottle) through a copse of gorse bushes, till the skin became roughened and immune to spines. It was an effective method but also led to Nocabs distinctive high-pitched squeal with which we associate them with today. Another effective and less traumatic way of achieving this end involved Nocab simply wallowing in pools of mud or peat bogs till they were completely covered, then to lie out under the sun till the mud-pack-like suit hardened against the skin, this method was known as 'makin Nocab' for some obscure reason.

Nocab loved to fight and soon the personal duels bloodily fought out in the isolation of fields and woods weren't enough to quench Nocabs' pride in his fighting prowess. Grand tournaments similar to the jousting fetes of medieval times were held, with galas tombola's and refreshment stalls for the spectators though the main attraction of course was watching two valiant opponents galloping in reverse at each other with their lethal tails pointing out at their assailant. It was a fascinating spectacle though because of hide-thickening there were few fatalities, the leathery skin being difficult to pierce. Trickery was called for and squirting faeces into the opponents eyes to hamper vision was allowed and also aiming thrusts at their opponent's tender areas. The contest was usually decided by which contestant keeled over first.

The jousting went on and on it was so popular, the victors treated as heroes and allowed privileges like the freedom of the best mudholes or priority over the choicest sows and were gloriously documented in the annuls of Nocab-lore.

At this point let me break off from the story and tell you about a certain splinter group of pigs who grew up during the time the fighting was at its zenith. This band of high-minded and enlightened Nocab saw fit to separate themselves from the main body of their fellow Nocab appalled at the blood lusting and viciousness of their brothers and sisters. Not only this, it had come to their notice that all the fighting was having a detrimental effect on their most prized asset, their straight rapier-like and lethal tail. Many Nocab after a particularly ferocious contest found that their tails as a result became bent or broken and their fighting days were prematurely ended.

The farseeing band of non-blood sport Nocabs who went under the campaign slogan of Save the Tail tried to warn their fellow Nocabs of the danger and possible dire consequences of it all . . . but alas to no avail, the fighting went on more intensive and furious than ever. Meanwhile the Save the Tail group sadly retreated into isolation and sanctuary away from the fighting and their descendants still exist today in wild, remote areas of the world and we know them as wild boar or warthogs.

For the rest of Nocab the fighting went on fiercer and more bloody than ever and as the STT group had predicted Nocabs' tail did become perceptively more bent and misshapen as the time wore on. But this fact was ignored (from where we derive the saying pigheadedness). The evolutionary process went on in its ruthless way until the fateful day arrived when Nocab noticed with alarm that their Nocablettes were being born with bent and even (horror upon horrors) curly tails.

Nocab's tail became the laughing stock of the animal kingdom and it didn't take long for the larger predators like lions and wolves to exploit this. Emboldened by the once-feared now curly tails uselessness it was no longer a fearsome fighting weapon and often it was only Nocabs speed that saved him from becoming prey to its enemies.

In those days of Nocabs' meteoric fall from grace it was then only a case of breaching Nocabs thickened hide. Many a Sabre-toothed tiger had slunk away ruefully with a set of broken canines after trying to bite through Nocabs leathery skin. Though once this obstacle was overcome underneath Nocab made a tender and tasty snack.

Meanwhile an even greater threat to Nocabs' existence had recently fallen from the trees (probably on its head) and was not only now discovering the rudimentary skills of throwing sharpened spears but while in the act of bashing two rocks together had discovered fire and an even more delicious way of serving up Nocab steaklets.

Well there you have it, I don't expect you believe this tale or tail but remember the truth is often more bizarre than fiction and by the way enjoy your bacon and eggs this morning.

Moral: It takes two to start an argument, three to make a war and four to have a decent game of Monopoly.

The Puncture

by

Roger Willacy

I woke well before the alarm was due as the beautiful summers morning lit the room. The birds were in full song as I drew back the curtains and let the sun in. The whole family rose without difficulty and we enjoyed breakfast chattering about the forthcoming day. I took my bike from the shed, waved goodbye and set off for my usual pleasant cycle ride.

Once off the estate I was able to cycle through the school yard to the 'chicken path', a public footpath that ran all the way to the bypass, the only obstacle of traffic on my entire journey. Once across, the whoosh of rush-hour cars faded behind me as I rode through two fields where the unofficial footpath had been worn away. This took me to the disused railway line, long gone after the Beeching cuts, but now regularly used by kids, dog lovers, cyclists and walkers.

I was at the top of the steep slope running down to where two lines once merged. Young BMXers and motor cyclists had worn a deep rut down to the flat but it looked formidable to a man of my age and on a cycle with dubious brakes. Cautiously at first, I edged over the top and with brakes full on, slid halfway before letting out slowly, faster and faster until the wind whistled through my hair at what seemed breakneck speed.

I didn't need to pedal until I reached the old station and under the road bridge which heralded the end of civilisation and the start of countryside which would see me all the way to the factory. This was the best part of the ride. Silence, bar nature, and with a slight decline in my favour.

I could see for probably a mile in front and seldom passed anyone at this time although I thought I could see someone in the distance today. Suddenly the smooth ride turned into a jerky bumpy one and I came to a stop. I looked down and saw a flat tyre at the back. I dismounted, cursed and crouched down holding the frame in front of me.

'That's tough, lad!'

The voice startled me and I lost balance falling backwards with the bike clattering away from me. I looked up and saw a chap standing in front of me. He wore an old brown suit that had seen better days. The trousers were too long and in folds over has battered boots. His collarless shirt was beneath a weatherworn face with white stubble and a misshapen handlebar moustache. He was topped by a broad old flat cap. By his side was a mongrel in even worse condition than the old man. I looked past him up the track but there was no one in the distance now.

'Didn't mean to mek thee jump, cock! Rough this track. . .ne thee maind, I only live theer. . .soon 'ave thee ont road eh?'

'No. . .er it's alright. . . I only work there. . .' I blurted but he was already pushing the bike into a field and towards a farmhouse. By the time I picked my self up and followed he was halfway across the field. His long strides took him through a farm gate and when I eventually got there he was gone. I spotted my bike over by a large green door on the farmhouse across the yard and went over.

'Hello,' I shouted.

'Hello,' and this time I knocked.

The door was not shut so I pushed it open.

'Hello,' I went in.

There was no reply so I walked into what was obviously a kitchen. There was a large table in the centre full of pots, and I walked past it and again shouted. As I did I heard a low grunting sound and looked down to see legs from behind the table. I peered round and saw an old lady lying face down on the floor. She was motionless but making slow hollow breathing noises. In her hand was a bottle and tablets were scattered around the floor. I rushed to the door on the far side of the kitchen and called out. In front of me was a long dark corridor with a small table halfway down. On the table was a telephone.

I dialled 999 and summoned an ambulance before returning to comfort the old lady. When I heard a distant siren I went into the farmyard to direct the ambulance. As they carried her on a stretcher a man ran into the farmyard. He was wearing wellingtons and overalls and at first I thought he was the man who led me here.

'Where did you get to?' I quizzed. It was not him.

'I heard the ambulance from across the field,' he panted. 'What is it?'

I told him of the old lady and how I had found her. He spoke to the ambulance man and said he would follow shortly.

'Thanks,' he said. 'How did you come to be here?' So I recounted the tale. When I finished he specifically asked about the man and then beckoned to me to follow him.

We went through the kitchen into the hall with the telephone and into an old fashioned parlour. It was quiet save for the ticking of a clock on the old mantelpiece. The table had a lace tablecloth and there was a piano in the corner. He went to the piano and took a photograph in a gilt frame from on top. In the photo was a man in a suit and an old dog by his side.

'Yes! that's him,' I exclaimed

'That's my dad,' he told me. 'He was badly injured in the war. When he came home he was never the same. I was only young then. . . hardly remember him.. .. he stopped.

'Remember him?' I quizzed, after a moment's silence.

'He died in 1955!'

Cloud Nine

by

John Higson

'Oh! hell,' I said, 'Why can't I do it?' Then I stopped, aghast. I can't say that in this place. Oh! Lord, I'm sorry. Another boob.

But by and large it had all gone very smoothly. Peter had checked my credentials and fingerprinted me when I arrived and then he had given me my clothes - a sort of white smock, very comfortable. And then he had introduced me to my section and all of them, the natives, seemed very friendly and co-operative. Mind you, one of them seemed a bit miffed when I arrived and mentioned a certain misdemeanour that had happened many, many years ago and queried my being allowed entry, but a very friendly fellow interrupted saying, 'Ah, yes, but what about the time you climbed to the top of that very very high tree and rescued the cat? And what about all the good works you did?' That silenced him. Yes, a nice bunch. Mind you, I was a little sad when a trio arrived and Peter said they couldn't come in: one of them was a great friend of mine and really he hadn't done anything very bad - he did batter his wife around a bit and he tended to get impatient with the dog and sometimes kicked it but that was all. Anyway, although there was a slight altercation, Peter eventually pacified them, patted them on their shoulders, and fitted them out with asbestos suits, saying 'You'll be wanting these,' before sending them away.

Since then I've been learning the ropes - well, actually there aren't any - the nearest thing is gold and silver strands which we wear around our waist - gold for outstanding merit, silver if you're just average. I suspect they'll soon be making a copper one for me! But there's quite a lot to learn - for instance, how to walk on fluffy clouds. It's quite difficult and if you don't do it properly you fall through and go for a proper cropper: it's all a matter of balance and thinking good thoughts.

And then there's the Harping School and after that the Harping Joinery Shop. Normally I would have been sent to both of these, but I've always been pretty good with my hands so I built my own harp. Admittedly, it's rather unorthodox and looks rather like a large boot and there were many ribald comments when I appeared with it, but the tone is very sweet and already the Big Man has commented on it. And as for harping itself - I've always been very musical so that was no problem at all and almost immediately I was appointed Head Harpster of my section and this allows me to skip the lessons which are usually a bit boring.

And flying was a bit tricky too and it was with some trepidation when I donned my wings. My chest is forty-two and I am quite heavy and the wings seemed so flimsy, but I needn't have worried - I soared up like - well, like a little angel and there was much rejoicing by my section - one wanted to thump me on the shoulders and congratulate me but very quickly I reminded him where we were.

But now the trouble is the ghosting. I can't do it. Why the - sorry, why the dickens can't I? And the miracling - what about that sort of thing? I'd love to do a

73

bit of that. But never mind, I have an appointment with the Big Man later on - at the moment He's at a symposium on cloud walking and is it possible to run - so hopefully all will be revealed later on. Thing is, I had a very lovely wife and we loved each other very much and I thought, well, if I could sort of ghost her then she would see me and we could have a chat - and even a snuggle. And I might even have a go at miracling her poor old knees - she suffers awful with arthritis. . .

Well, I've had a long talk with the Big Man and He's told me all about it and says that it's alright so long as I don't overdo it - don't go ghosting in old houses, there are enough of those already, and don't go miracling all over the place 'else there'll be nothing for the doctors to do and we don't want any more unemployment, do we? So tomorrow here goes. . .

I'm miserable. The clouds seem to be black - though I suppose they're not really - and the strings of my harp have broken and even though I've restrung it , all it does now is a sort of moaning noise. So I'm miserable. I ghosted my wife yesterday and she looked lovely as ever and our little house looked wonderful *but* I don't think she saw me. . .

Just a minute. A new entry has just arrived. It is a woman. *It is my wife*! 'What happened,' I asked, 'What happened?'

'Well,' she said, 'You scared me to death, didn't you?'

There was a crescendo of harp music and the whispering of many wings flying around and the clouds sort of fluffed up and were snow, snow white.

Vacant Possession

by

Jean Carroll

The house had been up for sale for some time. I was surprised at this as these little two up-two downers were usually snapped up straight away.

I couldn't resist tagging along when my son and daughter-in-law expressed an interest. They were both working now and, as first time buyers, should have no difficulty in securing a mortgage.

The woman next door let us in with the key.

'Smells a bit damp,' said Tony, but Ann was not going to be put off.

'It's only because it hasn't been lived in for a long time,' she replied. 'Look, there's even central heating, it wouldn't take long to warm up.'

I surveyed the modern radiators and gas fires obviously installed by a previous owner while in my minds eye I visualised the old black leaded range of the 1930's.

It had belonged to a little widow woman then. I remembered her well. I used to go to school with her daughter, Ellie, and many's the day I would return home with my friend and stay to tea.

Ellie's Mum would be out cleaning, like as not, to eke out her miserly widows pension. Ellie's brother Johnny, was fourteen and had a paper round after school.

I remembered a day in late November when the mists drew in from the river. It was Ellie's birthday and she was eight years old. My Mum had sent down some ingredients for Mrs Binns to make a cake. Such a nice woman, my Mum had said, and refined with it. Anyone needing a helping hand had not to look far when Nellie Binns was around. A mother in childbirth or a 'laying out', it was all the same to her. 'Salt of the earth,' my Mum had called her.

'Can we cut the cake?' I'd asked Ellie.

'No, we'd better wait until my Mum comes home.'

I could hardly see Ellie's face for the fast fading light as we sat in the dusk before the dying fire. Ellie heaped on more slack to back up the fire and I shivered as the last remaining heat melted away.

Suddenly a sound at the front door caught our attention, but when Ellie went to open it there was no-one there.

'Our Johnny's gone to the shop. He promised to bring me the 'Dandy and the 'Beano' for my birthday,' Ellie was looking forward to it.

A low moan was heard in the region of the doorway and a ghostly figure appeared to float towards us. I remember I was too frightened to scream and was visibly shaking.

In a moment the white sheeted figure had advanced to the foot of the stairs and the sound of hobnailed boots mounting the steps two at a time had brought us back to reality.

'Oh, it's just our Johnny trying to give us a scare.' Ellie had cried, relieved. 'I'll tell my Mum on him and she'll give him a piece of her mind.'

Just then Mrs Binns' key was heard in the lock and Ellie rushed to meet her mother, words of complaint hot upon her lips.

'Why, June, dear, your shaking, whatever's the matter?'

On being told the score Mrs. Binns stormed. 'I'll give that lad a piece of my mind alright, he'd better not show up here in a hurry.'

As if to defeat her words Johnny Binns at once appeared in the doorway.

'Happy Birthday, Sis, here's your comics. I've just come from the corner shop.'

Ellie shook her fist at him accusingly.

'You were here just now, Johnny, please say it was you,' Ellie for all her bravado held some misgivings.

'Must have been a ghost,' declared Johnny, winking mischievously while his mother frowned warningly.

'Now don't you go upsetting them any more, there's no such things as ghosts.'

I remembered her words clearly as if it were yesterday as I sat upon an upturned packing case awaiting Tony and Ann who had gone to investigate upstairs. I was quite familiar with the two small bedrooms they would find and the little square landing in between.

A bathroom extension had been built on downstairs and I considered it a great improvement on the old fashioned stone sink and privvy down the yard.

Tony and Ann were returning down the stairs now followed by the neighbour.

'It seems alright to me,' Tony was saying and Ann agreed.

'It's a wonder no-one has been interested, are you sure we are the first to view?'

'Oh, well, one or two have been in, you know how it is, the word gets round.'

'What word, what do you mean?' Tony was more demanding now.

'Oh well, I may as well tell you, you'll find out soon enough, There are some as do say that it's haunted, although I don't believe in such things myself.'

Ann's eyes were wide with disbelief and Tony openly scoffed.

'Come now, Mrs, you can't expect us to swallow that. How much is the agent paying you? I expect he wants to hold on to it till prices rise.'

The neighbour was on her metal in a minute. . .

'Ask anyone,' she said. 'Anyone round here will tell you about the sightings. I've seen 'him meself, climbing out the front bedroom window, shinning down the drainpipe, and going over to the corner shop. . .Then there's 'er with the scrubbing brush early in the morning. Who do you think keeps the front step whitened? It certainly isn't me!'

The neighbour was ushering them out of the house, turning the key in the lock, and as I glanced down the pristine cleanliness of the front doorstep winked back at me in the fast fading light.

My mind was trapped in the 1930's and how I'd lost touch with my school friend, Ellie, when she'd been evacuated at the beginning of the war. Some time later I remembered my mother telling me Mrs Binns had been devastated when Johnny, her only son, had been drowned at sea. . .But she went on cleaning her steps and rubbing up the brass as if her life depended upon it.

76

Eventually my mum told me that Mrs Binns had died, some said of a broken heart.

Sadly I remembered Johnny in his more kindly moods, when he'd bought us Spanish ribbons from the shop or an ice cream cornet in summer. His pocket money had been little enough without having to share it with us two kids.

Tony and Ann were piling back into the car now.

'It's a pity about the house, it would have been just the thing,' said Ann.

'G'arn, don't tell me you believe in all those old wives tales do you? I could put in an offer in the morning.'

'Don't you dare!' Ann almost snarled as Tony grinned mischievously at her.

On a impulse I told them to wait and I made my way across the road to the corner shop. . .The woman behind the counter must have been surprised when I asked her if she'd got such a thing as Spanish ribbons, but I was more surprised by her reply.

'Well, now you mention it, I do have some in. I keep them under the counter for a special customer. Come to think of it, he's due in about now. A young man in the Navy. He always asks me for them along with the 'Dandy' and the 'Beano'. Says they're for his little sister, though if you want my opinion, I think he reads them himself.'

The woman smiled as she handed me the Spanish ribbons and I gave her the cash.

No, I couldn't believe it. I shook my head as I walked out of the shop. Something, however, made me glance up to the bedroom window opposite where the net curtains were blowing out in the damp night air.

Through the kitchen window I could see the faint flicker of firelight as from a real coal fire and as I watched, incredulous, a little old lady came to draw the curtains cutting out my view.

In the bedroom above blocked against the light I could just discern the tall figure of a young man dressed in sailors uniform and I realised that Johnny and his mother had come home to stay.

Double Identity

by

Jeffrey Hill-Tout

The last man I expected to see that sunny summer afternoon was Jim Bowden. Behind him, as he stood on my doorstep, the trees in Berkeley Square looked cool and green. Then I remembered, he had been imprisoned for embezzlement and, of course, now he was free.

'Why Jim,' I said.

Bowden grinned through his beard. 'The very same, Joshua,' he replied in his genial way.

'Come in, Jim,' I said, 'come in,' and I led him into the living room and gestured to a chair. 'Scotch?' I said.

'Water, no ice,' he replied.

'Well, Jim,' I said, offering him a Corona, ' and what brings you to London?'

He didn't answer at once, just looked round my living room with an appraising and appreciative eye.

'I must say, Joshua,' he said, sipping his Scotch, ' this is a big improvement on that bachelor pad you had.' He puffed his cigar. 'Very nice.'

'The cigar?' I asked.

'That too,' he replied. He sat back in his chair and looked at me, his genial smile about his lips. 'I've come to London to find Madaleine,' he said.

'Madaleine?'

'That's right. Madaleine. I was going to marry her, remember?'

I closed my mouth which had fallen open in surprise. 'Of course, Jim,' I said, 'of course I remember.'

He turned and looked me in the eyes. 'But then,' he went on, 'Madaleine's dead, isn't she?'

'Dead?'

'That's right,' he said.

I took a pull at my Scotch. I felt I needed it. 'But what made you think she was dead?' I asked.

'Well,' he said, 'I heard she had a horrific car crash. From what I heard, she went over a cliff in Madagascar whilst you and she were on holiday there.'

I knocked the ash from my cigar, my fingers trembling ever so faintly. 'You heard that?' I asked.

His gaze wandered round the room again. 'Very sad,' he said. 'I was fond of Madaleine, you know, and she was very much in love with me. She'd have made me a good wife.' He looked me in the eyes again. 'As it was, she married you, Joshua, and left her house and her considerable fortune to you. You killed her for her money, didn't you Joshua?'

I was appalled at such a monstrous suggestion and I looked at him aghast.

'You believe. . .I. . .?' I asked incredulously.

He studied the dead end of his cigar, picked up the lighter on the table between us and relit it. 'I *know* you killed her, Joshua,' he said. 'You can't pretend with me. I saw you.'

'You. . .you saw me what?' I asked.

'I saw you tampering with the steering on her Rolls.'

'Nonsense,' I said, 'you were in jail.'

'Not so, Joshua. I was in Madagascar - out early - remission for good behaviour. I knew what you were up to. You'd blown the gaff on me to Madaleine about my embezzlement to get rid of me. I followed you to Madagascar. I saw you fix the steering.'

At that moment the door opened and my wife walked into the room.

'Hello, Jim', she said . 'You out of prison, then?'

The effect on Bowden was electrical; he sat bolt upright, his eyes bulging from their sockets, then he swallowed hard and grabbed at his drink with a shaking hand.

'Ma. . .Madaleine. . .' he said in a husky voice.

'You seem surprised to see me, Jim,' said my wife.

'Jim thought you were dead, my dear,' I said.

'Rumours of my death are greatly exaggerated, Jim,' she said brightly. 'Mark Twain, y'know.'

'Jim says he saw me fix the steering on your Rolls when we were on that lovely holiday in Madagascar,' I said. 'He thinks I killed you for your money.'

'He thinks *what*. . .?' she said, then she stopped. 'Oh, I see. . .' She shook her head slowly at Jim. 'Now, really, Jim. First it's embezzlement, now it seems, it's blackmail.'

'But. . .' stammered Bowden, 'you *were* killed. It was in the papers.'

'My dear Jim,' I remonstrated mildly, 'my wife is here with me and the Rolls is in my garage. You can see it if you wish.'

'But I saw you fix the steering,' persisted Bowden.

'I didn't touch the steering, Jim,' I said, 'I did have occasion to examine the radiator for a possible water leak. Other than that. . .'

Bowden frowned, perplexed. 'But. . .'

'Call the police, Joshua,' said my wife quietly.

Bowden jumped to his feet. 'No. . no,' he said hastily. I'll go. . . there's been a dreadful mistake. . .I'll go.'

When I returned to the living room my wife had built us both a drink. She smiled as I raised my glass in a toast.

I set down my glass and took her in my arms. 'I'm a very fortunate man, Laura my dear,' I said. 'I've got Madaleine's money, Madaleine's house and Madaleine's lovely twin sister.' I kissed her. 'The car in the garage was bluff, of course.'

'Of course,' said Laura. She sipped her drink. 'There's a French saying. . .'

'Yes there is, darling,' I said. 'It goes, 'the more things change, the more they remain the same' - or words to that effect.'

The Sword

by

Matthew Weir

The sword hung ominously in the air, as if suspended by an invisible thread. A great shaft of blue light radiated from its blade, stabbing at the darkness, creating shadows on the rough bark of the Oak trees that dominated the forest.

Arthur gazed up in amazement. In all the twelve years of his life, he had not seen anything to match the spectacle that befell his eyes at that moment.

Swords do not just appear out of thin air, Arthur thought to himself as he watched with wild curiosity the beautiful weapon bob and sway. And it was beautiful.

A golden hilt set with Emeralds and Sapphires, held the long, shimmering blade aloft. Arthur had seen many swords, but none to match the power and elegance of the one before him now.

He peered out into the blackness beyond the forest. He could just make out the lanterns on Camelot's battlements, fluttering in the breeze.

Mother and Father will worry for me, if I do not return soon, he thought. But however hard he tried, however much he wanted to, he just could not take his eyes from the sword.

He thought of reaching out and touching it, but then decided against it, ignorant of the power that it may hold.

The sword began to slowly turn until the tip of its blade was pointing in the direction of a cave, a small distance away.

Arthur knew he should be afraid but felt no fear. Only a sense of being privileged as the only one to set eyes upon this weird sight.

'Must I go into the cave?' Arthur asked sheepishly. He did not really expect an answer from a sword, but after witnessing its strange powers, if it did speak unto him, he would not be entirely surprised.

The sword didn't speak.

It sang.

A chorus of angelic female voices echoed from the light, filling Arthur's head. When they were lost into the forest, he stepped forward. The sword immediately floated in the same direction.

Arthur reached the cave's mouth. He stopped but the sword did not. It continued to glide forward, beckoning Arthur. He entered the cave gingerly.

Had the sword not been there, the cave would be in perpetual blackness. But its blue light glistened on the damp walls. The only sound was that of the occasional water droplet plummeting from the roof to melt into the darkness and puddles at Arthur's feet.

When Arthur looked up the sword no longer hovered in the air. Nor did it breathe its strange blue light. The light that now flickered on the walls was orange and ahead, Arthur could see a burning lantern fixed into the stone.

The sword lay in the outstretched hands of a dark-robed figure. The person's finger's were thin and on each rested a ring. A hood concealed the stranger's face.

'Who are you?' Arthur asked quietly.

'Do you fear me?' It was a deep, distinctly male voice.

Arthur shook his head. 'I have no reason to.'

'It is I who bewitched the sword,' the man added.

'You are a sorcerer," said Arthur.

The figure stepped forward, into the light. Arthur could now see his face more clearly. The man was old and deep wrinkles were set into his thin face and neck. A black moustache curled from his upper lip to his nostrils. He smiled and Arthur saw that he had very few teeth.

'That is but one name that I could hold, child. And it is one of the more pleasant ones.'

'Do you live in this cave?'

'Sadly, yes. Your people, in the village forced me into this life.'

'But why?' Arthur felt sorry for the man.

'Because I am different to them. I was blessed - though some may say cursed - with powers, beyond your wildest dreams Arthur!'

Arthur took a step back from the man. 'How do you know my name?'

The man sighed a deep and unhappy sigh. 'I know everything Arthur. And yet I know nothing.'

'You knew that I would follow the sword,' Arthur told him.

'Oh yes.'

'And enter this cave where I would meet you.'

'Quite right.' The man sprung lightly to his feet. 'You are destined for greatness Arthur.' He held the sword out. 'This sword will be yours one day.'

Arthur's eyes grew wide and he gasped. 'Mine. . .when?'

'When you become King,' he hissed.

Arthur fell silent, astonished by the old man's prophecy.

'Until then, the sword will remain hidden.'

'But how will I -' Arthur began.

'The sword will find you.'

'How can I trust you? How do I know that you are not just making this up?'

The man raised a long finger. A spark burst from its tip and grew into the shape of a giant egg. It hummed furiously. Arthur watched in amazement as the old man stepped towards it. He turned to face Arthur.

'If you trust me, you will follow,' he said confidently. Then he vanished into the light.

Arthur regarded the magical doorway with silent contemplation. He knew he shouldn't, mustn't go in, yet he felt compelled to. What if the old man is right, what if I do become King? he asked himself. Arthur hesitated only a moment before leaping through the light.

He was by a lakeside. The stranger was stood next to him. The moon's pale light rippled on the water's surface and small waves lapped at the pebbled beach on which they stood. A gentle breeze stirred Arthur's soft blonde hair into his eyes. He flicked it away before asking, 'Why have you brought me here?'

The old man placed a finger on his lips and pointed far out into the lake's centre.

Something stirred in the water. It was long and slender, rising gently from the black depths. Arthur could see now that it was the arm of a woman.

'The Lady of the Lake, Arthur!' the man cried. 'She is the keeper of the sword. It will rest in her hand until the day I spoke of.' He drew back his arm and with a grunt, hurled the great sword towards the arm. The pale fingers grasped the hilt and drew it back beneath the surface. The waters were again still.

Arthur turned. He was back in the forest. He scanned the darkness for any sign of the old man but he had gone.

'Wait!' Arthur yelled. 'Please come back!. I don't even know your name!'

It was then that Arthur knew he would see the old man again; he didn't need to know his name. Time would tell.

It always did.

Sheer Ignorance

by

Alan Toner

Things have really changed for me lately. In a big way. Unfortunately, the change has not been for the better, but for the worse. The *very* worse. I don't know what I have done to deserve all this, I really don't. I mean, as far as I can recall, I've always led a good life, I really have. I'm certainly not a lager lout or a mugger or anything nasty like that. Granted, I'm not a particularly religious person, and indeed haven't been to church for years. But surely God wouldn't see fit to punish me like this just because, unlike most Roman Catholics, I'm not a devout church goer. As long as you live a generally good life, avoiding all temptation towards evil misdemeanours, surely that's the main thing, isn't it? Talking of God, where on earth is he now, when I *really* need him?

So what is it exactly that's troubling me, you might well ask. Well, I'll tell you: people have started to ignore me. I can't stand it, I really can't. I *hate* being ignored. It hurts so much. And it's downright insulting! To think, one time people would always speak to me, and never excluded me from their little conversations, whether in the office or in the pub.

'What do *you* think about it then, Mike?' they would often ask, to which I would always reply with a loquacious and sensible answer, being the pleasantly sociable person that I am. But they don't talk to me anymore, oh no. Nowadays it's just the cold shoulder treatment. Incessant short shrift. Blimey, if ever there was a bloke totally sent to Coventry, it's me!

The fact that Diane has started to ignore me is hurting me the most. Dear Diane, the pretty typist with the long blonde hair, shapely hips and endless legs. Diane, the luscious beauty who always reminds me of Kim Basinger, my favourite actress, whenever I see her. Diane, the girl that I have fancied madly for months now and have longed to ask out for a date. Unfortunately, I *still* haven't gotten round to approaching her so, and considering the way she's been treating me lately, my chances of *ever* scoring with her really do seem to be looking pretty grim. Honestly, you should have seen the way she looked right through me when I passed her in the corridor this morning. Her ignorance was just like a belt in the face, it really was! I even said good morning to her and didn't receive even as much as a nod of acknowledgement! Oh God I'm hurt, I'm so hurt. And angry. Very angry.

But it's no use moaning about it all now. No use crying over spilt milk. What's done is done. Can't turn the clock back. I suppose I'll just have to try and grin and bear it, although it's going to be difficult, so difficult, to do so. Oh how I wish I had never sped along that narrow road in my car!

Diane has just passed me again in the corridor. Just like before, and just as I expected, she totally ignored me, looked right through me. Oh dear God, I can't take much more of this, I really can't.

Sigh. It's not easy being a spirit. It really isn't.

Fool If You Think It's Over

by

Stuart Carey

If Graham Adams had been telling this story, no doubt he would have claimed it was he who had picked up Carol McClean. That it was his chat-up line, his charm and his sexy smile that had got her to go with him. His mates would have laughed and probably believed him.

Standing at over six feet tall with a slim athletic build, longish black hair and an enchanting smile, Graham hadn't any difficulty with women.

Carol knew however that it was she who had engendered their coming together. The moment she set eyes on him she had decided he would be the one. The next one.

He reminded her of Tim. Tim of long ago. Her Tim.

It was Friday night and fate had taken her to the crowded bar of the Crown Hotel in the centre of Chester. Their eyes had met while he was in conversation with two other men. He had leaned forward for a better view. She had made an instant decision.

Within minutes he was by her side, using all his charm. She thought his chat-up line could have been improved, but the smile could have melted ice.

She allowed him to monopolise the conversation. Happy to listen to his illiberal opinions on women, the world as a whole, and this part of North West England in particular. From a man with less physical presence most girls would have rejected this almost arrogant approach.

Graham was charming though, had a wonderful laugh, and was nearly as good looking as he imagined himself to be.

When after an hour or so he had enquired about her life she had been vague. She told him she was single, twenty-nine years old, and because of her work, of no fixed abode. He accepted this with hardly a follow up question. She gathered from this that his intentions were not long term.

He leant towards her, as if to be heard above the din, instead of talking had kissed her lightly on the lips. She smiled, it was not unpleasant. The scent of his aftershave rekindled a memory which in turn made her stomach feel weak. He manoeuvred her to a quieter corner then kissed her again. This was the sort of place in which such behaviour was commonplace. She had chosen well.

A visit to the ladies where the noise abated somewhat, enabled her to freshen her thoughts as well as her sparse make-up. Carol smiled at her reflection as she adjusted her blonde hair.

He was laughing and chatting with the same two men as earlier when she returned to his side. He didn't introduce them and they left the bar almost immediately. Graham appeared to be the only scorer in tonight's game.

It was late when they vacated the now almost deserted hostelry. They giggled and shared little hugs and kisses, the cold night air bringing the effects of the evening's drinking to the surface.

His car was a new Mazda, exactly the same model as her own which was parked at Liverpool Airport. He looked offended, as though his masculinity was being questioned or threatened when she offered to drive. Carol did not push the point. If he felt he had to prove himself in this way, she'd take her chance. As it turned out alcohol was less of a danger to their safety than the fact that his hands spent more time on her than on the steering wheel. She allowed a little of this groping. Her resistance but a token.

Fifteen minutes later he led her into his small flat at a place called Backford. It was clean and tidy and not easily distinguishable as home to a bachelor. Once in the door Graham stepped up a gear. An urgent kiss, both hands going to her breasts.

'Hey slow down,' she chuckled. 'We've got the whole night haven't we.'

Reluctantly he removed his hands, 'I'll get some wine,' he said.

The wine was cold, white and dry, just the way she liked it. However it was he who consumed the lions share.

Chris Rea mumbled softly in the background as Graham undressed her in front of the fire. Kisses were laid on her neck, back and bottom. She turned getting herself into a more comfortable position. It was now the turn of breasts and stomach to receive attention.

She helped him out of his clothes, it became the turn of her mouth to do the exploring.

They made love with relish and delight. Twice she called him Tim during their coupling. Graham didn't care, this had been a great, if transient night.

Carol lay so quietly by his side he thought she had fallen asleep. He placed an arm across her lovely body then dozed contentedly. He awoke to the rhythm of her hand bringing his member back to its rampant former self. He groaned with pleasure as she nibbled and tweaked his flesh.

Tears welled in her eyes then drifted onto Graham's lower limbs.

'Tim,' she murmured faintly. 'Oh Tim, I do love you. Don't ever leave me.'

Graham felt a slight unease, but the impending climax from her now frantic movements overshadowed all rational thoughts.

Her timing was precise. His numbing pleasure literally cut short as the razor sharp blade removed his manhood. Carol stabbed repeatedly while grotesquely holding his severed penis in her free hand.

Graham remained incredibly soundless during all this carnage. Death being mercifully swift.

Carol stood for a long time in the hot shower. All traces of blood erased. Her blonde hair returning to its original brown under the fast flowing jets of water.

'Poor Tim,' she said as she stepped over Graham's mutilated torso. 'Poor Tim.'

The sleek white Mazda was leaving the motorway on its journey back to Bedford as the resonant jingle on its radio heralded the news. A bomb in Knightsbridge was the lead story, followed by a gruesome find in Chester. Police were already linking it to unsolved murders in Cardiff and Coventry. There was also speculation that the killing of television personality Timothy Beaumont in Cambridge in June of last year, could be connected. The detective leading the murder inquiry stated that there were many similarities. Not least of which was a missing part of the victims anatomy.

Carol parked the car in the driveway of her parents farm. She walked past the stables to the pigs enclosure. The contents of the plastic bag were soon devoured. Rubbing her hands together as if brushing off dirt, Carol felt a great release. She could now relax and forget all about Tim.

However, Cheltenham could be worth a visit in a month or two.

Felicity White

by

Carol McKendrick

Just being alive was embarrassing for Felicity White. She ate just chicken breasts from Marks and Spencer's and went out into the world only when protected by the safe zone of her cigarette smoke. Like a bride or a fairy she never seemed to need the toilet.

Taller, thinner, paler, darker than anyone else, she reminded me of a couple of saints I knew, one who lived only on Communion hosts and another who jumped out of a window to her death rather than have sexual intercourse. When I heard about the latter saint I thought 'Well of course,' so it wasn't surprising that I palled up with Felicity White.

Life had become steadily more embarrassing, school sandwiches without Tupperware or even tin foil, just decomposing paper bags. The facts of life, sanitary towels discreetly appearing in my bottom drawer. I prayed nightly I would never need them, or deodorant.

Unable to stop my body's natural progression I denied myself life as far as I could. When I met Felicity at nineteen then, I think my asexual air and the fact that I had never eaten a meat pie did give me a certain cachet.

We were at Liverpool doing Philosophy together, or would have been if Felicity had ever attended. Two weeks into the first term lecturers began to ask if Felicity White was present. She became as omnipresent and as elusive as the unicorns we constantly discussed, grazing on the campus for all to see, but only when we weren't looking. Until one day. One glazing epistemology lecture there was a sudden explosion, one of the swing doors was blown open, slamming so hard against the wall of the lecture theatre that the plaster cracked. A girl stood in the haze of smoke, one tiny hand still clenching the door handle, in the other hand her cigarette. Thick, dark, spiky cut hair, natural punk white skin. She looked like Keith Richard, which was ill by 1978. I knew instantly this was Felicity White attending her first lecture.

That evening I looked through the list of first year students and found Felicity was in the hall of residence next door. I went straight round and hammered on her door. She opened it and I saw over her shoulder into the room. The furniture was huddled into the centre, the empty wardrobe gaping open behind her. The walls were bare and the bed had not been made up. Of course, I had tried to put my minimalist stamp on my own room, rolling up the rug and taking down the lampshade but Felicity's room was in a league of its own. There was nothing to show that the room was occupied apart from the presence of Felicity herself.

'You're Felicity White,' I told her.

She let me in and I sat on her trunk which was behind the door. She stood in front of me, the electric light plunging into her navy blue hair. She told me how she loved the Rolling Stones and hated students and University. I said so did I.

The next day I went to Boots and along with my feminine hygiene products brought the latest Rolling Stones LP and a record player. I took the pictures off my walls and asked Felicity to my room.

By the second term I was going out with Robert and had a group of friends. What with the communal washrooms and complaints about the constant playing of my LP I'd moved out of the hall into a frozen green attic. I didn't see much of Felicity, she went home to her flat in London every weekend which she shared with her boyfriend. Sometimes though I'd see her in the Arts Reading Room behind a heap of philosophy books reading 'The Daily Mail'. We'd go for coffee, Felicity drank her's black and I had a three pack of digestives. She told me her family was a disaster, her father had vanished, her mother was odd and her brother an astronomer. I said I understood.

Gradually I saw more and more of Felicity. I skipped lectures and Robert and we'd go to cinema matinees and Marks and Spencers just before closing. I knew we weren't popular with the till girls but I hadn't realised what everyone else thought, until Robert told me.

Felicity and I had just been to see 'Manhattan', coming out into the brightness of the afternoon we met him. He nodded and carried on walking, he told me why later.

'You change completely when you're with her. I don't like you when you're with Felicity.'

It was as if Felicity was beside me. I laughed at him, swung my library books on my shoulder and went home.

Felicity and I scraped our first year exam's, only Robert had to resit.

When the second year started I was thrilled to see Felicity, she had told me she might not come back. This year I'd decided to live at home and commute from nearby Southport. Felicity was ensconced at The Feathers Hotel on Brownlow Hill at some sky high rate a night while she looked for a flat. After a week I asked her back to my parents house for dinner and to stay over. I knew it was only for financial reasons she accepted. So we checked out of The Feathers and headed for Southport with her suitcase and record-player. My mother says she will never forget that night.

I'd told them what to cook and not to fuss so we had our meal on trays watching 'Coronation Street'. During the adverts my father spoke.

'Felicity needs another couple of potatoes.' We all looked at Felicity's plate. She sprung up, the tray flying off her knees like an Olympic ski jumper, and she shot out of the room. We were stunned. My father at his broken crystal wine glass on the hearth, my mother at the roast chicken on the Chinese rug and me at Felicity's tears.

I ran upstairs after her, tapping on the bedroom door as I pushed it open. Felicity stood at the far end of the room with her back to me, sharp elbows on the mantelpiece her head bowed, black spikes of hair piercing through her child's hands. Her skimpy jumper, worn trousers and cracked plastic trainers pulsated with sobs. I tiptoed towards her and reached out my hand.

'Go away!'

I fled downstairs.

My parents and I crept up to bed at 11.00. The light was on in Felicity's room but there was no sound. I didn't go to sleep for a long time. My mother didn't sleep at all. She told me she had got up at 4.00, Felicity's light was still on but all was silent. When my mother finally dared go into the room with a cup of tea the next morning she was quite sure she'd find Felicity dead, blood and more ruined carpet. Felicity was standing by the mantelpiece in her jumper, trousers and trainers and told my mother she only drank coffee.

The second year passed much like the first. It was on and off with Robert and I hated every minute of my course but at least there were no exam's. Felicity found a two bedroom flat for herself and her record player. Her boyfriend started to come up at weekends and she told me I'd probably meet him. I never did.

On the first day of the third year, having worked as a waitress during the vacation, I went straight to Felicity's flat to check she'd come back. She told me I'd put on weight. I ate only Kit-kats during our final year.

Robert and I got Thirds and I told him I never wanted to see him again, Felicity got a Two Two and was over the moon. I bought her a man's trilby hat and helped her move out of her flat. In the two years she'd lived there I'd never been allowed into her bedroom and when I saw it for the first time that day, completely bare, it crossed my mind it had been like that the whole time. She gave me all the things she couldn't be bothered to take back with her and we struggled to Lime Street for the London train. I pushed the trolley along the platform, Felicity jauntily striding on ahead with the TV. Selecting a carriage she turned round and laughed. A box of soap powder had slipped and I'd left a shinning white snail trail of Persil all the way down the platform. I'd never seen her so happy. The train pulled out and I sat down on the empty trolley and cried.

We kept in touch. Felicity had given me her mother's address and my letters were forwarded to her flat. She got a job as a picture researcher and I started applying for jobs in London, there was nothing but trouble brewing in Liverpool. In November I finally got a job at the National Sound Archive, a chubby red brick house squashed behind the Albert Hall.

I hated it. The bird song man, the African drum woman, just rooms full of noises and silent experts who'd been there since dot. I was everybody's dogsbody and nobody spoke to me. I'd moved in with an ancient couple of former bakers, friends of friends of my parents. They kept a specimen of every year's Hot Cross Bun since World War Two in a glass case in the lounge and had no wastepaper baskets. I found the dustbin outside - empty and lined with scented drawliner. I started to take my rubbish to work in a carrier bag and wondered if I was going out of my mind.

Whenever I wrote to Felicity - care of her mother - she would always ring me and we'd meet up, but the time lag got me down and I had yet to meet her boyfriend or be introduced to any of her friends. I began to doubt their existence.

One Wednesday as I made for Harrods late night shopping I was suddenly outside myself, leaving my body and joining the unicorns in Hyde Park, I could see my own misery. I realised just talking to make-up girls would not suffice, I decided to go and visit Felicity's mother. Even if she was out, I could leave a note and be one day nearer Felicity and with any luck Felicity herself might be there, visiting. I turned round and headed for Notting Hill.

It was a quiet car lined road, the cars all drained grey in the white street light. The houses were enormous London ones with fat slug-like pillars crawling up either side of the front door and lots of glimmering door bells. Number 47 was no more nor less dilapidated than the rest. The communal door was open and I started to climb the stairs to Flat F. All the light bulbs worked and the lino was swept. When I reached the flat a man was coming out.

'Hello, is Felicity in?' I asked.

He looked perfectly normal, just surprised and perhaps rather quickly closed the front door.

'No, no she's not.' We stood looking at each other.

'I'm a friend of hers, Carol.'

'I'm her brother - Andrew, the astronomer, I'll tell her you called.' He was waiting for me to go downstairs, I did and he put the latch on the front door as he followed me out.

'Goodbye,' and he was gone, walking quickly into the dark end of the road. I headed back to the lights and traffic of Ladbroke Grove.

Felicity rang me the next day at work.

'You went to my mother's house.'

'Yes, I was so . . .'

'I said on no account were you to do this,' Felicity always spoke like a character from 'Guys and Dolls'.

'I know Fliss but . . .'

'We have to speak about this.'

It was to be that day, 4.30 at the Victoria and Albert Museum. It was always somewhere like this, St Paul's or Cleopatra's Needle but at least the V and A was convenient for my flexi-time.

I don't know what I expected. Felicity was already there, lurking behind a vase, when I arrived. I followed her up several flights of stairs when on a random, or perhaps pre-selected, landing she stopped and slid into a deep, dark window ledge. Her swinging trainers momentarily beating against the wood panelling, she stilled herself. Only the glass separated her hair from the mid-December darkness. I stood before her. She spoke.

'I cannot see you anymore.'

'What?' I didn't know what she meant.

'I do not want to see you anymore, you came to my mother's house.'

'I know, but . . .' She didn't let me finish.

'You don't understand my family,' her voice was rising, 'I do not want to see you again.'

'What . . .'

'I can't trust you,' she said.

'Why . . .' I started. And then I questioned everything. Why couldn't I ever have her address, see her bedroom, meet her mother, her boyfriend, her friends. Why? I'd accepted Felicity without question, like an SAS crack squad obeying orders, or a child interested only in self preservation. Why were we here now, in this ridiculous museum.

'Oh come off it Felicity,' I shouted. 'What's the big deal, what does it matter If I went to your mother's, what's the big secret anyway?'

90

I wasn't about to find out. Felicity slipped off the window ledge and quickly padded downstairs. I hung over the banisters watching until she became indistinguishable among a group of Japanese tourists.

And that was the last time I ever saw Felicity White. I wrote to her for at least a year and one day I got a letter in reply. Short and to the point.

'I do not want to see you. Why persist? The world is teeming with people.'

Why persist? Why Felicity? Because she was someone to skitter across the surface of life with, both of us too embarrassed to face up to what was underneath.

Pages From A War Widows Diary

by

Jerry Laeh Cim

I had waited so long, the countless times I had seen girls and women waiting at the train station with the look of longing and uncertainty on their faces and in their eyes. And hope please don't forget hope, such a small word that can conquer mountains. Yet today for some that hope to be banished like I had seen so many times, and each time doesn't make it any easier or soften that cruel blow.

I visited the station everytime the men came home those brave soldiers including boys. I don't know why I wanted to punish myself by doing this as it only made me upset and unable to concentrate on my life again, and remember such painful loss, without even your body to grieve for.

The Beginning:

I had met you just before this blasted war was declared and we like fools thought it wouldn't touch us, so naive and in love!

But one day you came home in uniform and though I remember thinking how smart it was and with a smile of admiration on my face, I felt it was only play acting, till you said 'Now I feel proud enough to die for my King and Country.' How that hurt my heart and I remember thinking: but what about me! I'm not ready for you to lay down your life so easily, so quickly, but I never got to say any of those words that my heart was begging me to say.

And on a beautiful sunny day you left me. It seemed so cruel so frightening and such a waste. And I cried, I cried for you, for me for everyone till I could cry no more, but sit stonily silent and pray you'd be home soon and safe.

I was glad I had decided to stay with your parents as it gave me comfort and company and a lot less time to think and brood. I also felt comfort in the fact you didn't feel alone too.

I was only thinking the other day, how we had argued over such silly things as children and how many we'd have and what their names would be and how it seems so trivial, so futile and pointless to argue especially when you love someone so much. Right now I'd give anything to hold you in my arms and agree to anything you said, my darling I love you.

I had received another letter of you they are so special and in my quiet moments I read them over and over again yet they are so few. And everyone tells me there's a war on you know as if I don't know my Husband my Beloved is out there fighting it. But I know deep down they are just as worried and do care.

Time and emotions are very fragile. I Love You.

My Darling, every day I try to write about things that you have missed and this war must seem so long to you as well. I know you appear cheerful and tell me to keep my spirits up but I do miss you so much. And I do think it's important to write your feelings down because I want you to know how I missed you and ached for you and most of all want you to be near me and feel your lips upon mine once again. I Love You, goodnight My Darling.

Today the telegram came. I must have read it a thousand times I don't want to believe it, missing in action what does that mean that you are dead, oh God forbid or have they left you, not gone back for you oh My Darling could you be so alone, left hurt please dear God keep him safe and bring him home to me.

It is 3am, everywhere is in darkness and tranquil yet such noise and horrors are happening around us I pray for you. I Love You.

I have cried so many tears and my heart is breaking, people have been so kind to me yet they have their own sorrows too how unselfish people can be at their own grief. Everyone needs comfort.

Another week has passed and not a sign from you at all. If I could at least get a letter from you I feel I would have something to live for my innermost thoughts are around you. God keep you safe my comfort is believing you will return. I Love You. The day is nearly over and I haven't written much I start to write and my eyes glaze over and I start to drift off and think about the happiness we shared, just you and me I see no others, I feel so alone!

My Love I Love You I have never stopped loving you in thought and prayer, my heart is so heavy and my burden no lighter. I talk to you every day I pray for you to hear me.

My time has been taken up listening to other people's suffering I feel it is the least I can do though I offer them kind words and comfort I feel no comfort and my nights are lonely without you by my side. I feel you being forgotten by others, yet I know they are afraid too.

My Love I cry but fear to grieve. I am afraid to go to sleep for fear of not thinking of you. I picture you in my mind and I see you so smart so proud yet so helpless.

So many men have returned, yet they have left something behind them. Such sadness. And everyone wants to be happy again. But I'll only be happy with you by my side.

I try to think positively and of all things we will do when this war is over! Will it be soon?

I hear shouting in the street below and fail to understand my own language. The war is over the war is over! everyone is shouting and crying they are dressed and in a state of undress. I'm crying but not with happiness I'm crying because I cannot share this glorious moment with you, where are you? My Love are you celebrating too? on the other side of the world.

So this war is over yet my war has just begun. You never did return and I never saw your smiling face again or felt your lips upon mine. I am happy for those who have returned to family and friends and feel saddened for those who have not I Love You.

I still write to you as though it was yesterday, yet now my youth has gone and I am scarred by life's cruel blow. I still wait for you and people think me an old fool. Such sadness that we never had children.

I never found you or knew where to lay down my grief and flowers. I do try not to think of my love so cold and alone, so brave but gone.

I still dream of you and as though it was yesterday, I feel you kiss me and hold my hand and wake up with tears in my eyes.

I've seen so many things change for good and bad but my sorrow for you will never go, as time to me has been no healer.

Janice Mouthed A Silent Word

by

Don-Paul Groom

The hedge separating the gardens hadn't been trimmed or cut for over four years. It reached up its grandeur massive. It spread wide pregnant with possibilities. It was home to a family of mice who darted to and fro between its dense roots. It was a metropolis for errant bloated spiders who grew fat from the pickings that were to be had from their invisible wavering death-traps. But most of all it was a wall. A towering screen that blocked sight and rumour of the house next door.

Janice was so glad that the hedge grew on her property as she hated having to tame something as fecund as nature. If the witch next door had her way the hedge would lose its beauty and become a mere privet, something cauterised and short enough for the witch to look over whilst walking along her path. Janice hated the witch next door. Janice would cringe everytime she heard the clanking of next door's gate. She would sit holding her breath expecting to hear the heavy footfalls of the witch coming up the path then the tap, tap, tap on the window. But so far today the footfalls or the tap, tap, tap hadn't come. Nor would they.

Hatred like most things that die has a base. A root or seed, the cause that creates the effect. Janice's hatred for the witch next door was planted years ago when the witch baby-sat for Janice's father whilst he was out or away on business. She had always known the witch who whenever possible filled Janice's head with educational contributions. Contributions that imprisoned a part of Janice's mind and left it starving. It soon began to find food however. The food was hatred and what a fine meal that was. Eventually the imprisoned brain became obese, bulging, threatening to break-out. Escape was impossible so soon the brain became sickened. It would gorge itself on hatred then spew a denser hatred out in a verbal projectile. It would become a violent accuser blaming the witch for its ills. It was right in a circular sort of way.

The witch never did understand Janice's outbursts of intense hatred. Why should she? To the witch Janice had been a normal girl who whilst passing through puberty had found it hard maybe a little embarrassing to talk to and relate to a woman twice her age. Janice often wondered if perhaps she was wrong in her understanding of the witch. Maybe it wasn't hatred she felt. . . just. . . just mere abhorrence for that nefarious corpulent female. Janice also wondered why she wondered such things only in the end to come full circle and reaffirm her hatred. If someone had asked Janice the reasons for her hatred she would smile and mentally run away from the question. For no one knew she hated the witch not even the witch herself. If she ever did bump into the witch in the street she would be polite and hide her hatred like she had taught herself to. Her bubbling ire would not be given vent until she was at home, solitary behind her own walls.

The witch would, on occasion, invite herself round to Janice's bringing a pie or some other hot delicacy namely gossip. It was never 'Gossip Gossip' just a tirade of anger that was repeated over and over and directed towards Janice's father. The witch hated Janice's father and so did she a bit. She still got angry with him even though she hadn't seen him for ten years. He had gone East and yes he had never returned. But he had been offered the chance of a lifetime, his daughter had just turned sixteen and the witch had offered to look after her. So with his only daughter's security confirmed he disappeared to the East and never came home. None of the anticipated letters ever came nor calls. Janice's father could have been dead. And who isn't angry with the dead? Or is it envy?

Janice left home at seventeen and by the time she was twenty-three she'd brought a house of her own. She was not in a relationship, she had a good job and she was happy. Happy that was until the witch moved into the house next door.

Janice contemplated murder that day but life and dignity got the better of her. She made out that she was pleased to see the witch and in a beaten dog way she was. She had missed her hatred.

The witch moved in.

The smiles became false.

The hedge was allowed to grow.

'Are you going to trim your hedge?' Inquired the witch in a friendly sort of way.

'No I'd rather not.' Replied Janice smiling.

. . . and grow. . .

'How are you Janice?' The witch asked, her fat face straining to peer over the hedge.

'Fine thanks. . . and you?' countered Janice holding back a laugh.

. . . and grow. . .

'Janice are you there? questioned the witch from behind the hedge.

'No I'm not.' Janice whispered to herself. Then she started to grin.

. . . and grow for four years.

Janice couldn't stop the witch from calling at the house so she would - depending on her mood, pretend she was out. Other times she would welcome the witch in. Inviting her to share food and drink and laughter. This happened twice a year: Janice's birthday and Christmas Day.

It was Christmas Day today and the witch hadn't arrived. Janice pondered this for a moment. She'd been dreading this day since her birthday. The witch had better be coming or else. By early evening the witch hadn't arrived and the turkey dinner had dried and died. By late evening there was still no sign and Janice thought of doing the unthinkable. Go next door and find out what the witch was up to. Boxing day came and Janice much against her own ideals left her house at first light. She wore her finest warm clothes and under her arm she carried an elaborately decorated box. She went to the gate of the house next door and lifted the latch then entered the pathway. The gate clanked shut behind her loudly in the post Christmas quiet. She ascended the steps leading to the front door and raised her hand to knock. The door was ajar. Gently she pushed the door and it swung quietly open. With trepidation and a colourful box she stepped into the hallway.

The hallway was a mess. Letters, coats, shoes, hats, umbrellas scattered about like a jumble sale. She walked forward and entered the lounge. This too was in disarray except this disarray wasn't from laziness or sloth but from hard work. It was very thorough this work. The house had been burgled.

Janice mouthed a silent word and moved to another room: this room had been raped too.

Janice mouthed a silent word.

Janice ran upstairs now screaming the silent word. She burst through the doors into the defiled bedroom and saw the witch, lying in a drying pool of blood. Her skull had been blown open for inspection and her once jewelled fingers had been hacked off for speed. Janice mouthed the silent word repeatedly:

'Mother . . . mother . . . mother . . .'

Lunch In The City

by

Sue Gerrard

Mike ordered another gin and tonic and glanced nervously at his watch again. 1.15pm - Julie was late and Mike was not amused. She knew how important he found punctuality especially under the circumstances, things were bad enough without her playing games.

The waiter brought his drink and asked him for the fifth time whether he was ready to order. Suddenly Mike felt his whole life was exposed to everyone in the restaurant.

1.20pm - there had better be a good reason why she was late, he thought. She knew he had to be back at the office for 2.30pm and it was on the other side of the city. All this secrecy was fun at first but after a while the constant looking over one's shoulder became a strain.

A thousand times he'd asked himself what he would do if his wife found out. Deny it all or brazenly admit he'd been having an affair for over a year.

One thing, he did know however, was that she'd never forgive him. Again he asked himself how he'd got involved and where was all this pleasure he should be having?

1.25pm - and Mike strained his eyesight and drained his glass but still no sign of Julie.

'Damn her,' he muttered and then glanced round the surrounding tables to see if anyone had heard him. But no, they were all too engrossed in their own conversations and suddenly he felt unbearably alone.

He was undecided whether to go or order another drink and decided on the latter. After all she had said that it was important that she saw him, when she'd rung this morning. But if she didn't hurry up, he'd be too drunk to listen.

He couldn't think what was so important. He'd made it quite clear that he'd no intention of breaking up his marriage for an affair - to him one affair was just like another. Girls came and went but nobody stayed forever.

No he'd worked too hard to build up a perfect marriage and Carole was definitely an asset on the social ladder he was fast climbing. She was quite attractive, but not so much that she would be the centre of attention at the 'home business' dinners he was fond of giving. She was an excellent hostess, good cook and was wise enough to know her place on every occasion.

It was a good marriage, but then Julie had never once asked him to dent it never mind break it up. She never complained about the broken dates or hole-in-the-corner arrangements he'd had to resort to.

In one way he felt cheated - if she cared for him, really cared then she would want him to leave Carole or at least try to prove herself a potentially good wife.

But no, she had never tried to compete with Carole and never even asked about the state of his marriage or even if he was seeing someone else. In short, she was just too easy going about the whole affair.

Still that was really all irrelevant now. His new promotion had seen to that, Mike had known as soon as he'd got the job that Julie had to go.

He just couldn't afford any scandal now - well not for the moment anyway. Maybe when he'd seen what the new department was like, found out what the other guys in the office were up to, well perhaps then he and Julie could get together again.

He'd known for a month now but just couldn't find a way to tell her. He'd made no promises but still he didn't want to hurt her any more than he had to. But time was running out.

'Hi darling, I'm sorry I'm late, have you ordered?' a soft, familiar voice broke his thoughts and he looked up to see his problem facing him.

God this isn't going to be easy, he thought, after one look at the elfin face framed with blonde hair.

'Where the hell have you been? I've been here for almost an hour and you know I have to be back at the office by 2.30pm. Have you no consideration at all Julie? I've got a terrible afternoon ahead of me, I've got to go through all the sales figures. I've had far too much to drink while I've been waiting, I'll never get them right. Honestly you interrupt an important business meeting to drag me across the city for lunch so that we can talk and you can't even be here on time. And no I haven't ordered.'

She just smiled and picked up the menu and flicked her eyes quickly over it - she could always make him feel in the wrong even if he knew he was right. She paused and then put the menu back on the table.

'I said I was sorry. I had to meet someone first and buy something very important. It just took longer than I thought and I got caught in all the lunchtime traffic.'

I don't believe it, Mike thought, here am I trying to decide our future and she's out shopping. He took a deep breath, he didn't want to cause a scene, he had to play up to her if he was, sometime during the next thirty minutes, going to tell her their affair was over.

'I thought you said it was important?' he coaxed.

Again she picked up the menu only to replace it on the table moments later.

'It is.'

Silence.

'Well, why the shopping spree?' he asked in what he thought was a reasonable voice.

'It's all part of the same thing. I really don't know where to begin. . .'

He would have taken her hands for reassurance if she hadn't quickly put them on her lap.

'Mike. . .' she began, 'I know we've come to mean a lot to each other. . .' her voice trailed off.

Oh God it was leave your wife time, this was his chance, his reason.

'Julie,' he started, but she interrupted him.

'Mike please listen this is important,' she paused, 'I can't see you again.'

His face was about to break into a smile and he almost breathed a sigh of relief. But then his pleasure at the news turned into indignation. How dare she - say that to him, he'd always been good to her as far as he could be.

'Why not?' he asked in a strained voice.

'Well darling . . . you see I'm getting married and well it wouldn't be fair, would it?'

Slowly the waiter approached.

The Watcher

by

Jonathan Weir

He was clever. He knew when to wait, how to wait and where to wait. He knew how to make an operation run smoothly and successfully. He had been biding his time since darkfall, watching the house with those large, haunting eyes. The occupants had no idea that they were being surveyed from outside by a stranger. Someone they knew nothing about.

But he knew their lives inside out. He knew that the father left for work at 8am everyday except Tuesday, and that he wore the same shirt for business meetings *and* social functions. The mother was always up first. She read the Guardian and liked cornflakes and coffee for breakfast. The eldest daughter saw a different boy every night of the week and favoured the colour black. She was always losing her car keys. The youngest daughter led a quieter life. She read a lot and drank mineral water. She was hooked on 'Gone With The Wind'.

He knew much more than that, more than enough, he decided. He would not watch them any longer. Tonight he would make his move.

He knew the house. He knew where every door led, what every cupboard contained. He was not worried about the house's alarm system. That did not present a problem.

No, his only concern was getting into the house. It was warm tonight, they would probably leave a window open or unlocked. Then he could simply stroll inside and help himself to whatever he liked. No problem.

The time passed quickly. Soon the lower floor lights went out and he heard voices. Then the beeps of the alarm box being set. The family had retired for the evening.

He saw the kitchen window had been left open. It was too easy.

He liked his lips and jumped off the window ledge, landing on all four paws. As always.

Anybody Seen Ann?

by

J Fairhurst

The jumble sale was due to start at 7pm but, as usual, most of the dealers were there by six or shortly afterwards. Bert had even arrived by 5.30 for this was expected by the connoisseurs of jumbles to be one of the better ones and you have to be early if you want to find anything good now people are parting with their bric-a-brac less rashly. Bert blames programmes like 'Going for a Song' for the public's increased awareness.

Nearly all those who frequent jumbles are not dealers, however, and Ann is one of this second group, the addicts. Some of them obviously need a bargain, others merely want one. For some the jumble provides a night out for 10p and a chance to talk to someone, just as queues for food provided chances in wartime.

Most of the regulars know each other by sight if not by name and will notice if anyone is absent. As usual Vera was holding forth as the queue waited. She'd been reading an article on second-hand books and it claimed that an early Agatha Christie was worth £2,000 in its dust-jacket but only £200 without it.

'Plain daft I call it,' she said, '£1,800 for a bit of paper. It's almost as mad as £25 million for that picture of sunflowers.'

'What's meant by 'an early Agatha Christie'?' said Louie, obviously thinking of the contents of one of the tables that evening. 'How early's early?' No one seemed to know so the subject was allowed to drop.

'Wonder what's happened to Ann?' said someone, for she wasn't there that evening, well not by 6.45 anyway, which was late for her.

Then they saw her. She's a big woman with dyed hair. Probably she's in her early forties, though she wouldn't be likely to admit it. In winter she's usually wearing a tight duffle coat and always she's carrying the large bag that's the mark of most jumble sale goers. That evening she was walking more slowly than usual and somehow she didn't look her normal self.

'Thought you'd gone to the mayoral ball instead,' said the life and soul of the party. Ann barely smiled and at first made no reply. Instead she turned to the man just ahead of her who was reading the local paper and said, 'Is that the 'Echo'?

'No,' was the reply, 'just the local.'

Ann didn't explain the reason for her question and didn't speak again for five minutes or so. Then, turning to the regulars, she suddenly said, 'I couldn't stand it in the house any longer. I had to come out even though me fellow's just died. I've known him over ten years and he's been to see me four or five times each week. I knew he was ill but he wouldn't let me go and see him at home cos he said his sister would be jealous of another woman. He hadn't been to see me for a week so last night I rang him. A woman answered and I asked how he was. 'My husband died this afternoon,' the woman said.

The regulars sympathised for the loss and also for the deception suffered and Ann brightened a little. 'Mind you,' she said, 'I've got another fellow as well so it might be worse.' And then it was 7 o'clock and the queue began to move into the hall.

Bert's early arrival certainly proved worthwhile for him as just behind the bric-a-brac stall was a hideous marble-topped washstand - well, hideous if you don't happen to know that such items fetch £200 - £300 at auction nowadays. Long gone are the times when people would buy them for 10/- or 50p, rip off the marble tops to use for flooring and chop up the wood for kindling.

Louie of course had made straight for the bookstall and she'd found an Agatha Christie dated 1955 - and it had a dust-jacket! - Pity she didn't know that by that date Mrs Christie was already a very well known and popular authoress whose books were being produced in large numbers and therefore are of no great value - dust-jacket or not. Pity too that she failed to buy a fine copy of the first edition of Ian Fleming's 'Casino Royale', his first book, that was also on the book table that evening. The little man who did spot it came away chuckling to himself and several hundred pounds richer!

In the excitement of the hunt people don't pay much attention to their neighbours unless somebody happens to get in the way. Then a few deft shoves with elbows or shopping bags are often employed, and Ann as a big woman is at a considerable advantage in this respect. This evening, however, she had little enthusiasm for the search and the only thing she'd found was a Jaeger sweater that looked too small for herself, though it might do for her next door neighbour. She'd paid the fifty pence asked for it without haggling and had just turned towards the exit when she saw him coming towards her - Bill, her fellow who'd died the previous day.

When a sixteen stone woman faints on a wooden floor there's quite a distinct thud even in the hubbub of a jumble sale. When she came round she'd been moved into a little office and Bill was still there.

'I guessed you'd be here,' he said. 'I only got out of hospital at teatime and my nephew's just told me what my sister said to you. I knew she was afraid I might get married one day. Well, after what she said, that's exactly what I'm going to do as soon as I can, that's if a certain lady called Ann will be my wife!'

The Cat Flap

by

Laurence Keighley

'I hate cats!' was the thought that constantly repeated itself inside Gerry Talbot's mind, as he struggled against the wind and rain. The local pet shop he was making for was only about two hundred metres from their home, but the rain was already penetrating his coat and soaking his inner clothes. 'Is this indirectly my fault?' he thought again; 'Am I getting completely soaked because of the new back door?' He shook these thoughts from his mind, where they were replaced by, 'It's the cat's fault.'

Gerry had bought the new back door on the insistence of Margaret, his wife. Buying and fitting a door was a job Gerry would naturally put off as long as he could, but on this occasion he had to admit the old back door was in a dreadful state and needed replacing. They travelled to an appropriate shop where they eventually settled on a pleasantly designed all-wooden door. The next day it was delivered to them, and watched by Margaret and Fluffy, Gerry fitted it. He did a decent job; he was always good at DIY. His wife was overjoyed with it at first, but then the cat intervened. Fluffy liked to enter the house at will, like all cats prefer to do. A cat flap in the previous door had allowed this, but as Fluffy demonstrated, by rubbing against the new door, there was no way through now.

Margaret loved cats. Ever since Gerry had met her she had always possessed at least one. She pandered to them, granting all manner of luxuries, so Gerry thought. Now a cat flap in the door was essential for one of Margaret's cats. How else would Fluffy be able to keep warm in the mornings after her 'nights-out?'.

Approximately four minutes ago, Gerry was verbally persuaded to visit the pet shop immediately, in order to fetch a relevant cat-door.

'Stupid, isn't it,' thought Gerry as he neared the shop, 'having to buy two back-doors for the kitchen!'

Regardless of this incident, Gerry didn't like cats. He found it a personal insult when, in his opinion, a cat tried to better him. Sitting in *his* armchair, nibbling away at his food carelessly left uncovered on the kitchen surface, knocking down his flowers as it rubs against them; the list was endless. All Margaret's cats saw *him* as the pet, the superfluous member of the family; there on sufferance. The present cat, though, was the worst; Fluffy was just that; a dumpy cat with a grey fluffy coat. It was unfortunate for the relationship between Gerry and the cat, that Fluffy permanently wore a cheesy grin on her feline face. To Gerry the expression said, 'Hiya, Gerry, just as useless as you always were?'

Gerry's hand clenched against the pet shop door handle, and he turned and pushed. A pleasant old-style bell rang as he entered and as the door shut behind him a thin, middle-aged man appeared. He smiled and proffered, 'Good afternoon, how can I help you?'

Gerry gave a quick glance round the cluttered shop, looking for anything resembling the flap. 'Hi there, I'd like to buy a cat flap, please.'

The man immediately nodded, crossed the shop and pulled two plastic-coated flaps off their wallhangings. 'How's these?' he said, showing them to Gerry. The first was much the same as the old, broken cat flap. An adequate size. The second was almost half as small and really looked as though it would not be big enough for Fluffy's frame. However, glancing quickly at the price-tags, Gerry reconsidered. The smaller one was more in line with the price he was considering paying. It would probably fit Fluffy. Gerry had read somewhere that cats are the most incredible contortionists, being able to squeeze through tiny gaps with the minimum of effort. Anyway, Fluffy owed Gerry no favours. All the cat did was sleep and eat all day. If the flap was slightly too small, a bit of extra effort to get through wouldn't harm it in the slightest.

His mind made up, he replied, 'The smaller one looks good to me.'

Unexpectedly, the man didn't agree immediately. 'These ones are for the smaller range of cats, you realise? If we're talking most domestic breeds, the larger would be the best.'

The man was looking at Gerry in an inquisitive manner, which reminded him of a cats stare. 'He knows I want it because it's the cheapest,' Gerry wildly thought. Any moment now he'll say, 'I hope your choice won't be to the detriment of your cat, sir. Cats are fine pets and ought to be shown the utmost of respect.' But instead, the man replaced the rejected flap on the wall, and crossing to the counter, bagged the smaller one. He smilingly asked Gerry for the money and before he knew it, he was on his way home.

'How could you be so stupid?' Margaret shouted. 'It's much too small for Fluffy. Look at her! She'll never pass through it.'

Unfortunately for Gerry, it was two against one. Fluffy's permanent grin seemed to have subsided the minute the new flap was unveiled and now her stare was fixed squarely on the guilty perpetrator. Gerry protested his innocence, mentioning contortioning cats and even that it had been the only one available. But this did no good at all, and Margaret stormed up to her bedroom, Fluffy inevitably in tow. Gerry stood fuming. Of course it was all the fault of the stupid cat. Causing friction between him and Margaret yet again. But as time passed, he began to feel more and more guilty about what he had done. How could he make it up to Margaret? Suddenly he realised.

Later, Fluffy made her way downstairs towards the source of the irritating noise. As she entered the kitchen, she saw the man who lived with her owner, kneeling at the half-open backdoor fitting her monstrous new house entrance. Tools lay littered all around the door. Outside it was raining, and some of it had entered the kitchen. Getting up with a grunt, Gerry suddenly noticed movement out the side of his eye. Spinning around he observed the hated cat. 'Ahh,' he uttered, 'has madam condescended to visiting this humble workman in order to approve her new door?' Gerry felt like saying something much more vicious to the cat, but he refrained, in case Margaret was within hearing distance. Right now, the cat had crossed the kitchen floor and was sniffing disdainfully at the newly-installed flap. 'Go through it, then,' said Gerry, 'it's the least you can do!' Fluffy obviously wasn't listening. She continued to examine the flap, walking round the door, carefully keeping out of the rain. Gerry suddenly acted on impulse and stepping forward, reached for the handle and firmly shut the door, pushing the cat out into the rain. 'You can either come back into the house through the flap,' thought Gerry, 'or stay out in the rain.' Actually this wasn't strictly true. There was a brick toolshed joined to the house, where Fluffy could enter under the door. But Gerry was sure the cat wouldn't be able to resist the temptation of re-entering the house. He wasn't wrong. After a pause of ten seconds, the catflap moved. Fluffy's head, then front paws emerged into the kitchen. The cat jerked quickly, obviously in an effort to pass clean through the flap. This didn't work. Gerry had been wrong. There was no way this cat was going to get through his flap.

Gerry wasn't too bothered at that particular moment, though. The sight of the stuck cat was making him laugh. After a while he was shaken from his reverie by a female shriek. Margaret had entered the kitchen and had obviously not shared Gerry's amusement at the cats predicament. 'Get her out! Get her out!' she screamed. Gerry's amusement was swiftly curtailed. Not wishing to incur his wife's wrath any further that day, he crossed to the door and opened it. The cat mewed forlornly. Seeing its back legs and tail projecting from the other side, made Gerry want to burst out laughing again, but this time he bit his lip. Three minutes later, with the help of gardening gloves, Gerry had succeeded in coercing the cat to back out of the flap. She mewed again to voice her displeasure, shot Gerry a vicious glance then disappeared into the rain.

'Glad to escape,' Gerry thought, as he removed his gloves. The cat had tried to claw and bite him of course, but Gerry was used to this treatment from his wife's cats.

Margaret's displeased voice broke into his train of thought. 'She's gone, and it's pouring. I hope you're satisfied. This is all your fault for buying such a stupid, small flap. I'm going out to Joan's for the evening. She'll be better company than you, by far. Make sure all this mess is cleared up by the time I get back. Honestly, the grief you give to me and Fluffy. What do we do to deserve it?'

Gerry thought of something very unpleasant to say about his wife's cat, but forced himself to bottle it.

Ten minutes later, Gerry was placing his tools back in their respective places in the tool-shed. He was feeling quite pleased about the way he had got one over the cat. 'Yep, Fluffy was made to look ridiculous tonight', he smirkingly thought, 'and it's all down to you Gerry. Well done!' The tool-shed door clicked shut. Gerry spin around horrified. If his tool-shed had been fitted with a standard tool-shed door, he wouldn't have batted an eye-lid. But the door to this shed was slightly different in that there wasn't a latch, handle or any kind of opening device whatsoever on the inside of the door. Stupid, but fact. When they bought the house, they inherited the tool-shed door. When you entered the shed, the door closed to. You wouldn't be locked in unless someone shoved the door shut. Thoughts flashed through Gerry's head. A burglar, kids, anybody! Someone had locked him in the shed in order to burgle the house.

It was getting colder all the time in the shed. It was getting dark but what light remained still allowed him to see the outline of the shed. This was because there was a foot's gap between the bottom of the shed door and the stone ground. A possible escape exit? Gerry didn't fancy his chances of getting through. He wasn't fat, but he was well-built. Looking around, he remembered his tools; Hammers, saws, small hand drill. He could always bash away at the door until he could get out. But two things eliminated this line of thought. One; although the door was wooden, it was quite thick; he could be ages powering his way through. And besides, even though he was trapped now, he still didn't want to break the door down. It'd have to be replaced and Gerry had had his fair share of door replacing recently.

He crossed his arms and hugged himself. He hadn't bothered to put a coat on, and now he had started shivering. He had to get out now. 'Help', he shouted at the top of his voice, 'Help, it's Gerry Talbot. I've locked myself in the tool-shed.' Gerry briefly thought how silly the sentence sounded, but the cold overrode it. 'Help! Help!' Ten minutes later, Gerry stopped shouting. His throat was hoarse but there was something else. He thought he had heard someone moving outside the shed door. He listened attentively, sure he had been right, but now there was no sound.

Gerry instinctively knew no-one was coming. He felt it. The next-door neighbours were away in Italy for the second time this year, whilst next-door-but-one housed an elderly lady with bad hearing. No-one was coming.

Gerry looked again at the gap under the door. he found that by concentrating on the gap and thinking of the possibility of staying the night here, the gap actually grew. He could squeeze under there. Of course he could!

Before he knew it, he had dropped to his knees and onto his stomach. Looking through the gap he saw both freedom and that the rain had eased off.

'Here we go', thought Gerry, and he began crawling under. As his head came through and rain hit it, it gave him fresh impetus. He crawled faster. Then the movement stopped. His belly was firmly wedged to the ground and his back could feel the door underside. The thought then occurred to him that he could get stuck, out here in the cold, but he sensed he was nearly through so he pushed hard. He seemed to be moving forward but then he made the mistake of breathing out. His stomach pushed the ground and his back pushed the wood. He froze horrified; he was stuck. He knew it.

Strange, but as the similarity of the cat's position to his own popped into his mind he simultaneously sensed the cat's presence. Turning his head to the left slowly, Gerry knew it would be there. It was. Fluffy was sat six feet away, watching him, with the cheesy grin fixed firmly in place. 'Laughing', Gerry thought.

He tried to shout for help again, but his throat was hurt from the previous shouting. he would be well and truly entrenched here until the morning, with only the laughing cat for company.

'And it was you who shut the door on me, wasn't it,' croaked Gerry to the cat, eyeing its bulk. 'Put your weight onto your front paws and locked me in. For revenge.' Fluffy grinned cheesily.

The rain increased in intensity. Gerry closed his eyes and leant a cheek against the ground. It was freezing cold. The cat got up and walked towards him. Gerry opened his eyes and saw it coming. 'It's going to finish me off! Going for the kill!'

Instead though, the cat veered away and settled down, four feet to the right of his head. Gerry turned his head. 'Got a better view now?' Gerry would have been full of hate for Fluffy, but at that moment he was too cold to feel anything. So he lay there whilst the cat continued to grin.

Sixteen hours later and Gerry recovered consciousness at visiting time. After registering that he was in a hospital he then noticed the streams of people entering his ward. He still felt cold but he was conscious of some warmth. Looking down at himself he was surprised to see layers of bed-clothes. 'Hypothermia?' he thought. It was at that moment he saw Margaret coming towards him. She looked worried, but George imagined he looked just as bad, for cradled in her arms was the last thing he wanted to see.

She reached the bed and started talking but Gerry wasn't listening. The thing he didn't want to see had been put on the floor, but now it jumped onto his bed. It looked at him and grinned, then it ambled up to his chest and looked straight at him. Gerry knew Fluffy couldn't speak but he knew what the stare said. 'Hiya, Gerry. I guess you'll be buying me the bigger cat-flap now!'

The Sympathy Man

by

John J Jones

George Oliver Duxbury drained his second cup of coffee, delicately dabbed his lips with a linen napkin and gazed disinterestedly at his bed-sitter his mind pre-occupied with his next appointments. The first was at 10.30 - name of Fenner.

Mr Fenner was a stranger to Mr Duxbury as were all his clients, although he always claimed he knew them intimately, a claim none of them was in a position to challenge. Mr Duxbury also gathered information about his clients to ease his way into the confidences of the bereaved and had discovered that the late Mr Fenner had been one jump ahead of the Fraud Squad. But Mr Duxbury was less concerned with his client's earthly activities as with his own immediate prospects.

He eyed his black three piece suit that was too long in the leg and too narrow at the waist with displeasure and shook his head. Perhaps he would be lucky today and land one that fitted him better. He dressed without enthusiasm for he was uneasy about his first appointment. There was something odd about it, something he should know. But there was no time for that. With a final check on the room he stepped onto the landing and pulled the door shut after him.

Mr Duxbury's business day had begun.

Turning into Noble Street he was relieved to see the cars parked outside the Chapel of Rest and broke into an undignified run. Once inside, his face fell into disciplined lines of sympathy and with artfully drooped shoulders he let the sombre world of bereavement close about him.

'Are you a relative, sir?' The sudden appearance of a tall man dressed in black startled him.

'Er, what's that you say?'

'Are you family?' The man frowned impatiently. 'Which side are you on?' Mr Duxbury looked bewildered. 'Come come, sir, you've got to be on one side or the other.'

Mr Duxbury was offended. Really! Did he look like a footballer or something? He was a Billy Bunter if ever there was one. Which side indeed! 'Friend of the deceased,' he announced grandly. 'Yes, friend of the deceased. Are you the undertaker?'

The man merely glared at him. 'Not here, only family. Everyone else straight to the crematorium.'

'Oh dear, and I'd promised I would . . . ' His voice trailed off in disappointment and he looked beseechingly at this unexpected obstacle.

'Look I'd let you in, but I've had my orders. Strictly family.' He looked hard at Mr Duxbury. 'Are you a distant cousin? Or perhaps a . . . ?'

'We're all brothers under the skin,' said Mr Duxbury wilting under the close scrutiny.

'Look, you wait here mister . . . ' The man's eyebrows rose enquiringly.

'Duxbury,' Mr Duxbury volunteered.

'Then you wait here, Mr Duxbury, while I speak to Mr Fenner.' Wraithlike he disappeared.

Why oh why hadn't he trusted his instincts? Mr Duxbury inwardly berated himself. They had never let him down yet, except that regrettable occasion when one unprotesting voyager had been dispatched from the wrong departure point. He was on the point of quietly slipping away when a thickset pugilistic-looking man in a grey suit and black knitted tie burst in on him.

'What the hell, I mean, what's the meaning of this outrage? Haven't you been told this is a family affair?' Mr Duxbury nodded dumbly fearing physical violence. 'Then how dare you come interfering, have you no damned decency?'

'I apologise intruding like this, Mr Fenner, but I've got to speak to you, your late brother . . . '

'So you're Charles,' he gasped. 'Where the hell have you been? You'd better come . . . '

'No, no, I'm not Charles. Your brother . . . well the fact is I'm here to offer my condolences and help. It's a trying time for everyone.'

'Right,' said Mr Fenner, 'Thank you for your sympathy, now why don't you push off?'

'I'm afraid you don't quite understand,' Mr Duxbury persisted. 'You see . . . '

'I told him the crematorium,' the undertaker complained, 'but he wouldn't have it.'

An ugly look crept into Mr Fenner's eyes. 'What's you're little game, eh? Are you putting the bite on me, because if you are . . . '

'Good heavens no! What do you take me for?'

'A nosy parker, that's what, and insurance snooper maybe, or just a dirty little crook whose got hold of the wrong end of the stick. Now why don't you go, quietly?'

Mr Duxbury sighed. It was time to apply pressure. 'I know all about the Russian gold consignment your brother, er, imported,' he said in a low voice. 'And the . . . '

'Go to hell!'

'I'll certainly go, Mr Fenner, but not I assure you, to hell.'

'Just a minute, not so fast. Who did you say you were . . . Duxbury?' Mr Duxbury nodded. 'Then wait here, right?' With that Mr Fenner disappeared only to reappear some moments later grinning weakly.

'Look you'd better join us, Mr er, Duxbury. Yes, well if you knew Tom.' Mr Duxbury heaved a silent sigh of relief. 'God knows it could do with a bit of class,' he went on. 'At least you look the part, not like that shower in there.' He leant towards Mr Duxbury. 'There's not a square of black among the lot of them, talk about showing some respect, that's a laugh. Molly, that's the wife, is taking it pretty bad though. If you could . . . '

'Of course, only to glad to help.' And once again, Mr Duxbury wondered what it was he should remember.

Curious eyes focused on Mr Duxbury as he sat beside the slight figure sitting on her own. He patted her hand comfortingly and smiled.

'Friend of Tom,' he whispered. 'Had to pay my last respects you know.'

Her eyes panicked. 'Tom. A friend of Tom's?'

'It's all right,' Mr Duxbury said, 'I'll look after you.' He felt his spirits rising. Things were shaping up quite nicely. Even so, he wondered who the other people were, and why the entire cortege was to go from the chapel of rest direct to the crematorium and not from the family residence? It was almost as though everyone had to keep the coffin in view from start to finish. But these were passing thoughts. He had achieved his objective. He was in the official party. His position was secure. He was content.

It seemed only natural he should assist Mr Fenner support his grieving sister-in-law into the waiting limousine and climb in himself.

Throughout the long slow drive to the crematorium Mrs Fenner clung to Mr Duxbury with unexpected tenacity. It was almost as though she knew he had no business to be there and was determined he should not escape the consequences. Mr Duxbury's stomach rumbled and he hoped there would be a decent buffet laid on.

How many such services had he sat through? Mr Duxbury wondered as the ritual ran its predictable course. At last came the moment of cremation.

It was as the coffin slowly retired and the gold and purple curtains closed to hide it from view that he heard a barely audible sigh emanate from Mrs Fenner and sensed her relax as though a great weight had been lifted suddenly from her shoulders. Poor woman, but how bravely she bore her sorrow.

The buffet was lavish and Mr Duxbury did it full justice. He was about to pay it a second visit when Mrs Fenner sidled up to him.

'I thought it was time we had a little chat, Mr Duxbury, don't you?'

He wasn't given the chance to answer and found himself being firmly steered towards a small anteroom. He waited with apprehension for Mrs Fenner to speak.

'Tell me, Mr Duxbury, how well did you know my husband?'

'Does anybody really know anyone?' he countered.

'When did you see him last?'

He was spared the necessity of invention by the noisy arrival of Mr Fenner smacking his great hands together and grinning broadly.

'They've all gone, thank God,' he said and reached for his wallet. 'Now, Mr Duxbury, shall we say, fifty pounds, and thank you for your, er, discretion?'

'Oh, but your late brother's clothing will be quite sufficient,' Mr Duxbury protested.

'Good God, why?' said Mr Fenner in amazement. 'You're not even the same size!'

'True, Mr Fenner, but there are those less fortunate who are. I try to help where I can. A Mr Clegg will call for; the things tomorrow, if that is convenient to you?'

Mr Fenner glanced at his sister-in-law then nodded.

'And now I really must go, another appointment I'm afraid. Thank you both for your generosity, and once again, my condolences.'

111

Mr Duxbury was halfway down the long drive when it came to him. Of course, he remembered now. It was a newspaper account he'd read concerning a Thomas Fenner who had been lost at sea from his luxury yacht.

But that was six months ago!

All My Hopes . . .

by

Erica Donaldson

I have joined the ranks of a well known brigade.

As yet I retain the status of a novicee, but I am assuredly progressing through the ranks of initiation and hope to have soon earned my wings in fully fledged distinction, as a member of 'the school round.'

You see, it is licensed to a certain predictability, that my days are destined to merge into one amalgamated cluster, 'a blob' which represents the entwinement of those light and dark hours - a passage of time, with few relevant distinguishing experiences, bar that concluding 'blip' -it is the gravitation towards my last 'pickup' on a Friday afternoon; a release from my constant state of stomach clenching distress by which my week is marked.

My life is assuming an automated directive.

I invite with a frankness that evolves with familiarity, a shuddering onset of cold that freezes my insides as, fearful of guarding myself against the stealing of a glance at those illuminous figures which beam at me whilst strapped in a fixed position of self indulgent torture in the driving seat of my car, those brightly cloaked, yet concise figures shine significantly as heralds of doom. They are an unavoidable precursor of a thrusting, booming fear attack expulsion, which initially cools from within, but transcends any normal time perimeters so that icebergs of panic quickly erupt from without my skin. The warm atmosphere of the car is pervaded by a condensing coolness - the air becomes heavy and my unlucky passengers are insulted into bouts of thumb sucking and other quiet comforters, 'Mama's late again.'

During the weeks which had preceded that first big day, my daughter and I had excitedly charged our batteries.

We had busied ourselves in determined preparation.

In pristine presentation at the featured proprietors, where the excuse of forced purchases thrilled us into delectable delights. We were willingly propulsed into the class of the leisurely 'millionaire elite' and mindful of our new-found status we carried ourselves in a suitably presumed grandeur (an albeit temporary exaggerated state) as we sought to amass those items enumerated on the uniformed list. 'Two of these, several of those, please' - we played our part well, and then at least, without conscience, we assured each other that at opportune future events, when the time would most certainly be called, we at least would not be found wanting.

Besides . . . I was almost certain that the bank statement would be some weeks away! Thus, we had indulged ourselves in the anticipation of frequent changes of attire, whilst hesitantly awaiting at the changing room door, the shop assistants return. Both mother and daughter, with escalating eagerness, each assuming significance over the other , in a mutual pride - One, anxious to let

113

loose the attribution of 'baby girl', the other-jealously shielding her growing child, intent to provide all that was within her realms to supply, and more, to ensure that her daughter might fit into a new and beckoning world. What niggles of doubt she may simultaneously have harboured as she bitterly decried the event which signalled that the time had come for her little one to enter an arena from which for the most part of their days, her presence would be barred and their separation would be inevitably sealed, she made a good attempt to shrug away. The countdown to this time, however, undeniably eats into the days, during which the allotted time to sew on name tags and to make those alterations to nonetheless, 'the smallest sizes which we have available, madam' will be made to suit. The days dwindle into the night preceding the big day. Without warning it seems, it is but a few hours before the momentous event is due to begin.

Already feeling the stress of the hour - exhausted by the special preparations attempted earlier during the day - an extra hair wash; the attention to immaculate cleanliness and grooming against which her daughter has shrugged and impatiently stamped her feet, protesting her indignation, until, in no less a spectacular dramatisim, she eventually loses her temper.

The teasing and cajoling into bed, earlier than normal, of an unlidded Jack-in-the-box - achieved with the ease of a frustrated practising magician - is taking its toll, draining all human energy, nonetheless, later, in the quiet, the ascribed seamstress role is set to, and extra caution to achieve a job well-done, is further hampered and aggravated, by the lack of availability to hand of all suitable tools.

I bemoan the fact, that yes, midnight is too late to catch the corner shops!

The day dawns.

From rising to breakfast, to achieving the timing in my head as to when we should be seated in the car, ready to open throttle onto the home strait - nothing goes right.

From the moment that that internal alarm fails to register the external signal which I instinctively reach to the bedside table to silence when it catapulted into action my early call, I sense a failure of my unwritten schedule.

Graspingly, I allow myself the satisfaction that, should this have been the 'dry-run' which I smugly neglected to arrange, then that this indeed would be but a hiccup open to correction.

Flummoxed, confused even . . . I begin . . .

I offer myself distractedly, a somewhat wry compensatory pat on the back: Membership to my new club is after all - sealed on entry.

The contract, I remember is unexchangeable.

Should I laugh or cry?

The slow moving bus (or do my eyes deceive me, is the damn thing actually . . . motionless) emerges out of a junction to block a speedy Gonzalez getaway. I slump in my seat and inadvertently catch sight of my presentation in the rear view mirror.

A mess!

Time to put on the lipstick with the one hand, to negotiate a grip on the real world with the other.

114

Hustling my daughter to the school gates - a brisk stretch, along which I scamper, in full view of others who needless to say are on their home run. They leisurely congregate to natter, or return to those coveted parking slots which have obstacled my own frantic efforts, prided as such parking spaces are, for the degree of closeness and easy access to the entrance gates which they offer. I cannot fail but to grudgingly applaud the practised veterans who assume in their stride their secured prizes for being early birds to which, after all they are entitled.

We walk past them and are welcomed within the ranks with an unexpectedly hearty nod.

We are easy to spot, one of us - immaculate and exact in her hitherto unworn uniform - a telltale sign of the latest entrant, the other a gawking duckling, significantly lacking in accessorised features, (an ability to allocate time to do this a visible mark of a higher position within the ranks.) She leads the pair in a reluctance to enter the confines of the school frontiers, by a hair's breadth.

They are only minutes late, although-

The class is already assembled.

Individually monopolised and correct school colours - their attention initially plunged in a sea of task orientated confusion - flip in co-ordinated swarm in our direction, as we present in the doorway.

Interlocked and damp palms, are released by the knowing smile from a head which parts that uniformed sea and rises to reveal a body comfortingly dressed in homely attire. She takes my daughter's hand, exuding calm-

'Welcome Isolyn . . . How are you?'

I am deserted by the warmth at my side.

Fighting back swelling emotions, I turn to quell what promises to be an embarrassing climax.

I am alone, but reassured, that she at least, will be fine.

The Captive Canary

by

Ronald E Good

Gene Mitchell woke up like so many times before out of a void of blackness seeing the two faces looking at him, impassive yet intent still. Where was he, who were these men? so many times waking out of unconsciousness briefly into light and back into darkness.

Many months had passed. He was trying to remember, but what was he wishing to remember.

The voice speaking quietly kept calling Gene, can you hear me? The face of the doctor was intense and searching for any recognition from him.

After many days Gene spoke for the first time. 'Where am I, who are you?'

The doctor replied, 'I am John Ferguson, you are at Chelford Hall recuperating from an accident.'

The next day, the other face came to see him and asked him how he was? did he require anything at all. Gene was trying to remember him but it seemed like a wall stopped him finding out. The man could see Gene could not remember him, he said don't try to do everything at once you're getting better now, I'll come and see you again soon. The man stepped into the corridor and spoke hurriedly with Dr Ferguson and went back to his office.

Gene, day by day grew slowly stronger and health was returning like dawn after the night. The doctor spoke to him everyday and eventually told him he had been involved in an aircraft landing accident in Belgium while on a US Forces singing concert.

Gene was allowed to walk round the bedroom now and he grew stronger everyday. He noticed the mark on his arm healing up now.

The man came to see him again and asked if he could bring him magazines or papers or cigarettes or anything. The man asked him, could he remember any details of his accident and did he know who he was. Gene looked hard and intently, something familiar about the grey and green eyes and the lips hard turned down at the sides, but he could not yet. The man smiled and the lips became a sinister frown, the eyes cold and icy. He patted Gene's shoulder, 'Don't worry old chap, you're getting on now, anyway one day at a time.'

Chelford Hall had extensive gardens and it was surrounded by thick belts of trees. It was a lovely place and Gene could see the spring flowers were just coming out.

The doctor and staff examined him carefully and seemed pleased with his progress. Gene slept better now and his broken sleep and weariness was leaving him.

One morning in the early hours he woke up with a jerk and sat up in bed. It was just before dawn. As his eyes focused he jumped instinctively as he saw two figures sitting at the foot of his bed. Instantly a voice spoke and said, 'It's alright Gene, Dr Ferguson here.' The doctor switched on the light revealing the man sitting at the foot of the bed holding a tape recorder.

'What's happening,' Gene said.

Doctor Ferguson said, 'We are monitoring sleep levels, don't worry you're doing well, go back to sleep now, see you later.'

At breakfast time Gene felt a little troubled and insecure, but kept this to himself. Later the man came and asked Gene, did he remember anything about the crash landing in Belgium. He explained he was their Administration Officer and kept all details of patients in Dr Ferguson's case.

Gene asked, 'Were you in the bedroom early this morning.'

The man said, Yes we are trying to help you all we can to recall your memory.'

The Administration Officer stood by the window looking out on the gardens and told Gene he had been on a singing tour of US Forces in Belgium, 20 September 1944, when the plane crash-landed due to malfunction of the undercarriage, and he had been thrown heavily and had severe concussion and loss of memory.

Gene thought a moment and asked, 'How long have I been in care and what day and month is it now.'

The Administration Officer said, 'It is March 1945, the Spring flowers are opening.'

Gene gasped and was speechless for a while. The Administration Officer looked at him, smiling, and said, 'We have been looking after you all the time like a baby, with instructions to see if you have everything you need.'

Gene was allowed to walk round the garden with two men assigned to him. Gus and Tex, nice guys. There were men who attended the gardens and men who looked after the woods, some carried shotguns to keep poachers out and unwelcome visitors.

No matter how Gene thought, he could not remember an aircraft crash-landing.

He was left to do as he wished between meals and his companions Gus and Tex became his pals.

Having been asleep a few hours after a fairly good day he suddenly jerked awake and sat up, looked through the semi darkness to the window where he saw two figures standing smoking. Thinking it might have been Gus and Tex, he quietly moved to the window to surprise them.

As he came close to the curtain he saw it was Dr Ferguson and the Administration Officer talking intently, the Dr said, 'Do you think we have got away with it Chris.'

Chris said, 'We'll have to go along with it a bit longer, it looks as if he may never remember again.'

Dr Ferguson said, 'Does this mean we can go home to the USA when de-mob comes? It can't be long now and I have a wife and kids waiting for me.'

Chris replied, 'Yes, you can go when a replacement who knows nothing of this set up can be arranged but I have to stay like the Gaoler.'

Dr Fergusan said, 'But can't you ever go home,'

Chris said, 'No, Al has selected me to keep the rearguard and the rest are going home. There are some big people in this, it goes right to the top.'

Chris said, 'I have to stay till Gene is dead, and remember you and all the others are sworn to secrecy for life.'

Dr Fergusan nodded in understanding, Chris said, 'If anyone ever opens their mouth Al will silence them forever, the Mafia has a long arm.'

Gene stood rigid, hardly daring to breathe. The two men walked slowly away. Gene returned to bed but could not sleep again.

Several nights later Gene fitfully sleeping, suddenly woke. He heard voices in the corridor and a voice saying keep it down, do you want to wake the whole house?

The hard voice. Gene suddenly knew who it was, it was General Al Burgoyne, US Army Iron Gut. Al the troops called him.

Al spoke to Col Chris Markland and said, 'This guy Gene will be given a new identity, he's been dead since Belgium, we had another body identified as his, he can't come back now.'

Gene shrank back from the door and sat on the edge of the bed drained, now his recall memory flooded back and he felt sick.

Yes up till 20th Sept 1944 life had been good to Gene Mitchell, singer, US Forces, Favourite, Base after Base ringing to cheers, Gene brought the troops a taste of Home.

The morning dawned nice and bright. Gene was awake but he wished he was not. Col Markland came after breakfast and chatted as he left and reached the door.

Gene said, 'Why can't you kill me and get it over with and you can all go back home?'

The Colonel stiffened and turned back in the room. He looked at Gene, a mask of Hate on his face.

Chris said, 'So you have remembered, for your natural life, you have a big friend in the US.'

Chris continued, 'You used to sing back in the Thirties for Les Gibson at the 'Black Cat Club'. Well Les is dead now, but his son in the State Department, he likes you, he's done well considering he was a two bit gangster and protection racketeer.'

The Colonel paused to let Gene take it in and then continued, 'Lee Gibson never forgot what you did for his dad. When you stayed with him at the club in the face of death threats from rival Gangs and once saved his life when shooting one night broke out and you stood between him, and a drunken gun toting gangster and bashed him over the head with a chair.

So now you know your life is saved by Les Gibson, and if anything happens to get out of control, I lose my life, the Mafia has a long arm.

118

'Yes Gene If you had not seen the Drugs given in Belgium to Gen Al Burgoyne you would be free as a bird.

'Lee and Al and me have been in crime since we started stealing Hub caps.

'I was the one that hit you so hard we thought you were dead back in Belgium, OK. Why did you have to walk in the wash room at that moment?

'But now you are officially dead and now you're John Erikson US special Forces Expert in Nuclear Science. If ever you try to escape you will be shot with a silenced pistol. All staff have instructions to shoot if you should fall in the hands of any enemy or foreign power, remember now there's a Cold War.'

Gene stared out of the window at the man walking in the woods.

So Chelford Hall was a prison for him and Col Chris Markland.

The month's passed and then years. Gene somehow made organised life and everything stayed peaceful, the periodic visits of officer's and sometimes Lee Gibson came to see him but Gene could not bring himself to like him although he gave him everything he wanted, including his old record Hits and Song Albums which were now collector's treasured items.

But there was no freedom, periodic visits, drives in blackened Cars, visits in disguise to Cinema and theatre with the everyready silenced pistols.

But an undercover drugs organisation within the US Forces in World War II was too hot a potato with High ranking officers and lesser minions in the Army, Airforce and Medical service was big business and men could make money on the European Black Market, fortunes twenty times over.

Yes, men living on the proceeds even today. Gene had seen the men at parties and knew drugs were big business. These were private parties but unwisely someone invited him to sing for them and he saw too much. When asked to keep quiet he told them to go hell and walked out but he was a marked man.

Sometime in the 1970's, Gen Al Burgoyne died in Sacramento of Cancer. Chris Markland came to Gene's room and told him the news. Chris looked crestfallen and sad, Gene thought that's one bastard dead. Chris shared a whiskey almost a human emotion from this Iron man.

Chris had mellowed a little over the years and looked upon Gene as, if not a friend, someone he could talk to. The staff changed as men's service time came to an end and they went home, Stateside.

In the early Eighties, Gene's heart began to fail although medication and doctors were always in attendance.

Chris realised they had both grown old together. He asked Gene if there was any favour he could do for him.

Gene thought; time's maybe getting shorter. He asked Chris could he through channels go to a music concert at an American Air Base, one he had sung at in the Forties, could he attend in the crowd. Chris said he would see about it.

The Bomber Base thronged with music enthusiasts. Gene remembered Norfolk very well, then he'd been the New York Boy with the Golden Voice.

On the platform the band was letting rip dressed in Period USAF uniforms. The singer dressed as Gene Mitchell, Captain Gene Mitchell was singing his old numbers.

Gene listened flanked by his ever constant guards and doctors, for a moment reliving those heady days, 1943, 1944 as if all his life had been encapsulated in those two years.

As the last song came up everybody was going out. Gene felt a sharp vice like pain take his breath away, he fell against his guard.

His men held him while the doctor examined him but after an injection he did not respond, the Dr said, 'Clear the way, this man's collapsed, back to Chellford Hall.'

Chris Markland spoke urgently on the phone, a transatlantic call to Pennsylvania Ave Washington and informed them that Gene Mitchell was dead.

Later Lee Gibson called Chris to say he'd be flying in to London and after calling at Grosvenor Square would come over to Chelford Hall.

A simple private service and cremation and Old Glory laid across the coffin, and the ashes returned in the Blacked out car to Chelford Hall. Chris and Lee talked old times Lee said, 'If Gene had been one of us he would have been the greatest singer in the world.'

In the morning as the sun was rising Lee and Chris stood by a tree in a clearing in the woods of Chelworth Hall. Lee sprinkled the ashes around the tree and put a notice on the tree, Gene Mitchell 1912 - 1987, stood silently for a moment, came to attention and saluted, and turning walked back to the hall.

Lee told Chris he would be going to Washington on the next flight and if he wanted he could come with him as his assignment was concluded.

Lee told Chris he could live on his estate in Oregon as he would be retiring from the State Department in Autumn.

Lee Gibson sat behind the mahogany desk looking through the window at the Washington Skyline, on his desk a photo frame with his dad and Gene Mitchell at the Black Cat Club.

The red light shone brightly on his phone as his secretary buzzed the intercom line, a voice said, 'Mr Gibson, the President is on line for you.'

Lee said, 'Thank you Claire.'

Lee picked up the phone and said, 'Mr President, Lee Gibson speaking,'

The President said, 'I hear you're retiring in the fall Lee, I'd like to thank you for your faithful service to our great country and could I drop in on your estate in Oregon sometime.'

Lee replied, 'Thank you Mr President and you will always be welcome.'

The President replied, 'Well I've known you so long Lee, I look upon you as part of the family.'

Lee stiffened momentarily at the word 'family' .

Lee answered, 'Thanks again Mr President.'

The President said goodbye and put the phone down.

Lee sat still staring at the photo frame and then burst out laughing and said, 'Part of the family eh?'

Huntly House

by

C L Jones

It was a beautiful moonlit night. A breeze whistled through the old, oak trees. She stood upon the balcony staring into the velvety, night sky, which was lit with a myriad of sparkling jewels. All of a sudden, the distant sound of horse's hoofs came to her ears, accompanied by the clanking of metal. She looked in the direction from whence the sound had come. The sound became louder. She could hear the snapping of twigs. Then she saw the head of what looked like a fourteenth century knight. The iron helmet and visor were clearly visible by the light of the full moon. As he came nearer, her heart began to beat faster. The small iron clad figure ventured out of the woods brandishing a sword. She was so frightened by the spectacle, that she retreated into her bedroom, closing the balcony windows behind her, and drew the curtains. Her heart thumped hard against her rib-cage. Her breathing was laboured. What was that apparition that had appeared before her? She told herself that it must have been her imagination playing tricks on her. Eventually, she took up the courage to go onto the balcony, just to make sure. This time, much to her relief, there was nothing to be seen or heard, but the bats and owls searching for food. She went back inside and went to bed.

She tossed and turned all night. Why did she imagine a knight? She was not even thinking about a knight. The vision haunted her. He appeared, with blazing, red, demonic eyes that shone out from the grid of his visor. The sword he held was blooded. He swept her up with his free arm, and rode away. She screamed, then fainted. When she awoke she found herself inside a dark, dank dungeon. She woke up from her nightmare in a pool of sweat.

She took a walk upon the balcony. It was now daylight. The morning bird chorus was clearly audible. She could smell the fragrance of honeysuckle floating on a summer's breeze. Then the scene changed, and she found herself in a banquet hall. Upon her head she wore a white, linen veil, which was held on with a circlet of gold, embedded with emeralds and diamonds. Her dark hair was styled in two bosses on each side of her head, over which were golden hairnets. Around her neck was a beautiful golden crucifix, which had a large, round ruby embedded in its centre, surrounded by small diamonds. She was dressed in a long flowing, trailing, scarlet gown. Tapestries hung from the wall. The room was filled with the sound of merry voices and music. A quartet of musicians, dressed in bi-coloured hoses and green knee-length surcoats, were playing tambourines and recorders. The people were all dressed in their finery with their fur-trimmed surcoats, and jeweled circlets. There was straw strewn all over the stone floor. Bones lay around the banquet table, where a handsome, young man sat drinking from a silver goblet. The room was illuminated by candlelight, which came from a chandelier, hanging from the ceiling. She felt somebody tap her on the shoulder. Turning, she faced a small, grey-haired servant.

'Excuse me yer ladyship, but I needs to talk to yer in private like.'

'Alright. I will meet you outside in the maze.'

They sat down on the stone bench that was situated in the middle of the maze.

'Swiftarrow sent me. He told me to tell yer to meet him in the 'Secret Glen' straight away.'

'Thank you Beatrice.'

She headed towards the stables, where a mount had been prepared for her. Then she rode of to the 'Secret Glen'. She had a vision of her beloved. He was a handsome figure, dressed in a chaperon, and a knee-length tunic, with belt. Upon his feet, he wore long, leather boots. His shoulder-length fair hair was untidy. As she rode thorough the dark, misty forest, brambles tore at her clothes. She rode until she came to a hill. At this point, she dismounted and proceeded on foot. Behind some huge oaks she found a narrow passageway. It was just big enough for a man to go through. It became broader as she carried on. The passageway came out into a small, wooded glen.

Swirls of mist impaired her vision. She could just make out the nearby shapes of the trees. The gurgling of the stream, was clearly audible. Following in the direction from whence it came, she came upon Swiftarrow. He was waiting for her by the stream. They embraced, kissing one another fervently.

'I have missed you Valerie.'

'And I have missed you my dearest.'

Just then the sound of horses hoofs came to their ears.

'They are coming from the other side of the stream!' Swiftarrow said. 'Let's get out of here.'

They both ran as fast as they could through the secret passageway. At the other end they were ambushed by knights on horseback. Then from out of the trees came arrows. Swiftarrow drew his longbow. She hid in the passageway with her heart in her mouth. Swiftarrow's bow twanged and the arrow hit one of the horses in the leg. He let another fly, this time it hit another in the leg. She screamed as a dark form grabbed her from behind. One of the knights had descended from his horse and was charging at Swiftarrow brandishing a sword. He drew his from its scabbard and counteracted the lethal blow. They clashed swords. Then there was a swishing sound as someone came from behind and decapitated his foe. He turned to find Lady Valerie gone.

The next thing she remembered, she was in the cell of her nightmare. The floor was covered in straw and there were vermin everywhere. She started banging on the thick wooden door.

'Let me out of here or you will be sorry!'

She could hear a chorus of harsh laughter. One of the men came up to the iron grating.

'You might as well keep quiet. No one's going to help you. The Earl will put a stop to that rabble, you'll see.'

Then there came the sound of footsteps. He turned and left. Then another face leered at her through the grating. His dark eyes were hard.

'Your lover might have defeated us, but I have you. He will come, and when he does, I will capture him. Then I will have him tortured, and his head paraded through the town for everyone to see, including you.'

'You evil fiend.'

He laughed harshly. Then came the sound of arrows being shot and the clash of steel. He turned and left. She looked out into the dark passageway. After a while she saw the familiar figure of Swiftarrow. He was dressed in a monk's habit.

'Swiftarrow you have come!'

He unlocked the door, and they fell into each other's arms.

'Quickly we must go.'

They passed dead bodies, until they got to the kitchen where they escaped through a tunnel that led under the moat. Once on the other side Swiftarrow's trusty, black steed waited. She got on behind Swiftarrow and held on tight.

She was woken by the daylight as the curtains were pulled back.

'Good morning, Miss Grant. Trust you slept well.'

'Yes.'

She handed her the breakfast tray and left. Then she put it down on the chair at the side of the bed. Putting on her dressing-gown she headed toward the French windows once more. She opened them, and walked outside, thinking about Swiftarrow. It all seemed so real.

Away With The Fairies

by

Lynne Moulsdale

'Do you know you have a Fairy Elephant on your back?', I was asked by the woman who stopped me on Lord Street.

'And pigs might fly in little green baskets', I replied without any idea of why I thought this appropriate. But what would you have said?

Now, if you know Southport, the seaside resort on the North West coast, then you will know Lord Street. This is the wide boulevard where many middle-class ladies come to replenish their already overstocked wardrobes, and to buy yet another pair of ill-fitting shoes.

It has an ageing population; an over-abundance of Nursing Homes and a collective determination to stagnate. Current medical thinking, however, threatens to replace its present image - it may even become an international centre for its unique management of what is, as yet, a little known disease.

The natives of Southport are known as Sandgrounders. This curious name arises because as youngsters they were never allowed to eat their sandwiches until they had been thoroughly ground into the sand. Regrettably it is now strongly suspected that this practice leads to an incurable condition later in life, the symptoms of which are frequent lapses of memory, hallucinations, distorted colour vision and acute paranoia. Sadly this eventually leads to death.

Inevitably, therefore, many people come to Southport to die but, before achieving their ambition, they frequently have many years to traipse their earthbound bodies around familiar haunts, their minds on higher things.

The strangest part of this ailment is that patients perform ordinary tasks well and automatically remember ingrained notions. For instance, they remember to eat now and again but never ever formulate a sentence without a verb. For this reason it has become know as the 'Southport Sentence', being, as you will appreciate, a life sentence.

Those afflicted randomly slip in and out of the various symptoms; have periods of lucidity, but no recall. This is extremely fortunate for their Doctors, who are saved the tedium of having to sound knowledgeable or the need to invent euphemistic lies.

Obviously this strange mental condition excites those in medical research but at the moment they have more questions than solutions. Why Southport in particular?

Experts are probing sand particles; some are considering the effects of certain pollutants; others monitoring the tides. (As usual, a few are wondering if their promotion chances might be enhanced).

Initially G.P.'s feared for their workload but the insular people of Southport, only too aware of their susceptibility, have organised their own system of care. They simply look after each other. Tenderly, devotedly, and when necessary, in those numerous Nursing Homes I told you about.

Maybe this arrangement could answer some of your problems. If, at the moment you consider yourself ineligible through sanity then this can be easily remedied. Why not come to sunny Southport, where you will find an enormous variety of sandwiches to take down to the shore?

Have you forgotten about the Fairy Elephant Lady?

Her amused smile was beginning to turn into concern as she said rationally, 'You have a child's toy attached to the back of your coat.'

She was right, of course, and she had said 'Furry' not 'Fairy'.

She looked at me searchingly before saying: 'Shall we return it dear, you must have brushed past it in the toy department.' She smiled encouragingly.

I feel I must tell you that I am not indigenous to this area, haven't eaten a sandy sandwich in years but that sometimes those pigs fly in little yellow baskets.

The Black Widow

by

Thelma Pennell

'What is it about her I don't like!' Audrey Cullen cast a swift sideways glance at the woman approaching along the suburban street before crouching down behind the spread of the privet hedge bordering the front garden.

'Has she seen me?' Perhaps she'll go by without speaking, but then she doesn't speak does she! Just smiles that awful smile!'

Stirring the crumbled earth with a small hand-fork she appeared to be totally involved with the task but all her senses were attuned to the rhythm of the approaching footsteps.

Were they slowing?

They stopped. She looked up. Over the low wall the woman in the black coat and hat smiled her slow smile before moving on.

Still feeling unsettled Audrey Cullen stared out of the kitchen window as she rinsed her hands, the image of the woman in black still potent in her mind.

'Who is she? Where does she come from, why has she suddenly appeared in the street? What is it about her that gets to me? Oh well, better get on, better bring the washing in before it rains!'

In the large garden at the rear of the house she gazed with pleasure at the newly-disturbed soil of the borders. So rich and dark after the flattening effect of the winter rains. She was pleased with her afternoon's work. How she loved this time of the year with its promise of things to come. She really was very happy here after a number of unsuitable house moves.

Looking back at the building she took in the neat brickwork and attractive gabled roof. The well-proportioned windows with sandstone lintels. Yes, this would most likely be her final home. There was no point in moving for the sake of moving.

Turning to take a towel from the line she recoiled at the sight of a large black spider nestling in the fold. 'Ugh, get off!'

A vigorous shaking finally dislodged the creature which dropped to the ground with an indolent air.

As she backed away it moved off slowly with a precise placing of each black leg.

Somehow she was reminded of the woman in the street.

Well, that's the garden ready for Spring, now to start on the house. With a sigh Audrey Cullen collected her cleaning-box and proceeded to check its contents.

'I bet I'm out of something,'she told herself. 'Let's see, wax polish, metal polish, something for the windows - ugh! no!' as her fingers probed the box a large black spider shifted position in one corner.

Once more, unaccountably she was reminded of the stranger in the street. Later as she wiped the skirting-board in the back bedroom she acknowledged her nerves to be still taut.

126

'Damn spiders, where are they all coming from!'

As she drank her afternoon tea she saw the tremor of unsettled nerves reflected in the liquid.

'It is silly to get so worked up but I do so hate them. They give me the shivers. I hope we're not in for a plague of them like that year of the ladybirds!'

Over the following days with the spring-cleaning proceeding satisfactorily she found her thoughts turning once more to the garden.

'The bulbs should be peeping though now, I'll give myself a break and have a stroll around the garden. Oh I do love this time of year!'

With a warm jacket over her working clothes she stood for a moment just breathing in the fresh air. The smell of damp soil and tang of young growth raised her spirits lifting her away from the oppression of mundane tasks. She closed her eyes, breathing deeply, filled with the joy of life - then she opened them to the enigmatic smile of the woman in black.

Turning away quickly as though intent on a positive task she went back indoors where she found to her dismay that she was trembling.

She did give me a fright, she excused herself. Creeping up like that and why does she stop anyhow? She never speaks, who is she? I must ask Nancy when I see her next. She's lived in this street all her married life and knows just about everybody around here!'

Somehow the sparkle had gone out of the day and the rest of the housework was completed in a contemplative mood.

She sighed as she put away the cleaning gear then went upstairs for a bath. I deserve this! she told herself as she poured a liberal amount of bath-oil into the water.

From the top of the pelmet the large black spider watched and waited.

'No honestly Audrey, I can't think who she could be!'

Nancy Cartwright accepted a shortbread finger and relaxed back into her chair. 'You say she doesn't call in at any of the houses in the street? No, oh well, it's a bit of a mystery! Anyhow Audrey your house looks lovely, as bright as a new pin. More than I can say for mine but what with working all week I just can't get up any enthusiasm at the weekend apart from a quick flick around with the duster!'

'How long have you lived here Nancy?'

'Well, let's see, it must be twenty-seven years because the Webbs who had your place were here for twenty-five years and you've been here for two. It's funny, the Webbs moved in within a couple of weeks of us twenty-seven years ago. I always got the impression they were settled for life but then Mr Webb took it into his head to emigrate. She never wanted to go, was dead against it. Rather odd person she was. Never had much to say, not much of a neighbour really! She always gave the impression of being entirely wrapped up in her home. I was very surprised that she agreed to go but then again I don't suppose she had much choice with him being the wage-earner! I never heard from them after the first Christmas. Twenty-five years as neighbours then they just vanish from your life. Well, thanks for the tea but I must get going. Got to pick up the plane tickets yet! Must say I'm really looking forward to two months in the sun!'

As the women moved to the front door a slight movement above the picture rail caught Nancy Cartwright's eye.

She decided against mentioning the presence of the large black spider. After all, when your neighbour has just finished telling you how they have thoroughly spring-cleaned it would scarcely be tactful.

It was unbelievable how quickly the house had been sold. Mrs Webb the purchaser hadn't even wanted to view the place saying she knew it well. A strange woman, the Agent thought, who had just scurried in and out of the office one day with an eagerness he couldn't comprehend in an area of like housing.

Audrey Cullen folded her farewell note through her neighbour's letterbox regretting that they weren't back from their trip but she'd be in touch with them again.

Walking back to the taxi ticking over outside her front gate she gave a last sad glance at the awakening garden. She regretted leaving it but you couldn't gear your life to a garden any more than she had found it possible to spend another day in that spider-ridden house!

As the taxi turned for the main road, the new owner, the recently-widowed Mrs Webb arrived to take up residence. Smiling her enigmatic smile she scuttled into her freshly-prepared home.

Not a cobweb in sight! She'd soon change that! Time to get weaving!

A Pregnant Pause

by

Janet Roberts

If it hadn't been for the wind, I would have been safely home by now and not sitting, shivering on the hard wooden bench in the police station.

I couldn't believe that only two hours ago I'd been busy shopping, minding my own business. Engulfed in my make-believe world, imagining what I would buy. I had pressed my face against the plate glass window of Babyneeds and peered myopically inside. I could feel the wind tugging at my coat and as I gazed dreamily at the cribs and babyclothes. The familiar longing for a child swept over me and for once I allowed myself the luxury of wallowing in a world of babies. I was brought back to reality by two giggling sales assistants inside.

'Look, she's at it again,' mouthed one, pointing in my direction. Their taunts and laughter hurt as I hurried away but not as much as usual, because I knew that soon, I would be having the last laugh.

Looking back, I can't recall a time when I didn't love babies. Even as a child playing games, I'd always wanted to be the mother. From an early age I'd had a strong urge to take care of others. I hadn't enjoyed games like catch or hopscotch. And I remember that I didn't like boardgames but was more than content to play with my dolls, whenever I could.

I'd once overheard my father talking to my mother,

'Dolls, dolls, it's always bloody dolls. There's something wrong with that child.'

'Leave her be. She's happy and she's not doing anybody, any harm. She'll make a grand mother if she cares for her own bairns as well as she cares for her dolls,' my mother had replied, defending me.

'Well, it ain't right. It's to the exclusion of everything else,' argued my father. 'It's unhealthy. Sometimes I think she's obsessed.'

I did grow out of dolls though, as I grew older.

But now the word obsessed was beating a rhythm in my brain, as I sat stiffly on the uncomfortable wooden bench. I stared unconsciously at the notices pinned on the board in front of me, as they fluttered in the escaped eddies of the wind, which now harnessed inside had turned into a draught. A strong smell of tea reached my nostrils.

'Would you like a cup, luv,' said the first kindly voice I'd heard in a long time. A young constable proffered a mug in my direction. I nodded, grateful for his tone rather than the tea.

Drawing warmth from the liquid, I thought, perhaps that's how other people saw me, as a crank with an obsession. It certainly seemed that way now. I'd thought that my maternal yearnings were natural. I'd assumed that most women had the same deep, built-in longings for a child of their own. It had been very hard for me to come to terms with the cruel God, who had given me these feelings but no way to assuage them.

When I looked back at my marriage to Tom, I couldn't deny that we'd been happy over the years. But we both felt an emptiness at the lack of tiny feet around our home. Years ago, after months of testing, the results had proved negative. There was no physical reason why we were childless.

'Cheer up love,' Tom would say, although I knew he hurt as much as I did. 'It'll happen one day when we're least expecting it.'

Good old Tom, he was always the optimist. And I would smile for his sake, inwardly feeling that it was my fault. It wasn't happening because I wanted it to happen, too much. It seemed ironical, that friends could produce hoards of children so easily.

Just recently, I had become so broody that it was impossible for me to walk past a pram. I would be drawn by some invisible force to peer into it's depths, admire the contents and wish for things to be different. I'd begun to notice that young mothers gave me strange looks before wheeling away their offspring. I understood the reason all too well. I would be fiercely protective of my own baby. You couldn't be too careful these days. But when someone I knew deliberately drew back her pram on seeing me and turned in the other direction, I was deeply hurt. I'd begun to worry that my thwarted love for a child was starting to overpower me.

But today everything was different and it would have been with a light step that I trod the high street, if it hadn't been for the wind. Anything light was in jeopardy of blowing away. And that's exactly what happened to the pram, that was parked outside the supermarket as I turned the corner. An enormous gust of wind bowled along the pavement, snatching and dragging at everything in sight. Its swirling rage filled the hood of the pram, and as the brake couldn't have been on properly, it started to move away, before I could stop it. With a gathering momentum, it rolled down the hill towards the main road.

My heart pounded with fear as I realised there was no one around, no one to stop and save the baby, only me. I wasn't very good at running, but that didn't matter now. I ran as if my life depended on it. The concrete slabs of pavement blurred before me. The pram was always just a couple of inches out of my grasp until with a gigantic effort, I caught the handle and brought it under control. As the sound of pounding died in my ears, it was replaced by an unexpected commotion. Turning, I hoped to see some help at hand but to my dismay I heard someone shout, 'Stop that women. She's stealing my baby.' Suddenly the deserted street was galvanised into action. People appeared from nowhere. A man dragged me away from the pram.

'Shame on you,' a woman shouted at me.

I could hear a police siren in the distance.

'The wind got in the hood and blew the pram away,' I explained shakily, looking for someone who understood.

People muttered and stared in disbelief.

'She's always hanging around prams, that one. Can't have any children of her own, so she thought she'd snatch one. Needs locking up, she does. Just look at her,' cried a woman I didn't even recognise.

Unkind faces jostled all around me. Someone leaned forward and spat at me, moisture hit my cheek and spittle stuck to my collar. The police car arrived. Overwhelmed by the crowd's violent reaction toward me, I allowed myself to be bundled unquestioningly into it.

And that's how I came to be in the police station, waiting to be interviewed. The sergeant carried a clip board as he walked toward me.

'Mrs Miller,' he said. 'Come this way please.'

As I rose to follow him, a door further along the corridor opened and out stepped Doctor Walker, swinging his bag. He was a good doctor, and his reputation went before him as being the best in the business. His genuine concern for those in need had earned him the respect of the town. He would brook no nonsense though and it was said that men would rather suffer the wrath of God than cross Doctor Walker. But he'd always been good to me and his surprise at seeing me again so soon was obvious.

'What are you doing here, Janice?' he smiled at me as he asked the question. 'I hope you've not been involved with this wretched accident.' He was waving his arm in the direction of the room he'd just vacated.

I shook my head, his concern opened the floodgates of the tears that I'd been fighting back. Seeing that I was too distraught to answer him, his gaze turned towards the sergeant.

'We have reason to believe that Mrs Miller tried to steal a baby,' said the sergeant looking uncomfortable.

'Steal a baby,' repeated the doctor, giving the sergeant a look as if he were deranged. 'Whatever for? Janice has no need to steal a baby. She's expecting one of her own soon. I told her so this morning when she visited my surgery. You'd better let her explain and we'll get this sorted out.' He steered me towards a chair. 'Now tell us exactly what happened, my dear,' he said encouragingly. And I did.

Afterwards Doctor Walker nodded toward the sergeant, 'There, you see. It was just the wind,' he said. He looked at me and winked. 'And you, my dear, will be having a lot more problems with that before your time is up,' he said mischievously, as he squeezed my arm and led me towards the door.

'I don't want Mrs Miller upset anymore today,' he called to the sergeant over his shoulder. 'So the young mother will have to thank her for saving the baby tomorrow.'

Doctor Walker liked to see justice done.

There was a pregnant pause, whilst the sergeant inwardly fought with himself over taking the doctor's orders.

'Yes,' he replied slowly. 'We'll sort that out tomorrow.'

And I thought to myself, if my pregnant pause had not been for so long, none of this would have happened today.

The Bird-Cage

by

Philip Burchett

'I'll buy you a talking parrot on my next trip,' said Jack.

'I'd like that,' said Jenny. 'But won't he be too big for the cage?'

'He'd be a bit on the large side, but he'd fit in. I'll teach him to say, 'Hullo, Jenny. The top of the morning to you'.'

'Don't teach him any of your horrid sailor's swear words.'

'I won't do that, Jenny. I'll only teach him to speak the Queen's English.'

Jack Masterson was a sailor, a junior officer on a merchant vessel that traded to South America from Bristol. He and Jenny Blackie were betrothed. Whilst he was on shore leave in England, they had been to a Rummage Sale, and bought a fine big bird cage, that stood on top of a thin metal support four feet high. The cage was intended for budgerigars, and was full of the joys of the small birds' existence: - mirrors, a tinkling bell, coloured beads, delicate perches, food containers. But it was so large that it could, exceptionally, house a parrot. The cage was now in Jenny's home. It would be an adornment of the cottage they would live in when married.

But the marriage was not to be. On Jack's next voyage his vessel was struck by Hurricane Louise. Jack, on all-weather watch in appalling weather, was one of three men assumed to have been lost overboard. 'Missing, feared drowned'. The bodies were never recovered.

Jenny was also lost - a lost soul that pined for a dead lover. Life offered her nothing that could fill the gap. Her tastes were not ordinary tastes, like those of her friends, who in any event were not close friends. Moreover, she was an orphan. Dancing, music, parties, church attendance, making pretty clothes - none of this was for her. If anything, her preference was for woodland walks, feeding the wild birds, and reading unsophisticated fantasies. Perhaps she was fey.

Two or three years passed. Then she had the strange notion of putting a model parrot in the cage, which still occupied an excess of space where she lived. The model she bought was a work of art and craftsmanship. It was about ten inches high, of wood, with a red crest, and a large red bobble at the end of its tail. The colours in which it was painted were the brightest of reds and greens, and its balance on a perch was perfect. It fitted neatly in Jenny's bird cage, and it seemed to belong, from the first day.

'Pretty Polly,' said Jenny. 'I wonder whether I might call you Jack. You look like a Jack - certainly not a Jill.'

So Jack he was, but hardly a Masterson, and because of that Jenny pined and paled. She came across a poem:-

But human life, at peace or strife,
Can die at greatest cost;
And sower, seed, the reft who bleed,
Be viewless, void, and lost.

She hardly understood it, but it seemed to fit her circumstances. Her prevailing sense was one of emptiness. Jack Polly was a help in a small way, but for the most part kept himself to himself. Yet his beady eye kept watch, and surprisingly attracted the view of a person, if any, in attendance.

Jenny took to her bed. Birchtrees, blackbirds, red admirals on the buddleia, and bookish fantasies seemed of less account, of diminishing significance. She was dozing one day, when a nearby voice spoke, interrupting her reverie.

'Hullo, Jenny,' it said. 'The top of the morning to you.' The beady eye was turned in her direction.

Jenny raised herself up. 'Jack,' she said. 'You've come back.'

'Of course I have. I haven't been very far away,' said the voice.

'It must have been two or three thousand miles at least,' said Jenny. 'And about ten years, I should think.'

'Don't suppose the space and time mattered much.'

'Oh yes it did. You don't understand. You try putting yourself in my shoes.'

'Perhaps we can make up for lost time.'

'Perhaps, but how?'

'Try joining me.'

'Are you really there - or here?'

'Yes, of course.'

'Prove it.'

'Right. Just watch me.'

In Jenny's eyes Jack Polly vibrated with a breath of life. He seemed to shudder, then somersaulted. Half-a-dozen somersaults were followed by a confident equilibrium. Jenny gave a shrill little scream, moaned quietly, had a spasm of hysteria, and sighed to momentary silence.

'Poor lass,' said a neighbour to a doctor. 'I found her on the floor over there by the bird cage. She spoke a few words to me, but she was rather incoherent. She kept pointing to the bird cage and the wooden parrot. 'Jack's come back,' she seemed to say. 'Jack. . . Polly. . . Jack. . . Polly. . . ' Then she smiled and passed out. . . and her breathing seemed to stop.'

Set Up

by

Robert McGrath

'Put that down and turn round slowly. I've got a gun in my hand and it's likely to go off if you make one false move.'

It was like something out of a cowboy movie, but I put down the video as gently as I could and turned round nice and slow, like the man said.

He was standing at the far end of the room, a small, thin, elderly man with fluffy grey hair trimming the sides of his bald head. He wore a washed out red dressing gown over old-fashioned striped pyjamas. His feet were pushed into scuffed brown carpet slippers, and his big toe peeped out of the one on his right foot.

The barrel of his shotgun pointing at me looked as big as the mouth of the Channel Tunnel.

'You're not much of a burglar,' he said, his weasel eyes glistening behind the lens of his steel rimmed spectacles. 'You made enough noise to wake Charlie Higgins, and he's been dead and buried for the last six years.'

He motioned nervously with his gun, 'Sit down on that chair and don't make a move. I'm going to call the police.'

I sat down on an old wooden armchair and gripped both arms tightly. I didn't like the look of the shotgun that he was still pointing at me. He picked up the phone and started dialling.

I put on my best whining voice, 'Give us a chance, mister . . .'

'A chance! Not likely! You were going to rob me blind. You weren't going to give me a chance.'

I was about to tell him the old story about having a sick mother and no job when he slowly put down the receiver.

'Wait a minute,' he said thoughtfully, 'I have an idea.'

'Go on. I'll listen.' At least it would delay the phone call, maybe give me a chance to escape.

He sat down opposite me and pointed with his gun.

'See that china figure. It's an heirloom.'

I braved the gun, crossed the room to the fireplace and picked up the statue off the mantelpiece. It was of a bearded man with a fish's tail. His long flowing hair was topped by a golden crown, and in his hand he held a long trident.

'Neptune?' I suggested.

'Neptune it is. My mother left him to me in her will. But he's only one of a pair. My sister, Mary, got the other piece, a mermaid.

'They are worth quite a bit by themselves, but together they'd be worth much more. I'd give anything to have them both.'

I guessed what was coming.

He nodded to the phone. 'You get me the mermaid, and I'll say nothing to the police about tonight.'

134

It didn't take me long to make up my mind. He was giving me a chance, and I was prepared to take it.

'OK. Where does your sister live. And how soon do you want it doing?'

'24, Hexagon Way. The lock on the kitchen transom is faulty so it can easily be forced open with a strong pocket knife. Even you should be able to manage that.'

'She goes to play Bridge on a Wednesday, that's tomorrow, and when she comes home about eleven, she is usually quite tired. Give her a chance to get to bed. Once she's asleep she won't hear a sound.'

'And what's in it for me?'

'Help yourself. She's got some nice pieces of silver. Just get me the mermaid and you can take anything you fancy.'

He looked at my hands and a pained expression crossed his face. 'Oh, and be professional, wear gloves. I don't want your fingerprints splattered all over the place, just in case they caught you and traced you back to me.'

It was child's play getting into the kitchen, just as he said it would be.

Holding my breath, I tiptoed through the hall, slipped the snib on the lock on the front door, and left it slightly ajar. That was my escape route in case she woke up.

I crept back into the room where he said the mermaid would be. The room was in darkness, but I felt I was not alone.

Apprehensively, I switched on my torch and shone it round the room.

There she was, lying on the floor in a pool of blood. Someone had hit her over the head with the poker which was still lying across her body. She would never wake up again.

'My God,' I thought, 'She's dead! Someone's killed her! Let's get out of here quick.'

Perhaps I still have some semi-dormant finer feelings, because it seemed all wrong to me to leave her as she was. Mechanically, I picked up the poker. I don't know why. Maybe with some idea of making her comfortable. Then all hell broke loose. The front door was flung open, the lights were switched on, and a couple of burly policemen burst into the room.

The bigger, uglier one looked at me standing over the body with the poker still in my hand. He spoke quietly, but with menace,

'Hold it there, son. You're nicked.'

The Interview Room was lit by one small, not too clean window. Its plain brick walls were painted in an unimaginative green. The dark brown floor covering had been chosen with the same lack of flair. I sat on a hard wooden chair on one side of a long, badly stained table. Detective Inspector Parker sat opposite me, a sheaf of notes in his hand. I had just told him my story. He looked at me in disbelief, as if I were a modern Hans Christian Andersen.

'It was a set up,' I protested, 'The old man set me up.'

He shook his head, 'George Watkins was devoted to his sister. Why would be want to kill her?'

'For the mermaid. He said it was valuable.'

'Then he said wrong. It's a nice piece. Interesting. But mass produced. There's quite a few of them about.'

I had an inspiration. 'What about her will? Have you checked her will?'

'Yes,' he said deliberately, 'She's left everything to him. But it's not much. Just the contents of her house and a few hundred pounds. Certainly not worth killing for.'

I was getting desperate. 'There must be more to it than that. What about her house? That should be worth a bit.'

'Rented,' was the laconic reply.

He stared at me unblinking. Those cold impersonal eyes they issue to all detectives never left my face.

'Then how would I know about his dressing gown and the hole in his slippers if I hadn't talked to him?' I argued.

'A lot of people knew about them. He was always wearing them. You could have seen him sometime bring in the milk, say.'

'Never!' Then I had a brain wave. 'Finger prints. My fingerprints should be on his video, and the arm of his chair. And don't forget, I handled his figurine. They could be on that too.'

He seemed almost amused. 'We've checked. But Mr Watkins is a very house proud man. He goes round his rooms a couple of times a week with a duster. No fingerprints.

'Let's face it, sonny, when we find an intruder standing over a dead body with a poker in his hand, we don't need an awful lot of imagination to work out what happened.'

He pointed a stubby finger at me, 'You are in trouble.'

Curtains! They were coming down for me. I was going to spend the rest of my life locked up for something I hadn't done.

As we sat there in silence, the door opened and young Detective Bromidge came in. He seemed quite excited.

'Inspector. We've just found out. Five years ago George Watkins took out a big insurance on his sister's life.'

Motive! The very word was written in neon lights flashing inside my brain.

The Inspector showed all the animation of an hibernating tortoise. But he echoed my thoughts, 'It does give him a motive.'

'And,' interrupted Bromidge, looking at me, 'We've found your fingerprints on the underside of the armchair. Watkins must have missed wiping them off there.'

He turned to the Inspector, 'It proves that the accused actually was in the house at sometime or other.'

Inspector Parker took a few long seconds to make up his mind.

'Go and search the house thoroughly. Look for a shotgun, and for any sign of bloodstained clothing.'

He turned back to me. Was it my imagination, or had his voice mellowed a little.

'Let's hear your story again,' he said.

Uncle Ned - A Man Of Many Parts

by

Douglas Griffiths

Uncle Ned was a pragmatist; not that he would put it quite that way himself, nor would it be advisable to tell him so, not after what happened to Charlie the postman who, by the way, considered himself a man of letters. He called Uncle Ned a chauvinist one night in the 'Boilermakers Arms'. Charlie was correct in what he said but unfortunately he failed to foresee the retired shipyard worker might misunderstand his meaning. Ned was on his fifth or sixth pint at the time. However, it was generally agreed that not much harm was done. The furnishing in the 'Boilermakers Arms' needed replacing anyway, and Charlie was soon back on his round with scarcely any sign of a limp.

Auntie Elsie would have agreed that Uncle Ned was a chauvinist, if she knew what it meant, which she probably did, come to think of it, as she had been to night school. She had been to literary appreciation classes, much to Ned's disgust. When she mentioned D H Lawrence he thought she meant, 'That Army bloke who used to dress up as an Arab.'

Ned was also a hypochondriac, another description which, if applied to Ned directly would be likely to have painful consequences. He would never take a holiday in case the water disagreed with him, which is surprising as he seldom drank any. Before he retired he always said he wasn't entitled to holidays. When pressed on the subject he admitted that he had been offered some time off in lieu but, as he said, 'Who the 'eck wants to go to Cornwall at this time of year.' He had also been advised by his firm to take his holidays at his own convenience, which he felt to be equally unhelpful.

After his retirement he had no such excuses, but still managed to avoid taking Auntie Elsie out anywhere. When she dropped subtle hints such as, 'Isn't it about time we went on a coach trip or something?' he would become very forgetful. He always protested that he had taken her to the pictures, 'not long ago', but could never remember the name of the film. He used this strategy a lot. Elsie said it was due to cooking with aluminium pans which, she said, gave you a disease which made you forget things. Whenever Ned got an attack of convenient forgetfulness she would shake her head and say, 'I must get rid of them aluminium pans.'

In addition to all that, Ned was an optimist. He did the pools every week hoping to repeat his one and only win of ten pounds, many years before. He had been drunk for a week. He was wild in those days. So was Auntie Elsie when she found he'd spent the lot. Auntie Elsie reckoned the pools were an expensive way to play noughts and crosses. She had him weighed up.

From time to time Auntie Elsie tried to involve Ned in more civilised pursuits than those which took place in the 'Boilermakers Arms'. Dominoes, she reckoned were dotty, and darts were pointless. She also had an opinion about snooker. Her own path to self-improvement lay in the Townswomens' Guild

137

where she learned flower arranging, keep fit and continental cooking. The results of the latter did not go down well with Uncle Ned.

Some of the meetings were open to husbands and other male guests but Ned was aghast at the slightest suggestion of his attending. He completely refused to take any interest in local history which he said he'd heard all about from his Grandfather. He said, 'The goings on in them days was no fit subject for a Womens' club.' Nor was he interested in gardening. His one, long-ago attempt to grow potatoes in an allotment had met with total failure. Auntie Elsie reckoned he'd planted them upside down.

One day she asked him to go with her to a wine-tasting evening. Then his attitude became one of crafty speculation. It appeared that Ned was also an opportunist.

'I might just manage that one, luv,' he said. 'I always reckon that 'usbands and wives should do things together, so long as I don't 'ave to eat that paella stuff again.'

'You always 'ave to bring that up,' said Elsie. But you could tell that she was pleased.

The meeting started well. The speaker described the characteristics of a range of table wines from sweet white through to dry red. He explained that a good wine need not be expensive as it all depended on 'the quality of the grapes'. Oddly enough, all the wines he recommended were available at very reasonable prices from the Cutcost Supermarket.

'This is a bloomin' advertising stunt,' muttered Ned, shifting his feet impatiently. 'When do we get to taste the stuff?'

Auntie Elsie, who had been shushing and nudging during the talk, lost the battle to restrain Ned as soon as the speaker's assistant began to pass around samples of the wine. Immediately he was at the front, sinking it by the glassful, and asking questions with urgent interest. 'What's this 'ere bouquet stuff?' and 'What's the point of gargling with the stuff!' He sank a few more glasses to show how he felt it should be done.

The speaker did not appear to resent Uncle Ned's philistine approach, but set about instructing him in the art of wine appreciation, drinking several glasses in the process. He was a true enthusiast. Bottles of sparkling wine were being uncorked like an artillery barrage. There was much laughter. It was a scene of great conviviality.

The ladies of the Guild were not amused. Many of them wanted to ask the speaker questions but found him being monopolised by Ned like some old crony. What's more the speaker was now becoming incoherent, rambling on about 'the colity of the gapes'. It was quite obvious that the meeting was going to be cut short.

After the speaker was carried out, an ugly scene developed. Ned, by then tipsy, made an attempt to take over the lecture, but a wall of hostile women advanced towards the platform.

Elsie, showing great presence of mind, as well as amazing strength and speed, frog-marched Ned out of the room. By the time she got him home he was distinctly glassy-eyed and rubber-legged. Her tirade about him, 'showing her up', and 'never taking him into decent company ever again,' was largely wasted. He couldn't agree more.

'Did you see 'em?' he slurred. 'It was like in that picture I took you to see not long ago, you know, the one with Stanley Baker in it.'

'That must 'ave been a long time ago,' put in Elsie acidly.

But Ned was not listening. 'No more women's clubs for me,' he declared shuddering. 'I'd sooner face the flippin' Zulu's.'

Another thing about Ned. He was a born survivor.

The Troubled Soul

by

K Farley

I came by myself on this fishing trip, not being in the mood for company. I was not a happy man. Fishing was not exactly the cause of my divorce. Not exactly, but maybe it could be called a contributory factor, as the cliché has it. I gathered that I had made my wife a fishing widow, and that I had no more romance in me than had one of the fish I was so keen on. She found someone else. I didn't ask what hobby he had. I headed for the west of Ireland, where I'd heard the fishing was good. And it was. I stayed at a farmhouse, where there was warm hospitality, and excellent food. On my first day fishing in a fast running stream, which they called a river, I had an almighty struggle with a salmon, which nearly pulled me down into the current. It took all my strength and determination to keep my hold on the wet rock I stood on.

Well, after that, in the evening, I felt I deserved a drink, and I drove to a bar on the outskirts of a small nearby town. This bar was in a large, gloomy shop, where there was a smell of oatmeal and cloves. I ordered a whisky, and went to sit in a dim and distant corner of the place. Ah, but the locals were not going to have that. Not being in the mood for company was not on, not in here.

'You'll be here on holiday?'

The old man sat beside me. Resigning myself to conversation, I agreed that I was.

'From England? I was there once myself. A grand place, surely.'

'I live in Leeds'

'I was in Liverpool. A fine city indeed, an' Leeds is an all, I'm sure.'

He was very affable. A pint of Guinness appeared in front of me, and two other characters joined us. As the time wore on, the conversation became more and more outrageous, of mysterious local happenings, past and present. There was no man here who had not seen some kind of unexplained apparition. They were heavily into the paranormal, though I'm sure none of them had come across the word. It was quite enthralling to listen to, and I gradually began to believe every word of their improbable, even miraculous tales. I mellowed, I even enjoyed myself.

The hours flew, and soon it was time to go. The farmhouse was a few miles away, and I was the only one going in that direction. I decided to walk, as I had had an amount to drink. How much, I wasn't sure. The car would be all right there until morning, wouldn't it?

'Indeed it will. But sure there wouldn't be any harm at all in driving. You'd meet nothing on that road.'

No, I had never driven drunk, and I was not about to start now. Off I set, in good cheer now, and singing to myself, something I'd heard my host at the farm singing. A catchy tune, I thought it, though when sober my taste ran to rock music.

'Its a grand night.'

I turned and saw a man walking along beside me, his face pale in the moonlight. I though him quite old, and his conversation confirmed that.

'Many's the time I walked this road, so long, so very long ago.'

'You lived here' I looked at him, and saw him clearly in the light of a full moon.

'I did. Ah, they were sad times then.'

He talked of the nineteen twenties, of war that split opinions among the people. He told me of how father went against son, brother against brother, of sudden ambushes, of houses burned down. Stories of comrades he'd loved being killed, of women shot dead protecting their husbands, of men on the run, hungry, afraid, hiding in the hills. And he spoke of a common enemy, the British government. Some old people talk, and you only half listen. But, in this case, you could see how awful a civil war could be. He gave a clear picture of it. I had known nothing of the history of Ireland until now. And what a mess it had been. So interested I was, that I hardly noticed when the moon went behind a cloud, and a drizzly rain came on. I seemed to reach my farmhouse in no time, and we wished each other goodnight.

The next morning dawned grey and wet, but that doesn't bother a fisherman. I wore my waterproofs and drove to a lake. The fish were plentiful that day. My session was relaxing and rewarding. Content, I made my way back to base, to a fine meal.

In the evening, the rain had stopped, so I walked to what I now thought of as 'the pub'. Good healthy exercise, and after all, I didn't expect to be in a fit state to drive back. Might as well face facts. I was on holiday, wasn't I?

I told my new acquaintances of my companion on the road last night. There was a moment of silence, and then, 'God almighty,' said the old man who had first spoken to me, 'where were you when you saw this man beside you?'

I knew this exactly.

'It was near a side path, and there were three trees together, rather a strange shape, like triangles.'

'It was himself you saw, the man who was murdered on that very spot, by his own brother. It was the time of the troubles.'

'The civil war?'

'The troubles. The killer disappeared after that. It was said that he did away with himself, from the terrible guilt that he felt. It was the troubled spirit of the man he killed that walked with yourself on the road last night. Sure, he's been seen before but he didn't speak to anyone until now.'

'You mean he was a ghost?'

I was incredulous, and I began to laugh,. It was monstrous. But I stopped laughing when I saw them crossing themselves in fear. Useless to say how a ghost couldn't have been so real, so chatty, so solid. They were sure of what they knew, and they were appalled at my experience.

'The troubles were a terrible time,' said the old man, 'but, sure there were real things, political matters. It's all very long ago, and we were fighting because of principles, not bombing innocents in other places, as they do now.'

141

He went on, after a pause, 'The soul on the road with you is a troubled soul. Now, what you have to do is to find out why he can't rest. Ask him when he comes again. For that he will. He talked to you. He has chosen you to bring him peace.'

Big deal, I thought, and I wondered if they were all crazy, in this far away place.

Time came to go, and I set off to walk, full of Dutch courage. I'd never seen a ghost, in all my forty years. The man who'd talked to me last night, he was real, of course he was. What nonsense about souls without rest. Only, I wasn't singing this time. There was no moon tonight, but an eerie darkness, and trees waved long arms and skinny fingers at me as I walked along.

'You're walking, I see, though you drive a car?'

Had I heard the words, or just thought I'd heard them? No, he was with me all right, and I explained that I never used the car after drinking, 'Good people are scarce,'

I added. Do ghosts like a joke, or have they heard all of them too often before? I could feel a presence, and see a vague form, but I couldn't see his face. Surely I wasn't talking to a spectre, a phantom, an emptiness? I didn't like to reach out and touch him. Supposing my fingers were to go straight through his arm? I shivered. The darkness seemed deeper. I could hardly ask him if he was a spirit. I had a feeling of cold, of dampness. I was sweating. I felt terror, and I began to freeze with it. No! I made a gigantic effort, I shook off my fear, and spoke. 'Is something troubling you?' I asked.

I thought I heard a sigh, and he said,

'Two brothers, twins. One shot the other, thinking him an informer. He was wrong. He took the word of a woman he was in love with, Katy. She preferred the other brother, and she was spiteful when he didn't want her. Maybe she didn't mean for murder to happen. She killed herself after that.'

He left me then, though I wasn't sure which way he went.

In my comfortable holiday bed that night, I tried to reason. A spirit and a body are two things. The dead have only one, a rotting body. Ah, but some people believe that the dead have spirit, that when we die, we 'give up the ghost'. All right then, but then you still have only one, you can't get the body back, and look human again, can you? Never. And all that information I'd had. It must have been from a real person. Over and over I went in my mind, over and over all that had happened. I lay awake for hours, and when I should have got up, I was deep in sleep, and I missed my fishing. Instead, I drove a long way, on deserted Irish roads. Then, I parked the car, and walked along an old bog road, and up a hill of crunchy purple heather. At the top, I could see for miles. The fields had hedges of fuchsia, and by the roads were clumps of rhododendron bushes. The peaceful scene soothed me, and I began to think how ridiculous it all was. Maybe too many drinks had given me hallucinations. I only usually drank in moderation, at weekends, with my fishing mates.

That evening, I was exhausted, and after eating I fell asleep on my bed, so I got along to the bar later than usual. A man stood at the counter, waiting for his order. He turned towards me, and my stomach did a somersault. It was my companion of the dark road. He nodded and smiled, and asked me what I would like to drink. So, he was real, and what relief I felt! The others sat over in the corner, looking at us.

'They thought you must be a ghost,' I said, nodding in their direction.

'I've been called some things in my time,' he said, laughing, 'but they think anyone is a ghost who hasn't been living here forever.'

'Someone was shot once at the spot on the road where we met.'

'I happen to be staying at a house down the side road. I like to take a walk at night. It helps me to sleep. I've been in Australia for many years, got nostalgic only in my old age. But I know a man was shot there. I did the shooting. My brother deserved to be shot. He was a traitor.'

'Oh, no,' I protested, confused now, 'he wasn't. You said so yourself last night.'

'I was in Dublin last night, came back this morning'

I looked straight into his face, and I heard myself say, 'Your brother was innocent. You took the word of a woman, Katy, a woman scorned by your brother.'

Well, that sounded like over the top dramatics, something from a Victorian play, and I half expected him to laugh. But, no. I could see he believed me . . . He said nothing, but stood aghast, no other word could describe it. Everyone there felt that something shocking was about to happen. He turned and ran, out of the place. Within seconds, I followed, and so did the locals. He had got into a car, whether his own, or not, I didn't know. . .We watched his reckless speeding, as he drove away from the town, and the car left the road, and crashed into a rocky hillside. It burst into flames.

I walked back much later that night, knowing that no ghost from Limbo would join me. He was shriven now. But what about the heavy load of guilt that the twin brother was having to bear, now that he too was dead, and a suicide? When would his tormented soul start searching for rest? Would he haunt the same road? And was I likely to be chosen again to be the honoured medium?

Oh, no. I'd had enough. First thing in the morning, I'd be heading home to Leeds.

Afwan

by

Shirley Baxter

Afwan was ugly! The small group of people, consisting of Bob and Sally Grant, their two children, Jane and Stephen, and Duncan Harvey stood surveying him, solemnly and silently, despising his ugliness. 'Go ahead, stare. I've seen that expression on countless faces before' thought Afwan, and stared back at them belligerently, with dull, vacant eyes. He was well aware of his appearance, filthy, dilapidated, unkempt and uncared for by anyone, including himself. He had no pride, that had been destroyed slowly and painfully by the human race - and time. He looked at the children, those small people, who could be so loving yet, sometimes, inhumanely cruel. Once, he had been young, stately and proud, admired and loved. Now he was dying, his spirit long since dead, his shell rotting. Youth's imagination was incapable of visualising a time when the old had been young. The old had always been old and the young would remain young they told themselves, blotting out the fearful future.

'May as well go in now we're here,' said Bob, leading the way through the rusty iron gate, hanging off its hinges and along the cracked, overgrown path. Duncan unlocked the stout oak door and pushed hard as the hinges squealed in protest at being disturbed. Afwan watched their expressions as they entered the house. Horror, on Sally's face as she observed the filth created by tramps, squatters, children. Curiosity, but hesitancy on the children's faces. Hope fading to be replaced by - something like defeat, on Bob's face. Duncan Harvey's expression was always the same, shame and embarrassment. He had been here many times with many people. This was only the third time he had managed to get anyone to enter the house, the others had taken one look outside and beat a hasty retreat.

'Go on, get out, leave me to die in peace,' thought Afwan, aggressively.

The group were walking from room to room, dreamlike, noting the rotting window frames and broken panes and the graffiti on the filthy walls. The children grew restless and ran outside.

'Funny, there doesn't seem to be any damp, except where the rain has got in through the broken windows,' Bob remarked.

Duncan seized his chance. 'Oh no, the walls are sound and the roof is good. It was built when things were built to last.

'Not like now,' thought Bob, 'craftsmanship and pride in workmanship had been abandoned in the race to satisfy the growing appetites of the endless homeless.' They entered the kitchen and for the first time, a tiny gleam of interest flickered in Sally's eyes.

'What a big kitchen, and look at the view from here. Oh Bob, it's got an old-fashioned inglenook and a utility room.' She stamped on the floor. 'The floors are good, I must admit,' she said, grudgingly. She walked around the kitchen for a long time.

144

The children came rushing in, flushed and excited. 'Mum, Dad, it's great! There's a wishing well at the bottom of the garden and an orchard, with all sorts of fruit growing and a big tree that we could make a tree-house in. We're going upstairs to choose our bedrooms,' they said, clomping up the stairs.

Afwan stretched himself, noisily, his joints creaking. He remembered children dashing up and down the stairs, the laughter, the tears, the warmth and love, all long gone. By the time the motorway, schools and shops had been built, not half a mile away from him, he had grown too old and dilapidated for anyone to want him.

The adults followed the children, slowly, up the stairs. Jane was in the first room that they entered. It was a peculiar shape, almost five-sided.

'This is my room because it's like a star. My bed goes here, my doll's house here and my wardrobe here,' she said, dancing around the room, indicating her preference.

'Come and see mine, it's got a washbasin and built-in wardrobe,' called Stephen, his face aglow. Sally and Bob stared at each other.

'You mean you like it here?' questioned Sally in disbelief.

'Yes, it's great, but it needs decorating. The garden's super, can't wait to build the tree-house. When can we move?' the children asked excitedly.

'Any chance of getting a grant to fix this place up?' Bob asked Duncan.

'Every chance, I've already approached the powers-that-be in case anyone was interested. I know you will think its sales talk, but it really is a good, solidly built house. It can be made beautiful and there's lots of land to go with it.'

They walked through the house again and then through the overgrown gardens. 'What do you think Sally? I know it needs a lot of work, its a mess, but I like it, it feels, well, friendly.' Bob's eyes pleaded with her. She knew that it was a challenge to him and that he would win. He was keyed up and excited.

'I like the privacy, not another house in sight. I love the kitchen, the amenities are close, but not too close, the children like it.' She put her arm through his and held him close. 'Tell him to knock a thousand off the price and we'll have it.' Bob hugged her.

'You won't know the place in a year's time,' he promised. 'Can you knock a thousand off the price?' he asked Duncan.

Duncan sighed with relief. 'I'm sure that can be arranged,' he said, shaking hands with both of them.

As they passed through the lopsided gate on their way out, Sally noticed some letters etched into the ironwork, Afwan. 'That must be the name of the house, I wonder what it means,' she said.

Bob laughed, 'Well, I'm not sure of the spelling, but while I was working in Saudi Arabia I learned that Afwan means 'You're welcome'.'

Sally looked back at the house. Afwan beamed at her. 'You know Bob, I think we are.'

The Wisdom Of Uncle Mort

by

Alan Ewing

The path at the side of Uncle Mort's house was strewn with various forms of plant life. Ivy climbed the walls which went up to a height of six feet on either side, Nasturtiums dominated the borders on both sides with a galaxy effect given in all the reds, yellows and oranges that were cast before the eye. Annual flowers in the form of Lobelia and Alyssum gave addition to the cottage garden image.

Next to these stood the Poplar trees reaching out into the sky, as each year a few more feet were added to their tall posture. A range of Forsythia caught the eye with the green of summer now having well taken over from the yellow of spring. There was not a weed to be seen in any corner and yet the impression was still of a garden untouched.

It was of course the view of Uncle Mort that a gardener has to work for the plants and not the other way around. You could not order plants about and have them appear like soldiers standing to attention. A garden needed the freedom to express nature and all that a gardener had to do was a touch here and there.

The path led to the garden proper at the back of the house, with a well manicured series of small sections of lawn interspersed with flowering borders. The scent of flowers and the buzz of industrious bees were to be found everywhere. This then led on to a second section of garden which contained the well dug borders of the rose bushes.

A third section revealed the vegetable plot with decorative features such as Sweet Peas thrown in for dramatic twist. It was right at the top of this section that Uncle Mort was to be found. An old shed containing lots of tools and other gardening items had in the middle of it a table and two chairs. It was within this dusty and homely scene that Uncle Mort and his niece Sandra were contained.

Sandra was seated on one of the chairs sipping a glass of Uncle Mort's home-made lemonade. Her Uncle meanwhile was potting up a fine Dahlia specimen with great attention. Sandra watched this portly man in a flat cap with the same fascination that she had felt as a child on first entering this shed twenty years ago.

'A lot of people have trouble with this particular plant,' said Uncle Mort. 'It's one of those you just have to labour with,' he continued.

The sun was beating down through both the door of the shed and the window. This had been by far the most glorious day of the summer so far and the ring on Sandra's finger sparkled in the sunlight as the sound of a blackbird singing carried its way to their ears. This happened to coincide with a sad expression on Sandra's face.

'It something the matter my dear?' asked Uncle Mort. 'It would not look from your face that all is well; a face like yours my love should be full of radiance and smiles on a day as beautiful as this. But what do I see? My angel appears to be carrying the troubles of the world upon her shoulders.'

Sandra's gloomy look lifted somewhat at these kind words spoken in those wise old tones that she knew so well. She had often through the years come to this shed for advice in times of trouble. She had always felt a sense of escape here from the outside world coupled with a sense of security within its atmosphere.

'Has there been some trouble with David?' her Uncle concluded. As usual Uncle Mort had been quick to realise the problem which his niece had brought to him on this latest occasion. He was like that with everybody though. If advice was needed then Uncle Mort was the person to see; you could be sure of a listening ear and sound guidance if requested. Sandra felt at ease and able to pour out her troubles. She and David had been engaged for six months now and there had been nothing but harmony in that time. Lately though there had been a restlessness about David: this had concerned the actual timing of their marriage date. Sandra had felt a long engagement of two years to be in order, to which David had at first agreed.

This arrangement had been fine up until about a month ago, when David had been asked by his company to accept a transfer to another part of the country. He had accepted straight away as the job was a better one with a larger pay packet. The transfer was to be in two months time, so he thought the best idea would be to bring the marriage date forward and could not see Sandra objecting to this.

Sandra herself would eagerly have brought the marriage date forward; but it was not so straight forward as that. Her parents, on a matter of principle, had insisted on paying all the wedding costs and they wanted these to be the best she could possibly have. It would though, take time for them to save up the money required to do this. So had come about Sandra's reasons for a two year engagement.

This then is where the point of trouble lay between David and Sandra. When David had told Sandra about his job transfer, with his idea to bring the marriage date forward, he had expected total agreement. When, however, he found reluctance to this suggestion, he was taken aback. Sandra did not want to put pressure on her parents.

The whole discussion had then collapsed into ultimatums. David began to make it clear that if the marriage could not be brought forward, then perhaps it would be better if it did not happen at all. Against this feeling of being pushed into a corner Sandra had replied that seeing as David could not wait a little while longer, then she too felt that maybe it would be better to call the whole thing off.

And so the couple had parted on these terms the night before. On awakening the next morning in a confused state, it had been the natural move for Sandra to make Uncle Mort's shed her first point of call. Assurance and advice could always be found there.

All this time Uncle Mort had continued to pot his plants, while listening to this tale about the sad turn in the young couple's relationship. He gave Sandra a consoling pat on the shoulder, as was his way, with a promise that he would give the matter some thought. Sandra thanked him for listening and then left for home.

A week later Sandra once again made her way to Uncle Mort's home. As usual she strode around the beautiful pathway and then through the various sections of garden with all their vibrant plant and insect life. She made her way down to the old potting shed where she found Uncle Mort in the middle of preparing his annual strawberry wine.

'Ah, hello my dear, I see that ring of yours is sparkling in the sun again. I trust that when this wine is ready to drink we shall be toasting a wedding sometime next Spring,' said Uncle Mort.

Of course he knew this to be the case, for indeed Sandra and David had agreed to be married the following spring. David was to go on ahead to the new town and sort out all the practical tasks such as a house, then later he would be back to marry Sandra, and then take her back as his bride to their new home.

This change in David's thinking had come about after a journey he had made to a place that Sandra had often told him about. Uncle Mort had demanded total secrecy about the fact that he had given David advice of any kind, and David was to respect this.

After Sandra had left him, Uncle Mort finished bottling his strawberry wine and then made his way into his house. On entering his living room he once again looked over the old teak desk that he had purchased from his brother that very week. It had cost a fair portion of his savings to buy the antique, but at least it meant that his brother could now pay out a little earlier then previously thought for the wedding of his daughter.

All things said and done, a spring wedding would be quite a treat to look forward to. There would also at some point in the future be young children beating a path to the old shed. Uncle Mort gave a sigh of contentment as he headed back to the shed, the place where he felt happiest.

The Gnomes Revenge

by

Carole Sexton

Jane was just closing her front-door, as she set out for the local shops, when an irate voice made her turn around.

'Have you seen my gnomes?' It was old Mr Parry from next door.

'Er . . . no, I'm sorry Mr Parry, is there something wrong?'

Jane looked over the hedge separating the two gardens, and to her horror saw the poor man's prize collection of stone gnomes had all been beheaded.

'Oh my goodness! how awful, who on earth could have done that?'

'I don't know, but if I find out, heaven help them,' raged the usually mild, elderly man. 'I've called the police, they said they would send someone around later.'

That afternoon Jane was greeted by her twelve year old daughter Rebecca, as she burst into the house after school, with, 'Have you seen Mr Parry's gnomes Mum?'

'Yes, the police have been here this morning.'

'Oh, I wish I'd been around,' she complained. 'Do they know who did it yet?'

They were still discussing the situation when fourteen year old Mark came in.

'Someone's done a Henry VIII to Mr Parry's gnomes.'

'It's not funny Mark,' admonished Jane. 'He's a nice old man, and doesn't deserve that. Those gnomes were his pride and joy.'

Chris her husband, unbelievably, had not even noticed the headless gnomes, until informed of the situation by the family.

'Well, I was rushing this morning, as I was a bit late, and it had gone dark when I came in tonight.'

The following day Jane was on her way to her creative writing class at the library, when she noticed the garden wall of a neighbouring house had been partially demolished. She continued on to the bus-stop, where while waiting, Jane saw the occupant of the house with the damaged wall approaching. Sharon Smith was a young single mum, who's husband had left her to bring up two children alone. These accompanied her now, one in the pushchair the other running alongside.

'Hello, Sharon, kids, what's happened to your wall? It was alright yesterday wasn't it?'

'Yes, and look at it now, some lunatic has half demolished it. I had a friend visiting last night, and I saw her off after midnight, it was alright then. Come here, Damian,' she yelled at her toddler son.

'It must be the same person who vandalised Mr Parry's gnomes.'

'This used to be a nice area.'

At that moment the bus arrived, and Jane had to cut short the conversation.

That afternoon Rebecca arrived home, first as usual.

'Mum, have you seen Sharon's wall? The mad vandal has struck again.'

'I bet it was Damian, he's a horrible little kid. He throws stones at the cat.'

'He's only four, Mark. I don't think he's strong enough to knock down walls, even if he's got the inclination.'

'This is getting serious though,' Chris confided to Jane later. 'Something should be done.'

'The police told Mr Parry, unless he catches someone in the act, or has proof of who it is, there's nothing they can do. He's got no idea who might be responsible, he's got no enemies.'

'As Sharon Smith's house has been attacked too, it looks as if it could be random, rather than a personal thing.'

The next day being Saturday, Jane, Chris and Rebecca set off for town, Mark having gone off to play football for his school. As Chris turned the car out of their drive they saw a man waving furiously at them from the pavement.

'It's Ray Lucas, from number twenty three. What's the matter with him,' said Chris stopping the car.

Jane wound down the window on her side, as Mr Lucas bent down to speak. He now roared in her ear.

'My prize rose bushes, some bastard has ripped up three of my best!'

'Steady on Ray,' said Chris glancing at Rebecca.

'Don't tell me to steady on, Barrett, I got first prize at the Horticultural Show with my Wendy Cusson's last year. You won't be so calm when something happens to your place. More of young Sharon's wall's gone too.'

'I'm very concerned,' objected Chris. 'In fact I think we should call a tenants meeting as soon as possible to discuss the situation.'

'Good idea,' said Ray slightly mollified. 'How about tomorrow evening, my place?'

Chris agreed to visit the tenants on one side of the road, which fortunately only contained about thirty houses. Ray Lucas did the other. The response was good, Chris reported back to Jane, most people agreeing to attend.

The following evening they all assembled in Ray's home, and he began the discussion.

'Two walls damaged again last night. Sharon's and Page's at number five.'

'I went out fishing at six this morning,' remarked George Carter, from number seven. 'Now I live next to Page's, and the wall was alright then.'

'Alright at six, you say, but it was damaged when I got up at eight,' replied Jim Page.

'That means its being done in the morning, not at night as we first thought,' said Chris.

'And on such a regular basis that it seems as if it's someone who either lives here, or has some reason to come here everyday,' suggested Jane.

'I can't see it being one of us,' replied Ray Lucas. At that moment the doorbell rang and his wife Margaret hurried off to answer it.

In came Sharon dragging Damian with her. 'Sorry I'm late and I've had to bring him, he wouldn't stay with the sitter.'

Damian raced across the room, as Ray seized a vase of flowers, and Margaret a china figure off the coffee table.

'I'll take him,' offered Jane lifting the child onto her lap.

'I think I know who it is,' announced Sharon dramatically. They were all agog.

'This morning Kylie had me up early, around seven. I heard a noise, so I rushed to the window. A lad was running away from my house, out of the gate, then he jumped on a bike and took off up the road. I looked, and there were more bricks out of my wall on the pavement.'

'You said you knew him?' asked Chris.

'I don't know his name, but he had a paperboy's bag on his back. One of those fluorescent ones, to be seen in the dark.'

'The paperboy,' said Ray in disbelief.

'He's certainly around each day, early in the morning,' said Jim Page.

'A new lad has started this week,' put in his wife Brenda, who had a part-time job as an assistant in the local newsagents. 'He doesn't seem a very nice type either. Mr Bailey had a complaint he'd beaten another boy up yesterday.'

'Well, I'm going to be waiting for him tomorrow,' said Ray.

It was decided several people would keep watch around seven the next morning, at varying intervals along the road. Chris took his turn, and was joined by Mark and Rebecca.

'You never get up this early so willingly for school,' complained Jane.

Concealed behind the curtains they watched and waited. At last, he arrived, propping up his bike against the hedge, he walked up the short drive and put the paper through the letterbox. The boy then proceeded next door. They waited until he disappeared out of sight. Deeply disappointed the children set off to school and Chris to the office, having seen nothing untoward.

Just before nine Jane was disturbed while washing up the breakfast things by a loud knocking at the front door. It proved to be Sharon Smith, with Kylie under her arm and Damian at her heels.

'It's happened again Janey, more of my wall and now Cooper's at number three too.'

'But half the men were keeping watch. How did he do it?'

Jane took Sharon in and made her a coffee to calm her down. When at last she left, somewhat pacified, Jane accompanied her to the door. They now both saw an open lorry bearing the name of a local garden centre, pull up next door at Mr Parry's house. In the back sat a giant-size stone gnome.

'My God, it's four feet high if it's an inch!' exclaimed Sharon, 'and it must weigh a ton.'

The two women watched the object unloaded with difficulty by two men, while Mr Parry supervised.

Jane remarked to him, 'I don't think I've ever seen such a big garden gnome before.'

'Yes, beautiful isn't he. Let that boy try attacking him, and see what happens.'

That evening Ray Lucas and some of the other men came around to Jane and Chris' to hold an inquest on the failure of the morning surveillance. After much arguing and everyone blaming each other, it was decided to try again the following day.

Chris was again in position before seven, joined by Rebecca and Mark once more.

'I really hope that we get him today,' complained Rebecca. 'I'm losing my beauty-sleep.'

'You certainly need that,' scoffed Mark. 'But I believe Mr Parry has a plan, so he told me yesterday.'

'What's that?' inquired Chris, 'first I've heard.'

'Quiet, he's coming,' warned Rebecca. 'He's going next door.'

Suddenly they were startled by the most tremendous crash. Chris ran out followed by Jane and the children. They found Mr Parry standing in his front garden surveying the spectacle of his gnome face downwards on the ground.

'Good grief, there's someone under it,' gasped Chris.

They observed a pair of young male legs sticking out from under the gnomes concrete base, the rest of the body was covered by the statue. Scattered around on the floor were copies of various morning newspapers. Mark now began to collect them up.

'They all have the addresses on them, I think I'll deliver them, then go round to the shop and explain what's happened to Mr Bailey. After all he'll need a new paperboy now, and I could do with a bit extra pocket money.'

'Well, this one won't need the job any longer,' agreed Mr Parry smiling pleasantly.

In The Eye Of The Mind

by

Doris Lamount

I remembered vividly that first week out there in that God forsaken hole. I'd been on an assignment for my newspaper nothing too special just the usual news thingies, or at least that's what I was led to believe. Indeed things had been pretty stable in that part of the globe for some years now.

However I felt a particular unease, call it sixth sense or journalistic nose indeed anything you please but I had it. Somehow I had a feeling that the old man back in his News-Editors Office had some kind of knowledge the rest of us didn't possess, or maybe he just had a hunch that all was not as it might seem to the rest of the world. He was a canny blighter that one a bit like a Jack-in-the-box, if you get my meaning.

Still, it suited me right then c'os all I wanted to do was get out of Britain for a few months and nurse my wounds if ya' like. My love life had taken a nose dive after three years with my steady girl friend Jancy.

Jancy had met this other guy while I was over in the Gulf the year before, she said he was just a platonic friend, personally I'd never believed in platonic friendships because in my estimation they always had sexual overtones.

However she kept telling me it was all in my flippin' head. . . like a lot of other things which were going wrong with our relationship. And, that my imagination would be the death of me, she had continued 'and if you don't get a job settling down here at home so we can marry and start a family I could forget her.'

Frankly the idea of a nine to five little number was out of the question as far as I was concerned. And basically just another nail in the coffin of our present time together, so I packed hastily and left the flat post haste. Hence when I received the *Dear John* the day before it actually came as a relief.

Trouble was you see I lapped up excitement like a sponge and anyhow I intended writing a book on my travels and experiences, one day. Then, and only then would I sit at a desk sip tea contentedly pat my kids on the head and make a fortune hopefully from my writings.

I smiled to myself at this thought; ha ha I'd have to find Mrs Right first wouldn't I?

Anyhow no rush to become entangled with a female at this stage I'd a lot more travelling to do and folk to meet before I settled down. The other thought which pervaded my mind was that I'd come to realise that lovely though she was, I had not really loved Jancy it had just become a habit being with her, and it was mainly my pride which was hurt certainly not, my heart. And what's pride at the end of the day?

To continue, I'd just sat down in the lounge of the small Hotel ready for afternoon tea, something I had been looking forward to all morning.

So taking the weight off my feet and stretching out my rather long legs I relaxed from the burning heat outside and it felt like bliss. The tea arrived, lemon tea very refreshing indeed. The boys back in Fleet Street know me as a bit of a health freak a bore in other words. I'm not yer' usual type of reporter propping up bars and swapping outlandish stories, and certainly no hero that's for sure.

I began to count slowly in my head, a habit of many years which helped me to relax. And came to the conclusion that I'd better get on with my plans for living my life my way and be philosophical about my break up with the still, lovely Jancy, send her a letter wishing her every happiness with her new lover and stop being so churlish. Right now I had this seemingly easy assignment to report on first.

The ceiling fan whirred steadily, waiters padded to and fro and with the gentle murmur of conversation in the background it all lulled me into a cosy frame of mind.

Suddenly, guttural voices and the stomping of boots intruded upon my reverie then there was a loud bang which seemed to echo forever.

My eyes flicked open, army personnel stood around the room demanding passports from the ex-pats sitting nearby, drinking tea quite peaceably. Then I too was confronted by a high ranking soldier who spoke to me in broken English. Or rather he barked at me requesting both my passport and press card demanding any other information I could give him regarding my presence in his country. Several of us were then roughly ordered out into the harsh sunlight. To be herded into trucks, pushed and dragged unceremoniously but protestingly away, destination unknown.

Eventually arriving at some kind of headquarters we were then shoved into small cell-like smelly rooms, bare except for one long metal bench fixed to the wall. The room was completely windowless and a feeling of chill pervaded one's senses.

Time passed slowly and the month's which ensued were traumatic. Interrogation after interrogation, endless questions beatings and humiliation. Sitting there in that miserable room with its confined space and whitewashed but stained walls I found my thoughts drifting back in time.

I began to discover that I could make an interesting game if I tried thereby taking my mind from the horror of spine chilling screams and my own dismal plight.

To my surprise I found that I could recall quite a bit of my life, so I learned to let my mind drift it wasn't easy I can tell you for the pain was intense.

The light stayed on for weeks at a time, then they would just turn them off for say roughly a week, so I would sit or lie in the dark totally disorientated.

Food, when it came was pushed through a low flap in the door which was then bolted down outside immediately. When I say food, I mean it was something sloppy and disgusting.

Time, was something I'd lost track of and I had no idea how long I'd been incarcerated. In the beginning I was convinced that I would soon be out and free and it was all a mistake a miscarriage of justice. Soon I knew better, I decided that some kind of coup was in progress.

I remember thinking, 'yes that's what it is,' and they, being either the ruling power or the opposition made no difference to me. Whoever it was 'they the bastards had me banged up for God knows what.'

None of their questions made any sense and I felt that I'd been mistaken maybe for someone else. I asked myself time and again when would my

She Wore The Dress And I Stayed Home

by

Alison Chisholm

Looking back, it seems funny to think that the whole thing started with the dress. When we were children we always dressed alike. Twins did in those days. We never resented it. We both rather liked the double takes and the careful looks. We cashed in on the fact that we were identical, and schooldays were a riot of confusion for the teachers and hilarity for our friends.

We shopped together for dresses for that party. Maddy chose scarlet taffeta, and I went for a sleek, more sophisticated line in a deep sea green.

Before we left the shop, Maddy announced she had fallen in love with my dress, and how did I feel about an exchange? I told her to forget it, and promised she could borrow it - but not for that party.

It was ironic that I had to stay at home. There was nothing seriously wrong with me, but I had a bout of summer flu - caught from Maddy, as ever. We shared measles, chicken pox and mumps as children, and any germ one brought home was passed on to the other even now.

Maddy was back at work by the time I started to feel rotten, and on the day of the party she was bubbling over while I felt shivery and weak, and ached in my joints.

I knew what she was going to say before she asked it. It was often that way with us.

'Yes, all right, you can wear it,' I said resignedly.

'Thanks, you're a dear. Are you sure you don't mind being left alone if I go? It's ages since I got together with the office crowd, and I still haven't met that new fellow - Pete, did you call him?'

I told her I didn't mind being left alone. I was glad she would be seeing her old friends. And that Pete was strictly my property. I'd had my eye on him since he joined the firm two months ago.

I knew Maddy would be the centre of attention. She always has been. When we were working together, even people who couldn't tell us apart gravitated towards her. We're not beauty queen material, but people find us attractive; only something indefinable makes her more attractive than I am.

When Maddy, who was always more ambitious than I, left to try her luck with a bigger concern, it seemed to get easier for me to make friends. And Pete, tall and blond and quite irresistible, was one friend I desperately wanted to make.

'It was heaven,' Maddy trilled as she banged the door a little after one o'clock.

I struggled to sit up in bed. 'You had a good time then?'

'Good? I've never enjoyed myself so much in my whole life. It was great to see all the girls again, but just after nine that new bloke came in, and I was knocked out.'

'New bloke? You mean Pete?' I could feel the apprehension creeping through me.

'Yes, Pete. Where were you hiding him? He is absolutely gorgeous.' Her voice drawled her appreciation, and her eyes sparkled with memories of the evening. 'He asked me to dance, and we had something to eat, and it was as if we had been waiting our whole lives to meet each other.'

She couldn't be serious, surely. I had been trying to get to know him for eight weeks, and in one evening . . .

'He's asked me out tomorrow, for dinner. And he said something about a concert at the weekend. He's incredible!'

I could hardly believe it. He had scarcely acknowledged that I existed; and yet Maddy, identical to me in every way, stole him from under my nose.

'He must have thought it was me,' I said, aiming at a teasing tone but knowing she must be able to detect the desperation.

Maddy was too absorbed to notice. 'Do you know, I think it could be the real thing. At last.'

She prattled on for another ten minutes, and then yawned widely and said she would fall asleep standing if she didn't get to bed soon.

I could hear the change in her breathing through the wall adjoining her bedroom. She must have dropped off as her head hit the pillow.

By that time I was too wide awake to get back to sleep myself. The more I thought about Maddy's treachery, the more anger swelled inside me. She knew, of course she knew how much I wanted Pete; and she had gone ahead and encouraged him, and then come home to gloat.

Maybe I was feverish from the flu, or maybe I had taken too much from her already. I remembered the time Maddy let me take the blame when she was careless with Mum's best china and broke half the cups by dropping the tray. I remembered when we were both learning to drive, and the pact that neither of us would tell which one backed the car into the gatepost and broke the rear light. I had kept silent, while she had dropped untrue hints. I remembered the funeral, when we buried Mum just a month after Dad had been laid to rest. Four hours later, Maddy had been out dancing.

The plans I made during that night were only half formed, and sounded like the merest fantasy. But in the days and weeks that followed, they grew like a cancer until they took over all my thoughts.

Maddy's infatuation with Pete was so intense I expected it to burn itself out. The trouble was, he was equally infatuated.

'Christmas Eve,' she called out joyously as she came in one night, after yet another date with Pete. 'Keep the date free - and you can dance at my wedding.'

'Your wedding? You're getting married? You and Pete?'

'In the absence of Robert Redford, yes,' Maddy laughed.

'You'll be my bridesmaid, and it won't be anything too elaborate. Just knowing I'll be with Pete will be enough . . .'

My mind raced as she talked through her plans. I had to be pleased for her. I had to show I bore her no malice for taking Pete from me even before he was mine.

I laughed and joked with her, and helped her make her plans. Then I dropped my own bombshell.

'You know, Maddy, I've been thinking a lot about what I would do if this happened. I might take up that offer I had to work abroad.'

'Well, so long as it isn't the Foreign Legion,' she joked. 'If you're serious, Pete and I could live here after we're married. What do you think?'

I swallowed the lump in my throat. 'Of course you could. And I could come and visit you from time to time. Yes, you know I think I might even do a bit of travelling first. I could perhaps manage a month or so before I settle, and than a complete change could be just the thing.'

Once I had dropped the idea casually like that, Maddy seized on it. It would be better for everyone, she decided. She and Pete could start married life in their own flat, and the holiday break would ease me through the first parting we would know in our lives.

It was good of Maddy to help me make all the plans. The funny thing was, she even chose to get married in my dress, the lovely sea green she had worn the night she met Pete.

I think I have covered everything. It was a stroke of brilliance to suggest we went alone to the airport. Maddy knew how devastated I was to miss her wedding, but my new career opportunity meant I had to skip the holiday and get to my post half way through December.

We were only ten minutes' drive from the airport when I asked to stop the car because I felt queasy. Thank the Lord for night flights. It only took a few moments. My handbag, suitably loaded with a brick, caught the back of her head as she bent forward, and I had her in the canal in no time. She'll be found, of course, and I shall weep as I identify my identical twin.

Pete has not noticed the substitution. It's a good job Maddy talked so much and with such little discretion. I know enough about her - and him - for him to suspect nothing. Nobody at Maddy's office has guessed either. Well, any little mistakes have been more than excused by Maddy's general dizziness and excitement about the wedding.

Funny to think I'll wear my new dress for the first time at my wedding. Mine. And Maddy's. And Pete's.

Sweet Revenge

by

Margaret Carr

The girl nestled into his neck and he squeezed the small hand in his. A few miles from town he had parked the car next to the gate leading to a meadow, and in the distance he could see the trees of the wood. They walked through the long grass feeling the warm early evening sun on their backs.

'You do love me, don't you Andy?' she asked.

He laughed softly. 'What a question - of course I do.'

'It's just that - well you know.' Her words were faltering and uncertain, 'This is my first time - and.' He gently released her hand and placed his arm around her waist pulling her tightly to him.

'I know, but don't worry, I'll take care of you.' She nodded and glancing up at his strong profile she felt reassured and happy. It would be all right, she knew this with all her heart. Andy was the person she wanted to marry, and she would when she was sixteen, hadn't he said so time and time again when coaxing and begging her, and now the time was right. Soon she would feel like a woman, loved and cherished. He kissed the top of her head as they came to the edge of the wood and was serious as he turned and asked her.

'Janey are you sure you haven't told anyone about our dates?'

A small frown formed on his tanned forehead and she wanted to assure him and to remove the lines which marred his perfect, handsome face.

'No. Nobody.'

'Are you sure?' he persisted, 'not your family, or what about your friend?'

'No Andy. I promised it would be our secret. I've told no one. Whenever I've been meeting you I've told my parents I was going to Susan's to listen to tapes. She covered for me because I did the same for her when she had a date.'

'Yes, but what about this Susan, have you told her about me?'

Janey had to convince him, she might lose him if he knew the truth and she couldn't bear that. After all she only told Susan in strictest confidence, and any way everyone would know when they announced their engagement on her six-teenth birthday. She knew her mother would be shocked and upset, but her dad would give in to her. Hadn't he always no matter what she wanted?

'I don't see that it matters. All this secret stuff having to walk miles from my home so I'm not seen getting into your car. I'm so happy about us, I could shout it to the world.' She saw his eyes grow cold and his jaw set, she added quickly, 'But honestly Andy, I haven't told a soul,' it was only a small lie. For a second dark eyes held hers and the look made her catch her breath, then he relaxed and his tone was caressing.

'You're my girl Janey and it's been our secret, but after tonight it won't matter any more.'

Janey nodded happily.

They pushed their way through the clinging bushes practically covering the rough path, and the girl held back shivering. Out of the sunlight she was chilled and the woods felt menacing.

'What's the matter?' he asked, 'are you cold?'

'No I was just remembering,' she whispered and was grateful for his comforting arm around her shoulders, 'I don't want to go any further into the wood, Andy,' a sob suddenly caught in her throat. 'It's in there those two girls were killed.'

Fear whitened her cheeks as the memory flooded back. Just eight weeks ago the first girl had been found and then two weeks later the next girl Marie. Both Sally and Marie were local girls and both had been raped and strangled and left in the undergrowth. Intensive police enquiries had followed and after carefully piecing together the clues and evidence there was now a nationwide search for a man in a dark car who had been seen near the area.

'You mean the girls who were murdered - the man must be an animal. But don't worry the police know who did it and he's probably miles away - and anyway I'm here to protect you. The bodies were found the other side of the wood a long way from here. From the look of the bushes I don't think anyone ever comes this way. Now relax - come on.'

Andy led her deeper into the wood, between the trees and thick bushes and over old stumps and roots. The shadows danced overhead caused by the gentle swaying branches and around the couple the trees enveloped them like a cloak.

An opening revealed a small copse completely surrounded by the closely packed bushes, and the ground was almost covered by bluebells and lilies of the valley. The scent of the wild flowers was heady, the air calm and still.

He led Janey to the foot of the ancient knarled oak and placed his jacket over the springy moss before she lay down. He kissed her lightly and was surprised at the sudden desire expressed in her demanding response. Their kisses became more urgent, as they were lost in their mutual passion.

The sun was beginning to set when Andy pushed his way through the heavy doors of the Red Lion Public House, and to the crowded bar.

'Same as usual, is it?' asked Joe serving behind the bar, and without waiting for an answer filled a pint glass with draught lager and placed it before the new customer.

Andy took a long cool drink and gazed with little interest at the assorted people filling the large room. One or two acknowledged him with a nod, but nobody joined him. Andy Simpson was known as a loner.

By the time the bell went for last orders Andy was sitting alone at a corner table sipping only his second glass of lager.

'Just another pint mate,' a thick set man stood at the bar where he'd been all evening and swayed unsteadily on his legs. 'Then I suppose it's back home to the wife. She reckons she can smell my breath as soon as I turn the corner into our road.'

Andy half listened to the man's loud voice, but his thoughts were elsewhere.

Joe the barman nodded and listened as he served another customer, 'Can she nag. Nag, nag, nag you'd think I was always in the pub the way she goes on.' He took a long drink. 'If it wasn't for my Janey I think I'd have left the missus years ago. Now there's a girl, no man could wish for a better daughter - and clever. Did I tell you she's top of her class at school. I reckon she'll go to college next year after her exams.' His pride in his daughter was obvious to all.

Andy slowly raised his eyes and stared at the man leaning against the bar. He knew Stan Loxton, not to talk to, he'd seen him around. A big foul-mouthed man, always calling his poor wife. If she nagged him then the fat slob deserved it. He deserved everything he got.

Andy ran his finger down the side of his empty glass and blinked hard trying to erase the face which sprang readily to his mind. How he'd loved Marie she was lovely and good. She shouldn't have died. He remembered how they had talked and planned their future together. First a nice little house and then a couple of children, it would have been great - but then their dreams had ended in her murder.

Marie told him about the man who harassed and pestered her and about the times he had followed her. Andy hadn't taken her concern seriously and if he had his Marie would still be alive. That same man had murdered his Marie - his lovely Marie. He knew he should have told the police, but over the weeks he was full of grief and remorse - and then he needed time to think and plan.

Oh yes it had been carefully planned and executed. It was just retribution, and revenge was sweet.

A few minutes later Andy walked to the door, he felt suddenly very weary. He tried to picture Marie, but the image was of Janey with her blonde hair the colour of ripe corn, and her long slim neck - she hadn't really struggled, well not for long. Had Marie struggled for long at the hands of Loxton? well now it was his turn to suffer. Oh her father would worry when she didn't come home, and then there would be a search. In time they'd find Janey's body - but not just yet.

A smile played around Andy's thin lips . . .

No, not just yet. . .

In The Eye Of The Mind

by

Doris Lamount

I remembered vividly that first week out there in that God forsaken hole. I'd been on an assignment for my newspaper nothing too special just the usual news thingies, or at least that's what I was led to believe. Indeed things had been pretty stable in that part of the globe for some years now.

However I felt a particular unease, call it sixth sense or journalistic nose indeed anything you please but I had it. Somehow I had a feeling that the old man back in his News-Editors Office had some kind of knowledge the rest of us didn't possess, or maybe he just had a hunch that all was not as it might seem to the rest of the world. He was a canny blighter that one a bit like a Jack-in-the-box, if you get my meaning.

Still, it suited me right then c'os all I wanted to do was get out of Britain for a few months and nurse my wounds if ya' like. My love life had taken a nose dive after three years with my steady girl friend Jancy.

Jancy had met this other guy while I was over in the Gulf the year before, she said he was just a platonic friend, personally I'd never believed in platonic friendships because in my estimation they always had sexual overtones.

However she kept telling me it was all in my flippin' head. . . like a lot of other things which were going wrong with our relationship. And, that my imagination would be the death of me, she had continued 'and if you don't get a job settling down here at home so we can marry and start a family I could forget her.'

Frankly the idea of a nine to five little number was out of the question as far as I was concerned. And basically just another nail in the coffin of our present time together, so I packed hastily and left the flat post haste. Hence when I received the *Dear John* the day before it actually came as a relief.

Trouble was you see I lapped up excitement like a sponge and anyhow I intended writing a book on my travels and experiences, one day. Then, and only then would I sit at a desk sip tea contentedly pat my kids on the head and make a fortune hopefully from my writings.

I smiled to myself at this thought; ha ha I'd have to find Mrs Right first wouldn't I?

Anyhow no rush to become entangled with a female at this stage I'd a lot more travelling to do and folk to meet before I settled down. The other thought which pervaded my mind was that I'd come to realise that lovely though she was, I had not really loved Jancy it had just become a habit being with her, and it was mainly my pride which was hurt certainly not, my heart. And what's pride at the end of the day?

To continue, I'd just sat down in the lounge of the small Hotel ready for afternoon tea, something I had been looking forward to all morning.

So taking the weight off my feet and stretching out my rather long legs I relaxed from the burning heat outside and it felt like bliss. The tea arrived, lemon tea very refreshing indeed. The boys back in Fleet Street know me as a bit of a health freak a bore in other words. I'm not yer' usual type of reporter propping up bars and swapping outlandish stories, and certainly no hero that's for sure.

I began to count slowly in my head, a habit of many years which helped me to relax. And came to the conclusion that I'd better get on with my plans for living my life my way and be philosophical about my break up with the still, lovely Jancy, send her a letter wishing her every happiness with her new lover and stop being so churlish. Right now I had this seemingly easy assignment to report on first.

The ceiling fan whirred steadily, waiters padded to and fro and with the gentle murmur of conversation in the background it all lulled me into a cosy frame of mind.

Suddenly, guttural voices and the stomping of boots intruded upon my reverie then there was a loud bang which seemed to echo forever.

My eyes flicked open, army personnel stood around the room demanding passports from the ex-pats sitting nearby, drinking tea quite peaceably. Then I too was confronted by a high ranking soldier who spoke to me in broken English. Or rather he barked at me requesting both my passport and press card demanding any other information I could give him regarding my presence in his country. Several of us were then roughly ordered out into the harsh sunlight. To be herded into trucks, pushed and dragged unceremoniously but protestingly away, destination unknown.

Eventually arriving at some kind of headquarters we were then shoved into small cell-like smelly rooms, bare except for one long metal bench fixed to the wall. The room was completely windowless and a feeling of chill pervaded one's senses.

Time passed slowly and the month's which ensued were traumatic. Interrogation after interrogation, endless questions beatings and humiliation. Sitting there in that miserable room with its confined space and whitewashed but stained walls I found my thoughts drifting back in time.

I began to discover that I could make an interesting game if I tried thereby taking my mind from the horror of spine chilling screams and my own dismal plight.

To my surprise I found that I could recall quite a bit of my life, so I learned to let my mind drift it wasn't easy I can tell you for the pain was intense.

The light stayed on for weeks at a time, then they would just turn them off for say roughly a week, so I would sit or lie in the dark totally disorientated.

Food, when it came was pushed through a low flap in the door which was then bolted down outside immediately. When I say food, I mean it was something sloppy and disgusting.

Time, was something I'd lost track of and I had no idea how long I'd been incarcerated. In the beginning I was convinced that I would soon be out and free and it was all a mistake a miscarriage of justice. Soon I knew better, I decided that some kind of coup was in progress.

I remember thinking, 'yes that's what it is,' and they, being either the ruling power or the opposition made no difference to me. Whoever it was 'they the bastards had me banged up for God knows what.'

None of their questions made any sense and I felt that I'd been mistaken maybe for someone else. I asked myself time and again when would my disappearance filter through to my boss? and what was he doing about it? 'Surely I reasoned *The Big Fella* would be in touch with the British Embassy by now.' I felt at such a low ebb by then it was all I could do to keep my sanity.

This I did with great difficulty, it was only the memories of my wonderful childhood, my late parents and great aunt Dora who had left me a small legacy and cottage that kept me going, for my only brother Steve had been killed in a crash several years before and I was alone with no remaining family.

However I knew that one day I could write of this experience, expose such cruelties to the world, and I was determined to survive. Eventually *they* stopped bothering me as my answer's were always the same, how could they be otherwise? One day the keys jangled outside the door bolts were drawn back grindingly. A figure in a smart navy blue suit strode in, he proceeded to open a briefcase reading reams of writings, sitting gingerly on one corner of my miserable shelf they called a bed. I remember how I sat as quiet as a mouse my hands clasped tightly wondering, 'What now?' With good reason to think that some new tactics were being used maybe some psychological one's this time round.

But no, to my surprise the smart guy looked me over rustled some papers into a tidy stack then spoke in perfect English 'Your name is David, David Spears?' the question hung in the air. Eventually I just nodded slightly as my lips were still swollen and my gums felt as if they weren't even there.

Still looking me over carefully before continuing, he spoke on as though he knew how cautious I would be, 'Your release is imminent did you know?'

What a foolish question I thought, but I refrained from commenting being too scared again. This time I shook my head from side to side.

'Well you are my dear chap.'

The very English way he spoke and the word chap sounded so incongruous coming from his sweaty demeanour. I said nothing. He continued 'You're to be sent to a rehabilitation Hospital for the war wounded and mentally ill. You've been very ill you know.'

'Have I?' I thought, 'you bastard you, you'll not get away with that one if ever I get released from this hell hole.' However I just sat quietly making no movement nor comment, it felt safer that way, 'Play along with them that's the name of the game,' went my thoughts at this juncture.

'Tomorrow a doctor will examine you then I will be back to escort you to the Hospital and we'll soon have you fit and well again to go back to your own country and family, you do have someone in your family we can contact don't you?'

Again I remained dumb shaking my head slowly from side to side this time, and thinking, 'Oh no you don't my fine fella,' you're not going to try and screw me up with that one either.'

He spoke on 'Yes my word we have been so worried about you, they say you were found wandering about without any identification then they brought you here for your own safety.'

I smiled inwardly at this point showing not a flicker upon my face, 'So that was the game a form of brainwashing hey; to cover up a monumental mistake, and it wouldn't do to harm a britisher and a reporter at that would it now?' Especially if they, were seeking financial aid or a back up to their coup.

'Politics' I snarled to myself 'shit if ever I get out of here alive I'll never go again to the mad unstable countries I'd had enough.'

Best be in Britain where every man can speak his mind even if no one listens, at least he wouldn't be dragged off and incarcerated for nothing. 'Perhaps,' I was thinking 'a nine to five wouldn't be a bad idea after all.'

I'd walk the green fields smell cut grass, live and love, feel the wind upon my face ruffle my hair, I almost broke down right there and then at the very thought of freedom. However I had the sense to remain impassive, and the sweaty man went away at last. I was left in peace to think, plan even, but really I had to prevent myself planning or raising my hopes too much.

I turned my thoughts to Jancy once again, maybe somewhere out there was another sweet girl like Jancy used to be, a girl who would lie close with scented skin warm and loving.

As I lay on my cold bed and transported myself to the realms of fantasy I knew that I needed love more than ever, in fact so badly by then I was close to tears, not a manly thing to admit but oh so true.

All I hoped was that this latest visit was not some cruel hoax they were good at that you know, subtle cruelties as well as the obvious.

One thing though which also helped me strange as it may seem and that was there was no one in England to worry about me, no relative that is.

It must be devastating to listen to constant rhetoric about one's wife or mother crying at home, that kind of torture can be as demoralising to say the least.

The next day, or was it several days after the sweaty man's visit; I'm not too sure being as we were once again in the dark, in other words it was lights out time.

Another man came to visit me, he said he was a doctor, 'But then who knows,' I remember thinking, he did have a stethoscope though.

Eventually I was transferred to this run down Hospital although I was still kept under guard.

And as the weeks went by and all visible scars were almost erased and yours truly was beginning to look reasonably fit I felt that at last my real release was perhaps nearing.

Negotiations were apparently in motion, I did not of course know any of this, until I was eventually and finally handed over to the British Envoy.

What deals had transpired Lord only knows but I do know this that I have old' Sam learing my boss, to thank for putting the wheels in motion and insisting that my assignment was purely on an environmental issue.

Britain's willingness to send aid to this troubled spot on the map had all been stage-managed beautifully, and so I was free . . . free at last.

I couldn't believe it until of course safely nearing British shores. Then, and only then did I breathe a sigh of relief and prayed fervently, for although I'd prayed in my cell, of course I did, this was different for I felt my God had listened after all.

As I sat gazing out onto the patchwork quilt that was the English countryside as we came in to land, I knew that for the rest of my life I would still be a prisoner, a prisoner of my harrowing memories in cell third on the left.

It brought to mind a saying my Dad used to quote . . .

'Stone walls do not a prison make: nor iron bars a cage.'

The rest you know, the waiting crowds, bands playing, the media the whole hulla - balloo for me; for me I ask you. Now I'm alone with my thoughts once more.